MOUNTAIN BALLADS
PART-ONE
NEPALI FOLK TALES

POORNASMRITHI

BLUEROSE PUBLISHERS
India | U.K.

Copyright © Poornasmrithi 2025

All rights reserved by author. No part of this publication may be reproduced, stored in a retrieval system or transmitted in any form or by any means, electronic, mechanical, photocopying, recording or otherwise, without the prior permission of the author. Although every precaution has been taken to verify the accuracy of the information contained herein, the publisher assumes no responsibility for any errors or omissions. No liability is assumed for damages that may result from the use of information contained within.

BlueRose Publishers takes no responsibility for any damages, losses, or liabilities that may arise from the use or misuse of the information, products, or services provided in this publication.

For permissions requests or inquiries regarding this publication,
please contact:

BLUEROSE PUBLISHERS
www.BlueRoseONE.com
info@bluerosepublishers.com
+91 8882 898 898
+4407342408967

ISBN: 978-93-6783-620-0

Cover Design: Sadhna Kumari
Typesetting: Pooja Sharma

First Edition: January 2025

AUTHOR'S NOTE

Every community in the world has a plethora of folk tales, each carrying a bit of the essence of the energy and practices that helped carry forward the tribe down the ages.

"Over the centuries, we have transformed the ancient myths and folk tales and made them into the fabric of our lives. Consciously or unconsciously, we weave the narratives of myths and folk tales into our daily existence."
- Jack Zipes

Like so many other communities and tribes across the world, the Nepali/Gorkha community (made up of many sub-tribes) has a huge oral repository of myths and folklore(s). They have been passed down through the ages and verbally, and therefore many of them have a little change here and there in the telling.

The Nepali/Gorkha are an ethnic group of tribal people that have populated the foothills of the great Himalayas for as long as time can remember. History drew lines among the foothills of these snow-capped giants, and the Nepali/Gorkha people can now be found in present day Nepal, Myanmar, Bhutan, Uttarakhand, Assam, Sikkim, Darjeeling and some pockets in the north-eastern states of India.

These tales belong to all the Nepali/Gorkha wherever they may be geographically. It is a gift from our ancestors to the world in the form of simple wisdom, tradition, culture, and knowledge of healing. It is what they left us to help find peace, harmony and balance in this world and co-exist with the rest of the inhabitants of this Earth.

Some tales are silly and whimsical made to entertain children. Some deal with plain simple good manners and act as a moral compass for humans, and others bear testimony to historic moments in time. The Nepali/Gorkha has many tribes, and each tribe has its own language along with its own religious and cultural practices. I belong to the Kirati Khambu/ Rai Tribe; I mention this here to clarify that Khambu/Rai means the same. Having been born and raised in the rural village in Darjeeling, I was lucky to have grown up hearing these tales.

My thanks to all the storytellers of my childhood for having passed on these tales. The demands of the modern world today have changed the fabric of tribal societies and family structures with the hope that these stories live on in the hearts and minds of our people. I have compiled whatever I could in the form of this book.

"The dreamer awakes, The shadow goes by.

The tales I have told you, The tale is a lie.

But listen to me, bright maiden, proud youth

The tale is a lie. What it tells is the truth."

Traditional folk tale ending

(Author can be reached via email: *poornasmrithi1974@gmail.com*)

ACKNOWLEDGEMENTS

ILLUSTRATIONS

1. Shri. Tseten Sherpa and his student Reena Rai (Dehi Art Gallery, Kakarvitta, Nepal).

THE CULTURAL EXPERTS

1. Shri. Dinesh Chamling Rai.
2. Shri. Kewal Chamling Rai.
3. Shri. D.B Dungmali Rai and Family.
4. Shri. Shyam Kumar Bokhim Rai.
5. Smt. Sheela Limbu.
6. Shri. Tope Ram Rumdali Rai.

All members of the Kirati Community Jhapa. (Thanks to them I was able to get the information about various practices within the Kirati Community).

THE STORY TELLERS

1. Kanta Bala Lorung Rai.
2. Gajra Singh Dungmali Rai.
3. Sakuntala Rai.
4. P.S. Rai.
5. Sukmaya Rai.

6. Gopal Rai.

7. Maan Bahadur Tamang.

(And all the story tellers I met in various places that helped me with different versions of the same tale or added the finer details of another)

THE 'HERBOLOGIST'

Shri Jigme Sherpa - who helped me identify the carious Himalayan plants and helped me with their local scientific names.

OTHER SOURCES

1. ***History and Culture of the Kirat People. Part I and Part II*** by Iman Singh Chemgonj. My deepest gratitude to this *'Ever Shining Bright Star'* of the Kirati World.

2. ***"Mundhum"*** by Shri Shiva Kumar Rai - Compiles by the executive committee of the Kirati Mundhum Philosophy Research and Documentation team.

3. ***History of the Kirata Empire*** by Shri. Jas Raj Subba (Pondhak)

THE MOTIVATORS

Mom, Misha, Tookie, Bala, Minkey, Abhinay Ghising, Ujjwalit and Issac. You know I couldn't have done it without you guys.

Thank You.

CONTENTS

1. HARINI: THE STORY OF A LITTLE GREY BIRD 3
2. THE FIG TREE (NEWARA) AND MAAGHAE SAKRANTI 15
3. HOW THE ROBIN GOT A RED BREAST 21
4. THE MAGNOLIA AND THE BAMBOO 27
5. ALL ABOUT A PIG'S NOSE 33
6. HOW THE LIZARD CAME INTO THIS WORLD 37
7. THE BUTTER AND THE FROG 41
8. THE DARJEELING WOODPECKER 45
9. THE HOUSE OF CINDERS 53
10. TREATY OF SAMENDEN 59
11. THE TWELVE HORSEMEN 65
12. CHARI BHUTLAE OR THE BIRD FEATHERED CLAN 71
13. THE SWALLOWS NEST 77
14. A TALE ABOUT THE MANGAR LANGUAGE 85
15. THE HALAESO, DHANASE AND KHOCHEELEPA 93
16. GARUDA MEETH OR THE EAGLE BROTHER 99
17. PILLAR OF POTS 103
18. THE BIRCH AND THE RHODODENDRON 107
19. THE TALE OF THE CAT AND THE TIGER 111
20. THE STORY OF THE BEAN 116
21. A STRANGE TALE OF LITTLE MEN 121
22. HOW THE BEAR LOST ITS TAIL 128
23. MORE ABOUT THE FOX AND THE BEAR 135

24. THE MOON, A COBBLER, AND SOME FLOUR 143
25. THE CREATOR SOME MILK AND SOME ALCOHOL 149
26. THE PRINCESS AND THE LEAF 152
27. BHADRAYO: THE VOICE OF MAN. 159
28. BREAD OF HUSKS (*Or Bhoos Ko Roti*) 167
29. SEERING AND LHARING 173
30. THE TALE OF THE MILLIPEDE AND THE GODSON 178
31. PLANTING SALT 183
32. MUKKUBUNG 191
33. STORY OF THE LAST SOKPA 203
34. HENKEBUNG AND THE TIGER BROTHER 207
35. SEEBAY – MY MYSTERY BIRD 219
36. HANSULAE AND PURULAE 223
37. PAARO HAANG AND SUMNIMA 233
38. A TALE OF THE FRIZZLED CHICKEN ......
    IN THE DAYS OF THE MAHABHARATA 242
39. TAYAMMA AND KHIYAMMA 247
40. BHAILO AND DEWSUREY: THE STORY OF AN
    ANCIENT KIRATI FESTIVAL 255
41. RIKKUPPA AND THE GREEDY CRAB. 267
42. THE CLEVER MAN WHO WAS NOT SO CLEVER
    AFTER ALL 279

1. HARINI: THE STORY OF A LITTLE GREY BIRD

Once upon a time many years ago, there lived a tribal princess in the hot plains. She had been blessed with great beauty and grace unfortunately for her, she had not been so lucky with her voice. Her voice was sharp and shrill.

Her father was a powerful warlord, and many chieftains would have gladly married her in spite of her voice but she insisted that she would only marry someone she chose. No one, not even her father, could deny her that right.

Her father had always known this, but as the years rolled by and she chose no one, he began to feel a little worried about her. There was nothing he could do but wait until his daughter decided whom she was going to wed.

The princess loved the outdoors, but she could not spend much time outside as her many aunts and mother kept telling her sitting out in the sun caused her skin to spot and darken, and she looked ugly.

Not that the princess actually cared, but the many aunts spared no effort in letting her know that it was already difficult having to bear her shrill voice every day. Did they have to suffer the pain of looking at an ugly face as well? She didn't like being told off for something she couldn't do much about, but then, like her old nurse always told her, Aunts would be aunts.

Higher up in the cold foothills of the mountains lived a pious chieftain of a place known to the plainsmen as Wallo Kirat. This chieftain was neither rich nor powerful, but he was blessed with gifts that only a few of his ancestors had ever been blessed with.

It was said that the gods had given him power over the spoken word, meaning his words always came true. He was also blessed with knowledge of healing herbs and minerals and had an uncanny ability to know exactly where such herb or mineral could be found. The gods had been very kind and had blessed him with great physical beauty as well, but they had not given him the gift of sight.

There were stories about how he had been born with perfect sight but he decided to give it away to someone who needed it. Some said he was born blind because the gods did not want him to see what evil Man was capable of committing. Some local legends said he lost his sight while assisting Paaro Haang find Sumnima. Whatever the truth may have been, the chieftain was indeed blind.

One day the blind chieftain decided to descend to the plains to collect a certain plant that grew only in the warmth of the plains. Accompanied by a companion, they made their way towards the lowlands, and their journey took them to the lands of the warlord.

Sure enough, within a day or two of him entering the lands, the warlord's spies reported the presence of two strangers from the north and how they had come looking for a certain herb. This was nothing of note as people did travel here and there looking for things they needed. However, the traveler's great physical beauty had caused quite a stir among the womenfolk of the land.

The warlord asked the spies to gather more detail about the traveller and on finding out that the traveller was a chieftain from the upper lands, when he heard about the chieftain's gifts of locating rare herbs and minerals as well as the blessings of the gods over the spoken word, the warlord wanted the blind chieftain as his son-in-law.

He wasted no time in speaking with his many sisters.

He repeated what his spies had told him about the chieftain, who was said to be kind and wise. Even though he was blind, he was blessed with such beauty maybe the princess would agree to marry him. The aunts said they would speak to the princess. She refused to even listen to the rest of her aunts' arguments once she learnt the chieftain was blind. She tossed her pretty head and announced rather rudely she was in no mood to listen to anyone trying to convince her to marry a blind man!

The warlord really wanted the gifted chieftain as his son-in-law but there was nothing he could do. He asked his sisters to think of something. The sisters came up with a clever plan. They asked the warlord to invite the traveller and give him permission to look for medicinal herbs by the lake near the palace.

He promptly agreed.

Unknown to the Princess, the Blind Chief and his companion camped near the lake because the chieftain wanted to gather some herbs by the light of the full moon.

It was a particularly hot night and the princess could not sleep. She lay tossing and turning in her bed. She decided to go out. Quietly slipping out into the cool night air, she decided to take a walk by the lake.

The moonlight shimmered on the surface of the lake and the cicadas kept calling out into the night. The princess walked by the shore enjoying the stillness of the night. She suddenly stopped…. There illuminated by the pale moonlight, stood the chieftain with a bunch of sweet flags in his arms (Commonly called Bojo). Softly he called out to his companion, " we have a visitor, lead me to meet her."

The princess found herself rooted to the spot and couldn't find her tongue. The chieftain approached and greeted her.

She could not answer. Her eyes had never seen such beauty and she could not believe her eyes.

The blind chief repeatedly asked her who she was and how they could help her. The companion also asked her what she was doing there at such a late hour. He asked her to go away, as they wanted no trouble from anyone.

Stung by his words, she hastily managed to stammer that she belonged to the palace and turned and ran away as fast as she could. Once she got back, she decided she would visit the lake in the morning. She could not get the handsome stranger out of her mind.

Early next morning she announced she was going to spend the day outside and unaware of the knowing looks between her aunts, she made her way to the lake with her friend. As she sat on her favourite rock by the lake, she could see the blind chieftain in the distance as the two friends sorted out the roots of the sweet flag.

She did not notice how quickly the hours passed. The sun had reached its zenith in the sky and it was rather hot. The princess and her friend moved to the shade of a big, shady tree nearby. As they sat in silence in the drowsy afternoon, they heard the blind chieftain and his companion approach the same tree from the other side. As the tree was very big, they could not see the two girls behind it.

The companion was telling the king all about the warlord. "They said he was very suspicious and dangerous but here we are enjoying his hospitality. It was very good of him to let us harvest these herbs from his own private lands."

"True," replied the blind prince. "It was indeed very good of the Chief to extend his hospitality towards us but I don't like the hot plains so much and I can't wait to go back to the cool hills."

"It is true" said the Haang. Up in the hills, life is hard and full of toil and here in the plains, it's easier, but that's about all."

"That's all that matters O Haang", replied his companion. "People want an easier life. Here the land is fertile and rich. Many kinds of food and fruit abound. People are healthy and happy and at peace. Who wouldn't want that?"

"You are right," said the chief, but I still prefer the simple sweetness of the hills. Have you noticed, my friend, our spring water tastes so much sweeter than the well water here that the honey gathered in the hills is much sweeter than the ones here, and the same thing about the corn?

"There is no convincing you, O Haang", laughed the companion. "What about the ladies here, are they not more beautiful than the ones in the hills?"

The Haang was quiet for a while and then replied half seriously, "I am a blind man. I would not know anything about a person's physical appearance but you know what? I would really love to hear a sweet and melodious voice singing in the hills. Now, if there is such a lady here in the plains, then my friend, I guess, I too would love this place as much as you do."

The companion laughed and said, "Well, here's to you finding your warbler in the very near future but for now, let me just take a nap to the cawing of crows."

The Princess who had been listening to this conversation from behind the tree, felt her heart sink. She had been feeling she had finally found someone she could love, even though he was blind. Her beauty was of no use because he could not see her; he could only hear her and her voice was really very shrill and sharp. She quietly waited till both had fallen asleep and slipped away.

After a few days, the princess received a rude shock when she learnt that the blind chief and his companion had left. Alone, she wandered the shore of the lake and shed many tears cursing her fate. If only she had a sweet voice.

One afternoon, she was sitting by her favourite rock watching the fish and there she heard a melodious song of a bird. She watched the tiny little grey thing warble to its heart's content as it fluttered from tree to tree.

As the songster finished its song, she clapped and said wistfully, "Lucky little creature. Why was I not blessed with your voice?"

She thought about her own voice and the Chieftain from the Hills and a sad tear rolled down her cheek. The little grey bird was a happy creature and a gentleman who didn't like to see anyone sad.

Hoping to cheer her up, he sang loudly for her. Many an afternoon, the little grey bird sang for the princess. His hope to cheer her up did not seem to work.

After some days, the little bird gathered up all its courage and approached the princess. "Why so sad, dear princess?" he asked her. "For three days I have sung of nothing but happiness and flowers, and yet you sit here every day, almost on the verge of tears. Why are you so sad o Princess?" He asked her.

The Princess having found someone she could unburden her heart to, narrated how she had lost her heart to the blind Chieftain. The little bird listened carefully.

After the princess had finished, the little bird cocked its head to one side and asked the princes and said, "You wish for a beautiful voice to speak with the chief who cannot see how beautiful you are, and this is what makes you sad."

"I know it will never happen", replied the princess sadly, "and this is what makes me sad. Some things were never meant to be." Two sad tears rolled down her beautiful face.

The little bird stretched out a wing and pretended to look up at the sky. All this crying was making him feel rather uncomfortable. He was a happy little thing who didn't think much about the great sorrows and truths of life. He just wanted to be happy and wanted others to be happy. He didn't like seeing such a beautiful creature sad.

Without thinking too much, he decided to help the princess.

He cleared his voice and said, "Well princess, if you really like my voice so much, I am willing to give it to you."

Before the surprised princess could even voice her surprise, he hurriedly told her he would exchange his voice for hers when the next full moon came around and that all she had to do was come to the lake all alone at night.

The princess could not believe her ears. How could that happen? Would it even be real? This would change everything. Would it? Could it really happen? Would he really give her his voice?

She thanked the bird many times and asked how she could reward him. The little gentleman, however staunchly refused to listen to any word of a reward. He gallantly replied that her happiness was enough for him and that it would be an honour to have been of help. "You will be the guest of honour at our wedding," exclaimed the princess. "You will be my friend forever."

Hurriedly telling the princess to be at the lake at midnight, the little grey gentleman flew hurriedly away.

As for the princess, the many aunts and her mother couldn't understand why she looked so happy. They had all thought she was sad to have heard about the blind chief leaving. Little did they know how she was weaving her dreams and wishes and hugging the secret of the little bird.

After all, no one likes being told almost every day that one has a really jarring voice.

After waiting for what seemed like forever, the day finally dawned, and the princess bathed, perfumed her hair, and changed into her favourite clothes. After offering her prayers to the gods and her ancestors for luck and strength, she quietly stole away to the lake. There sitting on her usual perch, was the little bird shivering in the cold. It had fluffed up all its feathers and looked rather odd, like a tiny grey ball.

"You have come just in time," said the little bird, "Now quickly wade out into the lake and pull out a root of the sweet Flag and wash it well."

The princess did as she was told and waded knee deep in the water to wash the root. As she turned to head back, the little bird called out, "Do not come back just yet, bite a piece of the root and chew it well. After you swallow it, wish for your voice to be given to me and my voice to be given to you."

The Princess bit into the root and chewed it and then made her wish. She waited a while and, when nothing happened, she slowly made her way over to the rock where the little bird sat. To her horror, the little creature lay on its side as it tried weakly to push itself up with its wing. The princess hastily wrapped the little bird in her shawl and blew her warm breath over it in a desperate effort to revive it.

After a few frantic minutes, the little creature feebly stirred and said, "Don't worry, princess. I will be all right. It's just that I feel a little cold right now." The princess was dumbstruck on hearing this because the bird's melodious voice had changed to a shrill screech. A hundred thoughts came flooding to her mind as she stood there speechless at the miracle. "I wish I could do something equally nice in return and make him look beautiful," she thought.

Softly in her beautiful newfound voice, she said, "Thank you, for the gift you have given me. I only wish I could do the same for you."

"That's all right, my princess," the little bird answered. "As long as your dreams come true."

"There must be something I could do for you," the princess cried. "I have taken the most beautiful thing you possess, and I have nothing to give you back. I wish I could at least make your feathers as colourful and shimmery as my shawl, then you would still look beautiful and I would not feel so guilty for having taken away your voice."

"Please do not feel guilty about anything," said the bird. "It is a gift I give you, willingly and gladly.", Here he trailed off because she was staring at him strangely.

"What is it now?" he asked her being a little worried about the way her eyes were becoming rounder and rounder.

Maybe it was because the moon that still hung directly overhead, and the fact the princess had chewed a lot of sweet flag roots and also because her long skirts were still very wet with the lake water wetting her feet.

Maybe the gods were kind enough to reward a good deed one cannot say for certain. Right before the princesses' very eyes, the shimmery blue-green colour of her shawl crept into the feathers of the little grey bird. The princess pointed at his wings, burst into happy laughter, and waded back into the lake with her hands joined in grateful prayers to the watching Spirits.

Confused at his friend's behavior, the little bird stood up and fluffed its feathers. To his utter surprise and delight, he saw himself all shimmery green-blue and beautiful. He was beautiful. He laughed and flew to where the princess stood in prayer.

"I'm beautiful," he said. "I am beautiful."

Needless to say, all ended well. The blind chief had a strange dream that he had missed a very rare herb by the side of the lake, and decided to head back at once. He went directly to the warlord's palace and made his request. The warlord granted him permission immediately.

As the blind chieftain and the companion approached the lake, they could hear someone singing beautifully. It reminded the chieftain of everything beautiful, and he fell in love.

The chieftain and the princess were married into the great delight of the parents, people, and many aunts.

As for the Little Grey Gentleman, he was now a beautiful blue-green bird and had many admirers. The princess did not forget her promise. He was the guest of honour at her wedding.

Years went by and the hills grew older; the story of the two friends grew old and dusty and eventually forgotten by the sons and daughters of Man; however, the little Verditer Flycatcher still hasn't. He tells his little ones this story and they tell their little ones this story.

Some of them still trust the sons and daughters of men enough, to nest in their homes. Some still live by the sides of lakes and ponds(See Story of Two Blue Birds)

They still remember the old bonds of friendship between them and us. Do we?

2. THE FIG TREE (NEWARA) AND MAAGHAE SAKRANTI

Many years ago, when the hills were young and man was still good, and the Spirits of the forests lived undisturbed in the land, there lived a Fig tree.

He was a beautiful tree with broad leaves and strong, gnarly branches; no wind nor storm could do him any harm, but he was not a happy tree.

He lived in the hills near a spring whose waters gurgled and bubbled in the early morning sun and murmured and hummed beneath the stars at night. Yet the Fig tree was not happy.

The Gods had blessed him with a fruit that tasted like wild honey but he was not happy.

"O, what is the use," he would often think, "The Gods have blessed me with so much, but what is the use of all this? When I am not able to thank him for all that I am."

"Man, and his sons thank the Creator each year and offer so many flowers and fruits and leaves and meat and fish and grain. How the fig tree yearned and yearned and yearned for some flower or even just a flower one tiny little flower, he could give Man to offer *his* thanks to the creator."

"What's the use of having fruit when Man goes far and wide in search of fruits but my fruit is not good enough to be offered to the Creator?"

"If only I had flowers, even if they were just tiny teensy-weensy flowers."

This was why the fig tree was never happy. He could think of nothing else. Oh, he would sigh, 'if only I had flowers to give to be offered to the Creator.'

Oh, he would sigh again and say, "I wouldn't mind if my flowers were very small and did not have pretty colours or didn't smell very nice. I just wish I had some."

Now, the Fig Trees wish travelled down his roots and infused the earth with it, the roots of the green grass picked up the wish and brought it out into the sunshine and whispered the wish to the warm day, waving their stalks in the wind.

The cool wind was blowing here and there and picked up this wish from the little blades of grass. They nodded each time the wind passed by and the wind picked up their drowsy whispers.

In turn, the clouds and the rain got to know of it too, and it wasn't long before the Creator learnt of the Fig tree wish.

It is said that when one hopes prays and wishes for a particular thing fervently, even the Creator cannot deny the wish. Like the old adage, "Wish for it with a pure heart and it shall come true."

So, it came to pass that the Creator decided to visit the Fig tree. He felt a little sad that the tree wanted more; after all, hadn't he given the fig tree big, broad leaves, hadn't he given it a broad and strong trunk. Hadn't he made sure that the tree had strong roots to withstand the harshest storms?

"Well," he thought, "Let me go and see what this is all about."

The Creator met the tree and spoke with him for a while. He was pleasantly surprised to know why the fig tree wanted flowers.

"Just one tiny little flower would do," the tree concluded, 'just so you are reminded once every year how grateful I am for all that you have done for me".

"I came here to speak to you and tell you to be happy with all that I have given you, but what you have said has made me think a little bit more," said the Creator.

As a mark of my love for you, you will bear one flower, just one flower in a year. It will be with you briefly and just as it blooms, it will come back to me, and I will remember you. Is that all right? Asked the Creator.

"Oh yes it would, thank you," said the fig tree.

"But no one will ever see it, no one is even going to admire it, is that all right with you?" asked the Creator.

"Oh yes it would," answered the Fig tree. "Just as long as I have a flower even just a small flower that would remind you of my gratitude, that would be more than enough."

"Remarkable," muttered the Creator to himself.

Many weeks passed and the cold nights heralded the winter in. The fig tree waited patiently for his flower.

One cold and frosty night the Fig tree suddenly awoke, the moon shone a little brighter than usual, but everything was silent. Then the tree realized a sweet scent had infused the night air.

There, among his broad leaves peeped out a little blossom. Silvery and pale in the moonlight, it stretched its petals out one by one, and the whole place permeated with its divine fragrance.

The Forest Spirits all arrived one by one to the Fig tree, drawn by the fragrance. Just as it had bloomed, the flower slowly disappeared.

The tree was very happy that the Creator had kept his word, and thus it came to be that the fig tree blossomed each year during the cold winter months year after year.

The Spirits of the trees and the rivers and the wind and the rain and all the others would come to visit the tree as it bloomed the magical flower in the night.

Word got around and Man and his Sons too came to the Fig tree. Man decided to celebrate his thanksgiving on the same day as the Fig tree. He cleansed himself in the nearby spring and took the blessings of the spirits who would have assembled to see the magical bloom. However, the fig tree bloomed only in the cold winter months. It became very difficult for man to find flowers and fruits so he decided to offer roots and meat instead. The harvest season being over, he did have rice, millet and buck wheat to offer, and so he offered millet beer, rice beer and fried buckwheat cakes and fried rice flour doughnuts called Selroti to the gods and to the Creator. This thanksgiving festival is commonly known as "Maagae Sakrati" but each tribe has its own name for the day.

Thus, started the tradition of offering thanks to the gods among the people of the hills. Over the years the sons of man kept moving around; they must have found it more convenient to plant a fig tree near a spring so that it would be easy for them to bath and cleanse themselves in the very early hours of the day and take the blessings of those gathered. This is why in many villages across the hills one will always find a fig tree just above the local spring.

The Fig tree being so blessed by the creator, Man made his offerings to the Gods and to the Creator in plates made of leaves of the tree locally called "Tapari" in the local language.

Every house in the hills still places their offerings on these fig leaf plates (taparis) and it is considered auspicious to eat out of such leaf plates during festivals and prayers. This practice is still prevalent throughout the hill even today.

3. HOW THE ROBIN GOT A RED BREAST.

Many years ago, when the hills were young, it was said that every living being coexisted in peace and that the spirits of the rivers and the trees walked among the man and beast. Man was wise as he could learn much about the earth through his brothers and man was happy.

The earth was happy and blessed, all living creatures with her plentiful bounty. It was during this time the Robin (a tiny little bird) came into being. He was just an ordinary bird, nothing very special about him except he could lift up the spirits of many tired souls with his sweet song.

He would fly from tree to tree busily feeding himself and would often burst into a beautiful melody that soothed many a traveller walking uphill. One day a strange man made his appearance in the hills.

He was a Son of the hills who was blessed with the second sight and knowledge of medical herbs. He had a headdress of porcupine quills, wore a white robe, had beads and bells crossed around his torso. He walked among the trees, streams, and woodlands collecting herbs and minerals he needed for his prayers and meditation, along with healing herbs that soothed the pain and fever of many a living being.

Surefooted and very strong, he could easily uproot the deep-rooted plants for their tap root, climb up trees, shin up steep rock faces to collect minerals, shoots, barks or fungus and moss. He was gentle and kind and could often be seen trying to heal a broken wing or a deep cut of animals and trees while on these gathering missions. This made the robin greatly interested in this human. He made it a point to follow the shaman whenever he could.

The shaman had come from a distant place to gather herbs. The shy, bright-eyed songster waited impatiently for the shaman to walk up the hill where he lived and gather his herbs.

He wanted to speak with the holy man, but he felt too shy, so the tiny songster would flit from tree to tree and sing his heart out to ensure the holy man felt no tiredness. The shaman forged through the woods for a few days collected the herbs he needed and left.

The Robin thought of the shaman for many days and understood the good the holy man was doing. He hoped he could see him again. After few months, the holy man made his appearance in the woods again. The Robin flew straight to him and excitedly welcomed the shaman forgetting his initial shyness. The shaman gently stroked the excited bird and soon the two became good friends.

The two became inseparable and it wasn't long before the Robin accompanied the shaman all along the hills and mountains. For many years this beautiful friendship lasted and the duo became very attached to one another.

One fateful day the shaman wended his way up high into the hills in search of Panchaule a herb whose roots that is known to cuts and wounds. This herb is species of orchid, the name Panchaule (meaning five fingers) comes from the resemblance of its roots to a tiny human hand.

Unable to find any, possibly because others had harvested the ones that were easily accessible, he kept climbing higher and higher, till finally he found the mountain orchid and collected as many roots as he needed. Night was approaching and the duo hurried down the steep path.

It is said that the Panchaule plant can cure any deep wound or cut but it is not advisable to carry the root around with you. This is because the plant takes great pride in its ability to heal deep cuts and wounds better than other herbs. It is said that the root, wanting to prove its mettle, would cause injuries to happen to anyone carrying it so that it would be used in healing the injury and be given a chance to prove how powerful an herb it is.

Maybe there is some truth in the lore of the Panchaule plant or it was just plain and simple bad luck; the shaman suddenly missed footing in the steep path and fell.

His body tumbled forward and rolled down for a bit before coming to a stop with a sickening jolt among the dark brown rocks. The Robin flew frantically to his friend below and called to him to wake up.

The unconscious shaman remained motionless, and still the little bird pleaded and sang and begged his human friend to wake up, but it was in vain. Night was closing in fast and the cold wind heralded an icy night ahead. The robin knew he had to seek shelter but he was determined not to give up on his human friend, so he stayed close to his friend and waited.

After a long time, the shaman stirred weakly and moaned. The Robin fluttered around in anxious joy. His friend was alive. The knock on his head gave the shaman a terrible headache, and he drifted in and out of consciousness. Perhaps the gods felt sorry for the two friends, and though it was quite cold, the icy wind decided to frolic in the valley below that night. The moon came out and illuminated the stark mountainside.

The Robin fanned the shaman with his wings and watched anxiously for his friend to recover. Sometime in the cold, frosty night, the shaman weakly muttered 'WATER' many times. The poor Robin took flight in the moonlight and looked around for water. He could not find any.

Upon hurrying back to his friend, he found the shaman lying on the ground, still muttering for water. The little bird was desperate to save his friend, so without further thought he plunged his beak into his breast and stood near the shaman's lips to slake his friend's thirst with his own blood.

Drop by drop, the blood ran down the shaman's lips. The Robin lay on his friend's face and waited for him to awaken as life ebbed away from his tiny body.

The golden rays of the morning sun gently nudged the sleeping shaman, who awoke feeling refreshed, and whole and to his horror, he saw his little friend the Robin lying on its side with the last of its blood congealing on its chest, struggling to take its last few breaths. He tasted salt in his lips, wiped his mouth and saw blood. He understood in a flash how the bird had given up its life to save his.

The shaman swiftly opened his bag of herbs (that had come to no harm during his fall as it was secured against his waist with his waist band.)

He called upon the spirits of the mountains and muttered prayers to them constantly as he took out the Pachaule root and crushed it on a rock and ground it to a thick paste. Gently holding the tiny bird in his hand, he applied the paste onto his friend's wounds. While applying the paste, he prayed aloud to all the spirits of the mountains, woodland, rivers, stream and to every living breathing being around for the life of the little creature with such a giant heart.

He called out to The Supreme Spirits of Supta Lung (Great Spirit of the Sky), Bakha Lung (Great Spirit of the Earth) and to Dhe Lung (Great spirit of the Space between the Earth and Sky). He beseeched them to witness the great sacrifice of the little bird and to bless him and heal him.

The Spirits heard him and sent their blessings.

It wasn't long before the bright-eyed songster stretched out its wings and burst into a song of happiness and of life. The Shaman was happy to have his little friend back. Offering their thanks to the Great Spirits, they carefully made their way home.

The Great Spirits watch and see everything they say. The dried blood never came off the Robin's breast and ever since that day he carried the rusty brown colour on his chest that remind us of his selfless act even today

Thus, it came to be his offspring too carried the mark, and to this day an ordinary little bird with a reddish-brown breast still flits from tree to tree, watching humans with great curiosity in their fields and gardens or walks in the woods.

If you should ever chance upon to see an ordinary brown bird with a grey head and a reddish-brown breast, you will know you are looking at a descendant of one of the most selfless creatures that loved man.

Man has changed a lot from what he used to be. He has forgotten old truths, old pledges, and old friendships, but the little Robin still warbles and sings for us cheerfully among the woods, streams and hills.

4. THE MAGNOLIA AND THE BAMBOO

Once upon a time in the hills, lived a chieftain. He had a beautiful wife whom he loved very much. The lady was very kind and noble, and the people loved her much. It wasn't long before they were blessed with a son. The people rejoiced and celebrated the birth of the young chieftain with feasting and dancing for many days.

The little boy was a delight to everyone, and the chieftain would often say, "If only I had a daughter, my happiness would be complete." His wish was granted, and a beautiful baby girl was born to them. The chieftain, happy with his family, made sure everyone else was happy. Peace and prosperity prevailed. Thus, they lived for many years, and then one day, the queen fell ill. Although the chieftain offered a great reward to anyone who could cure her, his efforts were in vain. The lady died one night, leaving the chieftain with his two orphan children. The people mourned their loss and the chieftain shut himself in the palace and refused to see anyone.

Many months passed, but the chieftain remained in the palace. Though he met his councillors, he still refused to go out and see how his people were. So profound was his grief that the alarmed councillors were at a loss as to how they could help their beloved chieftain. Finally, they came to the conclusion that if their chief took another wife, he would feel better. They went in a group to the chief and advised the chieftain to marry again.

"Never," said the chieftain, his brows clouding with anger, and the councillor s were silent, but not for long. They thought that if the king remained unhappy, then he would neglect the state and there would be no peace. They approached the chieftain once again and asked him to think about their advice.

"No," he said and frowned. "But your majesty," said an old councillor. "If you do not marry again, then who will look after the motherless children? Who is going to teach the prince about compassion and kindness, and who will teach the princess about virtue and strength of mind? How will the princess learn to be a good spouse and a good queen? The state needs a queen, and your children need a mother. I pray you think deeply about this."

Faced with this angle of argument, the chief was silent. He then said, "You will have an answer tomorrow."

The next morning the chieftain called the councillor s and said, "I thought about what you have said and am willing to remarry. If you can find a lady worthy to be mother to my children, then I will marry her."

The councillor s searched far and wide and finally found a princess who they thought worthy enough. It was said she was beautiful, brave, strong and clever.

The chieftain and the princess were married, and the councilors thought peace would prevail once more.

The new queen was not what the councilors had thought her to be. She was very beautiful with raven black hair and beautiful brown eyes but she was also wicked, vain and selfish. She wanted to get rid of the little prince so that when she had a son, he would rule the state.

She was angrier still when she saw the princess, who was as beautiful as her mother, was going to grow up into one of the prettiest girls in the hills. She hid her true feelings towards the children when the chieftain was there. Whenever he left the palace, she ill-treated them and made sure they were never happy. If she knew about anything that gave them any happiness, she got rid of it using some pretext or the other.

One day the prince, unable to see his sister suffer, asked the chieftain to intervene and ask their stepmother not to trouble them so much. The chieftain, who had now fallen under his wife's spell, felt like the children resented their stepmother for having taken their mother's place.

Gently, he explained to them that their stepmother was not a bad person. "You must try and please her always. She does love you very much, but you don't love her in return. Do not displease her in any way; she only wants what is best for you. That is my wish."

Realizing that the wicked stepmother had now captivated their father completely, the prince and his sister waited until the chieftain went out on a hunt and decided to flee. The prince made his sister swear she would never ever come back, as he feared for her life. He also swore an oath that he would never leave her side as long as he lived.

They rode deep into the dark forest and lost their way. Tired and unhappy, they dismounted from their horses and fell asleep on the forest floor. The forest spirits had pity on the two orphans and cast a spell on them. When they awoke, the brother and sister found that they had been transformed into two beautiful, slender plants. There they lived in happiness with the pure forest air and rain to nurture them. They were finally happy.

Meanwhile the chieftain came home to find his children missing. He sent out orders to his soldiers to search for them everywhere; he promised huge rewards to anyone who could give him news about his children. He sent out a proclamation he would behead anyone suspected of harming his children and raged and wept and worried, but no one could locate the missing children.

It was only a matter of days before someone whispered to someone else that the children had actually chosen to run away and wished not to be found. This was soon relayed to the chieftain. He had all the maids rounded up and questioned. He got to know about the queen's cruelty and how his children suffered her ill treatment in silence. The maids all said that the children had run away because of the queen.

Wild with anger and worry, he had the queen brought before him and questioned her. Frightened by the chief's anger, she confessed. The angry father had her beheaded. He blamed himself bitterly for not having listened to them. He spent many years looking for them, but he never saw them again.

The grief stricken father decided to work for the good of the people and immersed himself in his work, hoping time would heal his pain. He worked ceaselessly for the good of his people and tried to avoid war with his neighbors. The lands prospered, and the people were happy, but the chieftain still waited in vain for some news of his missing children.

Many years later, a party of the chieftain's army passed through an unfamiliar part of a forest and saw a slender tree with many white-scented blossoms. Next to it stood a tall cane-like plant, sturdy and strong. Having never seen such beautiful plants before, the captain decided to take a couple of the fragrant flowers and show them to the chieftain.

He reached out to pluck them and was surprised to find that the tree suddenly moves its branches away from him violently. He tried again, but the same thing happened. He was surprised. He wondered what it was and asked his soldiers to pluck the flowers. His soldiers tried but met with the same result.

Suddenly the bamboo, the tall cane-like plant next to the tree, spoke and said, "Dear sister Chaap (Magnolia), give the soldiers, one of your flowers. They may be our father's soldiers but they are innocent of the wrong that was done to us. Let them have a flower, and they will be gone."

"No, I will not let a single blossom of mine enter the palace of our hard-hearted father," replied the Magnolia Tree. "When we left that palace, dear brother, did we not promise each other we would never ever darken the doors again? Wasn't it you who said the Chieftain is under the spell of his wife and there was no room for us there?"

The captain was dumbstruck and left behind his soldiers to guard the plants; he rode as fast as he could to fetch the chieftain.

The chieftain arrived in great haste, unwilling to believe what he had heard. He tried to pluck a flower from the tree. When the branches moved away, he realized what the captain had said was true. Humbly addressing the tree, he said, "Dear tree, I know you are no ordinary being; let me have a single blossom and you shall have whatever you want."

"Why, dear father?" mocked the Magnolia tree. "You, who did not see the truth and grant your children a little happiness, what can you give us now?"

"The forest is a happier place than your palace," said the bamboo. "A single blossom from my sister's hair is far more precious than all the wealth you can dream of. Go back to your queen, and leave us alone."

The chieftain embraced the two plants and wept. "Forgive me," he begged. "Come back, dear children; I'm old now. Do not punish me for what I did so long ago."

"No," said the brother and sister together. "Forget us, dear father, and go in peace. Our life is much simpler now, and we are very happy."

The chieftain begged and pleaded, but in vain. The children refused to go back with him. They agreed, he could come and visit them once in a while but they said that they were happier than ever in the forest and he had to go home alone.

The chieftain passed a decree that the two plants be left strictly alone; anyone foolish enough to disobey his orders would have his head cut off.

The chieftain died, the tribe moved away and time marched on, but the legend still lives. Even today in the hills, people do not bring green bamboo into their houses, as they say it brings death to the house. As for the magnolia blooms, they are left in peace because people still believe the gods themselves would not accept the blossoms if used in prayers and ceremonies, and ill luck follows those who are stupid enough to bring Magnolia Blossoms inside the house.

The two plants, protected by this legend, still grow and flourish under the blue skies in the green hills.

5. ALL ABOUT A PIG'S NOSE

Long ago, when the world was young, all animals could talk and think just as we can today. At that time there lived a young farmer in the hills. The Creator had said that he was to till the land and grow food for his family. For this task, the ox had been asked to help him.

It was a very hot day, and both man and beast were very tired. Nevertheless, they toiled hard. The hot sun beat down mercilessly and not a breath of wind could they feel. To make matters worse, the yoke rubbing on the poor beast's back made it quite raw. True to his nature, the ox did not complain but kept on working. The farmer also did not see the sore back, because he was busy thinking how lovely it would feel to rest under a shady tree and drink a pot of cold water. As the day wore on, the poor ox suffered terribly and it was a blessing indeed when the farmer finally unyoked the ox and set him free.

Without saying a word to the man, the ox walked on into the forest, until he came to a tree.

"Friend, Owl, it is I the bull. I have come to ask you for something that will heal my back."

The owl, a wise old bird, poked his head out of the tree hollow and hooted, "Whooo! Send the pig to the Creator. He will prepare an ointment for you."

"Thank you," lowed the ox and walked on to the mud pool where the pig was wallowing happily.

"Dear friend, what brings you here?" asked the pig, pushing his nose towards the ox and taking a good sniff. (About the nose, I almost forgot! In those days, all pigs had beautiful upturned noses perched on the tip of their snouts and not flat like the ones we see today. This pig was no different.)

"Dear friend pig, see how I suffer. Please ask the Creator to prepare an ointment for my sores. See how they bleed," replied the ox. Feeling sorry for the ox, the pig pulled himself out of the pool and set off towards where the Creator lived. On reaching the place, he was pleasantly surprised to find the Creator home. "I know why you have come. Here, take this, and give it to the ox and tell him that his sores will heal soon." Saying this, the Creator handed a packet of leaves to the pig. The pig bowed and left.

On his way back, he thought about the packet and wondered what was inside. Curiosity got the better of him, and he wondered and wondered and wondered some more till he couldn't help himself and he opened the leaf packet.

Inside the packet, he found some pale yellow-brown paste. He pushed his nose towards the paste, as was his habit, and sniffed it hard. At that moment, he stumbled and fell nose first to the ground.

He picked himself up hurriedly and brushed off the leaves that clung to his coarse fur as he looked around for the ointment. But he could not find it. He looked everywhere but the packet was lost.

Feeling very sorry for himself, he sat down and thought about what he was going to do. Suddenly, he realized that something was stuck on his nose. He tried to brush it away, but it would not come off.

He soon realized what it was. The leaf with the ointment had stuck on to his nose. He knew that he had to get it out before it was too late. First, he tugged at the leaf and then tried washing it off, but that was no good. He then turned and twisted and jumped and rolled and frisked and yelled but it did not help. The leaf stubbornly stuck on and did not come off

He rubbed his nose on the ground and then against tree trunks but all he was able to do was rub two holes in it, which served as his nostrils. After that, he had to stop because this nose began to hurt.

Now the pig had a large, flat nose in place of his beautiful one. How ashamed he felt and how sorry he was to have opened the packet. Afraid the other animals would make fun of him, he buried his nose in the ground and wept. Even today you can see the pig hiding his nose in the ground on pretext of looking for grubs.

As for the ox, he waited and waited, but the pig did not come. So, he went to the farmer's wife with his sore back. The kind lady applied a paste of turmeric and oil and some local herbs and very soon the ox was as good as new.

But the story of the pig's nose got around, and even today, in many villages, the pig's nose is considered a source of medicine. They say that if you apply a paste of the pig's nose to your nose, you will never even suffer from nosebleeds. People who suffer from nosebleeds are advised to rub the pig's nose on the grindstone with a little water and put the paste into their noses (about 3 to 4 drops each). They say it works, but I would advise you, dear readers, not to try these remedies, because after all, it's only a story. Isn't it?

6. HOW THE LIZARD CAME INTO THIS WORLD

Long ago, in the far-off hills, there lived a man with two wives. Though the man worked hard, they never had enough money to live in comfort. The elder wife, a plain, hard-working woman, would often say, "If we all do our share of work, I'm sure we would prosper."

"What do you mean by that?" The younger wife would retort, "Just because you are plain, I don't see why I should not try to make myself beautiful. You are jealous of me and that is clear." She was immensely proud of her looks and especially her long black hair. Not a single day would pass by without this lady oiling her tresses and combing them for hours. Whenever the elder wife got angry with her for spending too much time tending her tresses, the younger wife would toss her head and say, "Don't you know , black hair is a symbol of prosperity?"

"Prosperity indeed!, if you did not waste so much time on your appearance, then perhaps you could help," the elder wife would snap. "You are jealous of me, you plain, ugly woman," the younger one screamed, and then they started bickering and arguing, while the poor husband went into the forest to look for some peace and quiet.

Once, the wives quarreled for two whole days, the husband, tired of the constant arguments, decided to do something about it. He gathered all the money he saved and calling his two wives, and said, "I have decided to go to a distant land and earn enough money for the three of us. While I am away, look after the house and please don't quarrel amongst yourselves." He divided his meager savings into three parts. Picking up his share, he set off towards the setting sun. The younger wife tossed her pretty head and taking her share of the money, set out for her parents' house.

The elder wife sadly shook her head after the departing figure and stayed home. With no one to quarrel with, she found that she could devote more time to household affairs. With her share of the money, she bought a pair of goats and began to sell their milk. Their fields, which had so far been barren, soon began to yield vegetables and roots. Slowly, the elder wife began to see better days. She now had five cows, a neat and clean hut, a beautiful garden, and fields that yielded a plenty of crops. She also had a couple of farm hands to help her. Many years passed, but there was no sign of her husband. Patiently, she waited for him to return.

Meanwhile, the younger wife, who had gone to her parents' place, was having a wonderful time as well. Her parents had died a year after her coming and had left their daughter a tidy sum and a beautiful house. However, unfortunately for the lazy woman, there was no one to tell her to work and earn. So, all she did was sit in the sun and comb her hair. The farm began to show signs of neglect, but the young woman was having a wonderful time and did not notice that the weeds overran the garden, the livestock died, and the fields lay barren. She did not care at all. She was so happy that she could now spend days admiring herself in the mirror, and nobody would tell her to work in the fields or fetch water.

In the distant land, the man had done quite well and decided that he now had enough money to live in comfort and to provide for his wives. Collecting his earnings, he started homewards, wondering how his wives fared.

When he reached his house, he stopped, hardly believing his eyes. There, in the place of his broken-down hut, stood a neat little cottage. Busy farmers worked in the fields. Surprised, he walked to the gate and looked around uncertainly. Then he saw his elder wife, busily weeding the pretty garden. She too espied him and welcomed him. He was very pleased by her hard work and how she had brought such good changes to the farm. Looking around, he asked for his younger wife. Sadly, the elder one told him how she left for her parents' place as soon as he had left.

The next afternoon, the man decided to go and see his younger wife. He walked on until he reached her village and made his way towards her house. When he arrived, he stood rooted on the spot because this is what he saw: the roof had caved in, the fence broken down, and the garden choked with weeds. There was his wife sitting in the sunshine, oiling her hair. She turned and saw her husband standing there and greeted him happily. The man was not pleased to see the once beautiful home in such a terrible state. He could see that she had done nothing but waste her time in making herself look beautiful. He thought about how hard his elder wife had worked and of the troubles he had faced in a distant land, all while this vain and lazy woman basked in the sun.

Stepping back, he cursed her, "Since you love to sit in the sun and do nothing except oil your hair, may you turn into a creature so ugly that no one will ever give you a second glance!" He was a son of the hills, and having gained the blessings of his ancestors, the man's words took effect at once.

The lovely young wife was transformed into a lizard. Her shiny black hair vanished, and all the oil she had applied to her hair now glistened on her ugly back. Looking here and there, the lizard, true to the nature of the younger wife, ran out into a patch of sunlight and sat there basking in the sun.

The man turned around and went home to his hardworking elder wife, where he spent the rest of his life in happiness.

7. THE BUTTER AND THE FROG

Once there lived in the hills, a frog. He had built his home near a little village pond and spent his days sunning his handsome green body in the sun.

One day, a farmer's wife was busily churning butter, "whirr …whirrr …whirrr …." the churn sang merrily and pale soft yellow mass of butter started to form.

No one actually saw it happen but they say the lady accidentally tipped the butter churn and the butter rolled out merrily down the hill, straight towards the pond.

SPLASH!

The frog leapt from his stone in fright. He saw a lump of pale-yellow mass floating in the pond.

Curious as he was, he gathered his courage and swimming up to the lump, he touched it gingerly with his finger.

"Ouch! You nearly poked my eye out," said the yellow thing angrily.

"Serves you right for nearly startling me out of my skin," retorted the frog.

"Anyway, what are you?"

"I'm a lump of butter; that's what I am. Now, please help me out of this container." The frog towed the butter away and set him on a stone in the shade.

"Thank you, friend," said the butter. "Now I think I'd better get a move on."

The frog, who had taken an instant liking to the soft yellow mass said, "Where are you going? Perhaps I can help you."

"I need a cool place to rest," said the butter. "It is very hot here."

"Come with me," said the frog, hopping away towards his home. You will find my house a very cool place to live in. You can stay with me if you like. He hopped on for a minute or two with the butter following closely. Here we are."

The butter liked the place and accepted the frog's invitation. The two of them stayed together happily. Every day after sundown, the two friends would go out in search of food, prepare their meal, and share it.

One day the butter said, "Dear friend, why don't we take turns to look for food while the other stays back to prepare the meal? That way we won't feel so tired."

The frog agreed, and from then on, the two friends took turns to go out and forage. The one who was left behind at home did the cooking. A few days passed under this arrangement when the frog realized that the meals prepared by the butter tasted far better than his own cooking.

"How come you are such a good cook?" asked the frog one day. "The meals you cook are very nice compared to the meals, I prepare."

"No, it is just that when you go out to eat, you feel hungry, and hunger makes any food taste nicer," replied the butter.

The frog kept quiet and said nothing. The next time the frog had to go out foraging, he hid himself near the doorway, determined to find out the secret behind the delicious meals.

Unaware his every move was being observed, the butter lit a small fire and placed the cooking pot on it. When the pot was just warm, he hopped into the pot and slid around the pot, letting some butter melt and quickly jumped out. He proceeded to prepared the rest of the meal as usual. Satisfied with his discovery, the frog went out to gather food. He could hardly wait to prepare the next meal.

Impatiently, he waited for sundown so that the butter would go out. Finally, the sun set and the butter set out. The frog excitedly lit a huge fire and set the cooking pot on. When the pot was hot ,very very hot…. he hopped in.

Later….much later, the butter returned home. Looking around, he saw no sign of the frog. He walked up to the fireplace where the fire had died out and looked into the pot. There was his friend stuck to the pot, burnt, charred and black.

Realizing what had happened, the butter sadly shook his head and said, "Poor silly frog!"

Taking the frog out of the pot, he buried him near the pond. He took a long last look at his friend's grave and carrying the cooking pot with him, the butter set off in search of a new house.

8. THE DARJEELING WOODPECKER

Many years ago, in the hills, two little girls were born in the village on the same day. One was born to the headman's wife. And the other was born to his poor cowherd's wife. There was much merrymaking at the headman's house to welcome their daughter, and the headman's wife sent food, money, clothes and gifts to the poor little child born to the cowherd.

The cowherd's wife also worked in the headman's house, and the two girls grew up together. The headman's wife was a kind soul and allowed the little girl to become friends with her daughter. The two girls were great friends. They shared a lot of time together. It did not matter to the two friends that one was the daughter of a poor man and the other had a father who could give her whatever her heart desired; many remarked how the two sometimes looked the same and had the same mannerisms and also the same merry voice.

Many said they could have been twins. The girls didn't mind and didn't pay much heed to all this.

Many years passed, and the headman decided it was time for his daughter to get married. After all, many people had been flooding his home with informal requests asking if they could formally come and ask for his daughter's hand.

His daughter deserved the best, and so he took his time looking for the right boy. Someone who would pamper his little princess and take care of her, He finally chose the son of a wealthy family, and in due time they came to ask for his daughter's hand in the prescribed way.

The bride's price was settled and the agreement was finalised on an auspicious day with the groom's side arriving with a huge red rooster and the girl's side presenting them with an equally large plump hen.

Amidst laughter and games, the girl's side poured out a little oil in a wok, added turmeric and presented the groom's representatives with all the necessary utensils, spices and herbs to prepare the chicken; however according to tradition, they did not give them knives, plates or glasses.

The groom's men who had already come prepared for such eventualities, swiftly set about putting up a hearth and cooking the chicken. The liquor that was offered to them, they brought out their own mugs they had carried and drank out of it. After a while, the chicken was cooked and the men took out the banana leaves, they had carried from home and used them as leaf plates.

Amidst many jokes and laughter, the groom's men had to finish eating both the chickens; no one from the bride's side would help them finish it. Then food that was prepared for the "guests" was served by the bride's kinsmen. The groom's men valiantly continued eating their portion and finally managed to finish it all. This was considered a good sign.

This way the bride's kinsmen had a good laugh, the ice was broken and everyone became good friends so that they would all be able to enjoy the wedding as friends and make things work out amicably during the wedding and later.

The wedding went off without a glitch and the parents bade their daughter a fond goodbye. The two friends parted and amidst tears and embraces, the bride promised her friend that she would come soon and visit her home after a year and take her friend to visit her new home.

The new bride and groom settled down into their new life and were happy together.

Time went by and many came to ask for the cowherd's daughter's hand. She however flatly refused. Her mother told her repeatedly that no prince was going to come and ask for her hand as she was not the headman's daughter, but the girl refused every suitor and declared she would never marry, and she waited for her friend to come home.

Sure, enough the following year her friend arrived. She was pregnant with her first child and was very happy to be home. Her husband took his leave the following day and promised he would be back to take her home with the child.

The two friends were delighted to be back together and spoke about many things. The headman's daughter missed her husband, and often spoke about him and how kind and thoughtful he was.

She also described the various places they had visited and the wonders she had seen. The cowherd's daughter listened with great interest, drinking in every word. The two went for long walks and laughed and giggled like before. It was almost as if they had never been apart.

Soon a son was born and the family rejoiced. They sent word to the husband who arrived in great haste and was delighted to see his baby and his wife. He was so happy and excited and said that he wanted to take them home right away.

His mother-in-law, smiling at his enthusiasm, gently advised him that his wife was a mother for the first time, so she needed all the help she could get from the womenfolk of the household. Looking after a baby was not all that easy, so could he leave her behind for a few months? When the new mother was a little more capable, they would send the child and the mother back. The husband was crestfallen but agreed as this was a normal arrangement in every home. He stayed for a few days and showered his wife and baby with love, attention and gifts. With great reluctance, he took a leave and promised his wife he would visit as often as his work allowed.

The cowherd's daughter devotedly nursed her friend for a few months and helped her with the baby. The new mother felt confident enough to go back home and asked her friend to accompany her. She sent word to her husband not to take the trouble to come and fetch her as she would be escorted to her husband's house by her own kin.

On the day of her departure, the headman came down with a nasty cold and his daughter insisted that no one was to worry about her and that she and her friend would travel together. She said she was worried about her father's health and asked everyone present to take care of her father. She said she wanted regular updates on his condition, and with that, she took leave of her family.

The two friends made their way to the husband's village and decided to take the less travelled short cut through the forest. They walked and walked and had a very pleasant day together.

The headman's daughter stopped by a river and washed up. She laughingly told her friend she did not want her husband to think she had lost her looks and would take some time to look nice.

She said they were close by and that she wanted to look her best. She changed into the new set of clothes she had brought along for the occasion and took out her new ornaments to wear. Her friend stopped her and said she would do her hair first and then she could wear the ornaments last.

The two sat by the river, and the cowherd's daughter combed out her long black tresses. They were both silent. The young wife was busy thinking of her husband and how happy he would be to see them. The cowherd's daughter was silent, wondering why she did not have the same fortune as her friend? Why she would never be able to be this happy, with a happy home and a rich husband who doted on her? After all, she mused. Didn't many say they could have been twins? Then how come one had so much good fortune while the other had nothing?

She looked at the chuckling baby at her beautiful friend who was dreamily staring at the water. Without thinking much, in a fit of jealous rage, the cowherd's daughter pushed her friend off the rock. A loud scream, a dull thud as her head hit the rock below and then a splash as the waters carried the body away. The deed was done.

The cowherd's daughter stood on the rock and stared at the water for a long time.

She was shaking with rage. She had hated her friend for as long as she could remember but had hidden it well. She hated not having things and that her father was not as rich as the headman. She hated this little spoilt brat who had to be fussed over all the time. Life had been so good to her friend, but it had nothing to give her; it was not fair. So well, now here she was trying to set things right for herself. She looked through her friend's belongings and quickly changed into her clothes.

She did her hair and wore the ornaments and looked in the small mirror. Well, she did look exactly like her friend, didn't she?

She gathered the baby in her arms and made her way to her friend's home.

In the excitement of seeing the baby, the husband's family didn't notice much about the subtle change in their daughter-in-law. The husband did.

He was too nice to say it out loud but he found something very strangely unnatural and unpleasant about his wife. He did not feel comfortable around her and took pains to generally stay away. He also found it strange that his wife left the baby in the inner room as she slept next to him and did not wake up when the baby cried.

The wicked woman had decided she didn't want the baby after all and decided to starve him to death. The second night, the baby cried due to hunger as she slept blissfully unaware; the husband got up and rocked his baby to sleep. The baby refused to sleep and wailed in hunger. He placed the baby in the cot and went to wake his sleeping wife when he heard his baby gurgling happily and chuckling, so he settled down for the night and the baby gave no further trouble.

On the third night, the baby wailed late at night. His wife kept on sleeping, and after a while he heard his son laughing and chuckling.

He stealthily made his way into his son's room and there he saw a little bird hovering around his son feeding him something from its mouth. The bird flew out as soon as it saw the husband enter the room.

Puzzled and worried by all that he had seen, the husband hid himself in his son's room the following night. When the baby started wailing, the bird he had seen in the night flew in and soothed his son in a human voice. "Sleep my baby, it murmured. She cannot harm you as long as I am here. Drink this sap and stay strong, my son."

"Some sap under your little nails to keep you happy during the day." "Sleep, my son. She tricked me and killed me but the gods have been kind to you. I have come back to look after you," saying this bird flew in and out of the room several times and fed the child sweet sap.

After the child fell asleep, she stood over the sleeping child fanning him with her wings. A few hours later, when he stirred, she fed him again. As dawn was breaking, she deposited a small amount of sap under the sleeping child's nails. "She is trying to starve you but that is not going to happen, my son, she murmured. The sap I have left for you under your nails will keep you from feeling hungry during the day," saying this, she flew away.

The stunned husband waited for sunrise and checked his sleeping son's nails. There he could see small amounts of milky deposits. In his dream, the child moved and sucked his thumb contentedly.

In a fit of rage, he dragged the impostor before the entire family and made her confess. The cowherd's daughter knowing her evil designs had been found out, confessed everything and begged for mercy. The husband got the village elders to decide her fate. She was branded a murderess banished forever from the land and no one would ever help her or trust her as she wandered around.

The husband waited the following night for the bird and told her what had happened. He cried and begged the bird to stay with him and the bird agreed. She came every night to feed her son and to speak with her husband. The child grew into a young, strong lad and lived happily with his parents till the end of their days.

Whenever white patches appear on people's nails, it is believed the person will get a gift from the gods, as it is a sign that the mother left some sap for the person while he slept.

The sap sucker bird in the story is called the Darjeeling pied woodpecker, and it can be found in the hills of Darjeeling. It can even be seen feeding its young with tree sap whenever it is available. It is said it even dips insects in tree sap first before feeding it to its young, though I can't say I have seen this myself.

9. THE HOUSE OF CINDERS

Once upon a time there lived a little old man and a little old woman.

They didn't have much, so they built a house of cinders and lived there in peace.

One day the little old man wanted to eat 'phullawro'. (a fried delicacy made of buckwheat flour). He mentioned this to his little old woman.

The little old woman always tried to keep the little old man happy, so she searched for some buckwheat that grew by the side of the river.

After she had collected enough grain, she sat down by the huge smooth stones by the river to make some flour.

The little old man wanted to help, so he went into the nearby forest to collect dry firewood. Humming merrily to himself, he went deeper and deeper into the forest thinking about how wonderful the "phullowros" were going to be.

The little old woman was a very good cook, and he knew she would make some mint sauce to go with the dish. He remembered how nice the mint sauce had tasted with the pumpkin flowers the little old woman had made the day before.

'Mmmmmmm", he smacked his lips. He would make sure the little old woman had the driest wood to cook with.

The little old man suddenly found himself seized roughly by the neck and shaken like a rat. His eyes rolled in his head, his teeth clattered violently, and he felt as if all the bones in his body had come loose.

"Oh dear," he thought, "I think I must be in a very bad dream." Then suddenly, he found himself sitting on the grass with a great big thump.

After the world had stopped spinning around him.. He looked up to see a VERY BIG and a VERY ANGRY BEAR looking down at him.

"Man", the bear snorted angrily, "Man... and son of man.... what business brings you to my part of the forest."

Now the little old man was not terribly scared of bears and so he boldly replied, "Your part of the forest, you say? I didn't know the forest belonged to anyone."

"It does now," roared the bear. "This is MY part of the forest; I learnt it from YOU, O Man and Your Sons. You have taken so much from everywhere. You claim parts of the forests too. You even build fences to keep the others out."

"You claim what grows there as yours alone. If the deer so much as dares to nibble a handful of grass within your fences, you chase him away with a terrific din. If the mole digs his tunnel within your fences, you dig him out and kill him."

"I have learnt much from you O Man and with that very same right I say this is MY part of the forest and you have no business being here."

The little old man was quiet. He knew that the bear was right about Sons of Man fencing in land that didn't belong to them in the first place.

He also knew it was wrong on the bear's part to stake claim to the forest, but when a Very Big and a Very Angry Bear is looking down at you, one doesn't exactly care to argue.

"You know, you are right," he said, "but you must forgive me. I do not have any fences, nor do I chase deer and kill the mole. I just live in a house of cinders with my wife and I have come here for the first time today."

The little old woman makes very good 'phullowros'.. "Hot and crisp and soft inside", he smacked his lips. "I thought I would help her by collecting dry wood for the fire. If you say this is your part of the forest then I will just leave the wood here and go home. The little old woman can cook them another time."

With that the little old man turned smartly away and started walking back to where his home lay.

'Now... just a minute," called the bear, who had been thinking about the 'phullowros', he didn't exactly know what they were but they sounded delicious.

"Just a minute......did I say you could not take the firewood with you??"

The little old man kept walking briskly and didn't look back.

The bear rushed up to him and blocked the path, "Did I just say you could not have the wood?" he demanded.

"No, you did not," answered the little old man, "but you did tell me this part of the forest belonged to you and you shook me hard enough to get your point across."

"So, I do get the point. This is YOUR forest and I have no business collecting firewood here."

"I didn't say that. All I said was this is MY part of the forest and that makes all that in here mine." snorted the Bear.

"So, you are giving me the wood then?" asked the little old man.

"Yes, Yes," replied the bear eagerly. "But , in return I do expect some of the 'phullowros' that your wife is preparing. I have heard that Daughters of Man make very good food, better than what we eat."

"I guess you heard right," said the little old man once again remembering all the nice things the little old woman cooked.

"So, if I let you keep the wood... can I taste some of what your little old woman makes?"

The little old man thought this was a fair deal and agreed at once. The bear helped the little old man carry the bundle of wood to the edge of the forest.

"Remember to keep at least a dozen for me," said, turning back into the woods once more.

The little old man helped light the fire and the little old woman started cooking.

The 'phullowros' were delicious and the two of them had a wonderful time eating the piping hot fried buckwheat cakes with mint sauce. Between the two they soon finished the lot. It was only after the last 'phullowro' had been eaten then the little old man remembered the bear.

"Oh my goodness, now what shall we do about the Bear's share!" he exclaimed.

"What Bear? What Share?" asked the little old woman.

The little old man quickly told her all that had happened in the forest.

The little old woman shook her head sadly and said, "I guess the Bear will shake you up again, and I guess he will shake me up too. Our bones will rattle and our teeth will chatter and the world will spin around for quite some time ... I don't think I would like that very much."

"No, you wouldn't," agreed the little old man. "I wouldn't like it at all either."

So, the little old woman thought of a plan. She made the little old man collect a dozen round smooth stones and smeared the leftover oil all over them. Carefully arranging them in a plate, she left the plate on the hearth.

Next, she fetched a huge pot from the potter who lived not far away and the two of them climbed into it.

As darkness fell, the Bear thought about his dinner and slowly made his way towards the little old man's house. He moved quietly in the dark and entered the house of cinders. He sniffed, yes there it was the delicious "phullowros" ready for him to eat.

He reached out and put all of them into his mouth together.

Inside the pot the little old man burped softly. His tummy was finding it hard to digest all those oily buckwheat cakes.

The bear broke his teeth on the stones and spat them out with a great rattle.

"Faugh," he thought. "If this is what Man and Sons of man eat, then they must have very strong teeth. It is a good thing that the Man I met this morning did not challenge me to a fight, I would have surely been beaten. I better go away before he finds me here."

The bear, feeling a little afraid slowly turned to leave.

Inside the pot, the little old man was desperately trying to hold back another burp, it was trying very hard to get out.

In the dark, the Bear gently bumped into the large pot The little old woman screamed loudly and the little old man burped. It was a VERY LOUD AND LONG BURP.

The pot shattered into many tiny pieces and the house of cinders blew away.

The very frightened bear fled as fast as his legs would carry him. He only stopped when he reached his den. His ears were still ringing.

'Goodness me!' he thought, 'not only does Man and the sons of man have very strong teeth, they also have powerful roars that cause stones to fly and houses to be blown away'.

That was the last time the bear tried to lay claim to any part of the forest.

As for the little old man and little old woman, they went looking for a new home and decided to live in a tree hollow where they lived happily till the end of their days.

10. TREATY OF SAMENDEN

Once upon a time, there lived a brave hunter. He was cunning and shrewd, and could hunt and trap great many animals for his food. This hunter lived in the low-lying hills, and unknown to him, a Sokpa (Yeti) had his home and hunting grounds in the steep hills above.

One day the hunter was tracking deer and having found fresh tracks, started following them. The tracks led higher and higher towards the steep hills but the hunter doggedly followed. The hot sun beat down and the hunter was tired and thirsty. Nevertheless, determined to get the deer, he kept on going further up into the mountains. Suddenly he stopped and drew back. There in a clearing, on a huge boulder sat a shaggy Sokpa devouring the deer in greedy mouthfuls. He espied the hunter and raised his hand in a sign of welcome. Realizing that he was seen, the hunter stepped out and greeted the Sokpa in return.

The yeti was frightful to look at, with shaggy fur covering his whole body and long, heavily muscled arms and legs. He had very sharp teeth and an ape-like face with a very flat nose that spread across his face. The hunter, though a brave man, felt a slight chill of fear tingle down his spine, but he looked at the creature on the face and pretended he was not afraid.

He pointed to the remains of the deer and then pointed at himself, meaning to say that the deer belonged to him. To his surprise, the creature angrily replied, "What do you mean the game is yours? It strayed across my path and thus became mine." His shaggy eyebrows drew together in a dreadful frown. His eyes glowed, and his wide nostrils flared.

The hunter thought, "He thinks because he is strong and big, he can get away with another man's game but I will not give up without a fight." Calmly, he continued, "If you think that your strength lets you rob another man's meat then I say you are but a common thief." Stepping up to the boulder, he said loudly, "I challenge you to fight me and show me how strong you are." The yeti was very annoyed, but said nothing and kept on chewing the last bits of flesh from the deer (which by now was reduced to a pile of bones).

The hunter brandished his club and jeered, "Afraid are you, you big, greedy thief?" Now the yeti grew angry when he saw the hunter taunting him, and getting up from the boulder, he threw back his head and screamed out the awful hunting cry – "AAAAIIIIIIEEEEEE." The hills rang with the sound, and an echo answered. The forest stood still. The hunter was not impressed. Swinging his club, he clubbed the Sokpa in the ribs and the duo began to fight.

They hurled boulders at each other, they tore up trees and used them as clubs and missiles, and they flattened the hills, as they fought in the mountains. They grappled, fell, tumbled, and yelled.

For fifteen days and fifteen nights, they fought without any rest. On the fifteenth night, they were both so exhausted that they were forced to rest. While they rested, the hunter thought, "Oh dear, now I am really in trouble. This creature is bound to get back his strength and that will be the end of me." The Sokpa thought, "No one has fought so bravely and so well. It would be a good thing to make friends with such a brave man."

The wild creature spoke up, "You know, brother hunter, I thought I was the strongest creature alive. But now, I see that you are just as strong. It would be a shame, to let an opportunity for friendship go to waste. Let us be friends and divide the hunting grounds between us so that there is no further dispute." The hunter agreed and said, "Let us go home and come back here to decide this matter fairly." Each went home and slept soundly as tired men who have fought for fifteen days and fifteen nights' sleep.

On the appointed day, the hunter gathered some berries and potatoes and yams and went to the spot where they had decided to meet. He waited for a while humming a tune and wondered if the great ape had forgotten about the meeting.

After some time, the yeti came along the forest path. He set down his offering for the hunter - a blue sheep, found only in the mountains, and a delicacy for the Sokpa. Not to seem unversed in the laws of hospitality and friendship, the hunter pushed forward his offerings. The two solemnly accepted each other's gifts with respect.

It was a grave matter, and both were very quiet. The hunter lit a fire and skinned the sheep. The creature sat on his haunches with his shaggy arms crossed. The hunter roasted the meat and buried the potatoes and yams under the hot ashes to bake them. The giant ape, used to eating raw meat, thought it was a terrible waste to burn the food, but he kept quiet.

After the food was cooked, the hunter asked the Sokpa to divide the hunting grounds. For an answer, the Sokpa picked up a huge triangular boulder and lifting it high above his head, brought it crashing down into the ground with all his strength. Only the tip of the boulder, about a foot and a half, remained above the ground.

The hunter said, "All the lands that fall below this rock are mine, and those above are yours." The yeti nodded and, the deal was done and they both sat down to eat.

The Sokpa offered the meat to the hunter and the hunter offered the baked yams and potatoes to the Sokpa. Having eaten raw meat all his life, the creature carefully sniffed at the baked potato. The hunter said, "Eat it; you'll like it."

He took a potato in his mouth, and trying not to pull a face, he chewed it carefully. To his surprise, he found the taste strangely pleasing. "There, you see;" said the hunter. "You'll like it even better after you eat another." He pushed the pile towards the Sokpa who happily ate up every single potato, and gobbled up the yams and berries as well. The hunter then offered him some meat, but the Sokpa politely declined, as it was bad manners to eat what one had brought as a gift.

"Do you want some more potatoes?" Asked the hunter, and the great ape nodded eagerly. "Then open your mouth and I will feed you myself," he said. The Sokpa opened his mouth and waited. The hunter had placed some smooth round stones in the fire while baking the potatoes, and now those stones had become white-hot. Picking these up, the hunter rammed them down the poor Sokpa's throat, causing the simple creature to die a horrible death.

The hunter buried his enemy and became the lord of all the hunting grounds in the hills.

Though this took place many years ago, the story of the Sokpa is not forgotten. The place where the treaty rock lies embedded in the ground is known as the "Sokpa Dhunga" (meaning the Yeti Stone). You can still see it today at a place called Samenden.

The people of Samenden still go to the Sokpa Dhunga and offer flowers and leaves to pacify the spirit of the Yeti, who was deceived. The people also say that sometimes they can see a shadowy form of the Yeti flitting across the hills calling out mournfully to the mountains.

Samindin or Sameden as some pronounce it, lies above Siri Khola village. One can get there by going to Rimbik and then to Siri Khola. The very popular Sandakphu Trek starts from Rimbik and any of the locals can give you directions to Saminden, if you wish to see the Yeti Stone even today.

When I was there at Saminden, many years ago, I did meet a father and son duo who claimed the Yeti still existed. The father said he had seen the Yeti walking among the trees just above the Sokpa Dhunga (Yeti Stone).

The son claimed as a teenager he and his friends had gone to the forest to collect wood and they had seen huge foot prints leading towards the hill top. He said the foot prints measured roughly about two feet and the space between the prints was around five to six feet. He didn't exactly tell me the measurements but drew them on the ground for me. I really didn't know what to believe.

11. THE TWELVE HORSEMEN

The plains reeked of slaughtered corpses and the sun blazed upon the blood-soaked ground. Dharma had fled the land of Sindh.

Guests were no longer respected. Wang Huen Tse, the Chinese emissary had escaped narrowly and taken shelter in Too Faan (Tibet). His faithful band of men lay dead upon foreign soil, never more to see their land. They had never expected the assassins.

O-la-na-shung (Arjuna) The corrupt and shrewd minister who had managed to murder the sons of Srivardhana (Harshavardhana) had usurped the throne.

When Wang Heun Tse had arrived in the land he had been kept in the dark about the death of Harsha. The usurper had been almost successful in murdering the harbinger of peace. The emissary was not going to let the usurper go unpunished.

The King of Too Faan had been a powerful warlord and was known for his determination and military prowess. It was believed that he had asked the Chinese emperor for the hand of a Chinese princess. When the emperor refused, he declared war upon them. The emperor of China finally relented and wed his distant niece, the Lady Wei Chun to him.

Later, it was said that the warlord had a dream of another beautiful princess in the city of Yabu Yagal (Kathmandu). He sent his emissaries there with offerings of gold on a hundred horses.

It is also said that the Lichhavi king of Yabu Yagal, flew into a terrible rage and refused to give his daughter to a barbaric warlord who now called himself a king.

The monarch told the emissaries there was no law, no dharma in their land. It was a land of hungry ghosts, while in his land no one ever went hungry, and dharma reigned, and the sound of the flour mills never ceased.

The war lord had sent three letters written in gold on blue paper pleading his case eloquently in the language of the King. Each time the king refused a letter was handed to him.

Legend says that the Laichhivi king was finally won over by such humility, persistence and eloquence. He agreed to wed his pious daughter Bhrikuti to the warlord. The princess Bhrikuti and her entourage were escorted up to Mangyul by her father and entered Too Faan riding on her elephant, clasping a sandalwood idol of the Tara. The princess had taken Dharma to the barbaric land of Too Faan.

As time went by, the warlord learnt the way of Dharma from the beautiful and pious Lady Wei Chun and Lady Bhrikuti and became famous in history as the mighty Tibetan king Songtsen Gyampo.

Wang Huen Tse approached the mighty king for assistance, and the King, outraged by such a breach of trust and open insult to the Chinese emperor, sent 12000 men and asked the King of Nepal to help as well.

King Narendradeva, who once had been overthrown after his father's death and had to live in exile in Too Faan owed much to his generous brother –in- law who had helped him re-establish Lichhavi rule in Nepal. He was only too happy to extend his support to his benefactor.

He immediately put up 12 divisions of cavalry of 7000 men each, at once and asked for them to be led by King Songtsen Gyampo's own commanders. He also extended great honor and kindness towards Wang- Huen -Tse.

War ensued and the plains of Too-po-ho-lo (Tirhut. Bihar) ran red with blood. The 12 cavalry divisions were headed by skilled commanders from King Songtsen Gyampo's own army. Under their leadership, the skilled Laichhavi archers created much damage to the enemy. The fierce onslaught of the twelve thousand strong warriors was just too much for Oo-La-na-shung's army; they could not stand the attack for long.

The Oo-la-na-shung made good his escape and left his soldiers had to face the ferocity of the barbarians. It is said that over 3000 soldiers were beheaded and ten thousand were drowned in the Bagmati River. Never before had the plains of Too-po-ho-lo seen such a bloody massacre.

Oo-la-na-shung launched another attack a few days later but was captured. His followers were beheaded at once and he was taken to the Chinese court to answer to the Chinese Emperor himself.

Wung-Huen-Tse was rewarded with the post of a councilor, at the Chinese court.

King Stongsen Gyampo asked the twelve commanders of the cavalry to stay back and mingle and live with the locals of Nepal. They were to make the land of Lady Bhrikuti their home and help maintain law and order and peace.

The Twelve commanders bowed to the wishes of their monarch. In order to show the citizens of the land that the 12 commanders were skilled in the art of war and were capable of protecting them, the 12 commanders held a festival where people could come and watch them perform amazing feats of arms.

The day began with skillful riding and handling of horses and then amazing feats of archery while riding a galloping horse. The people were suitably impressed, and then the twelve horsemen dismounted, and an expectant hush filled the air.

The Leader of the commanders, Moktan, stepped forward. He walked to the center of the field carrying a heavy metal bar. Amidst cries of wonder and amazement, he lifted it high in the air and with his bare hands, crushed it into a ball of twisted metal.

Bal was next. He seized an iron spear and flung it hard against a very tall and dusty, dry rocky cliff. The spear penetrated the hard rock smoothly, and lo and behold, clear fresh water rushed out of the hole in the cliff. The people were amazed.

Up stepped Bomzan, his long hair fluttering in the wind. With a smile on his lips, he carelessly removed the thick gold necklace from around his neck and stretched it easily into a thin golden wire with his bare hands. The people cheered but not done with that, he wove a beautiful basket with the golden wire, and once he was done, he collected water from the very same spring that Bal had created. The weave was so perfect that not a single drop of water could make its way out. Amidst roars of approval and whistles, he walked off the field to make room for the next commander.

Ghising walked to the spring and followed the runoff, where it joined a lake nearby. With just a wave of his hands, steam started rising from the surface and swirled heavenward. People cried out in fear. Steam billowed upwards and collected high above the surface of the lake and hung there like a huge white cloud. Within minutes there was no sign of the lake; only a huge dry crater marked the spot. High above the dry crater hung a thick white cloud like a fluffy cotton boll that had just burst into bloom.

Theeng, the next commander stepped up. Seeing the look of horror on the people's faces, he turned towards the cloud and with a few muttered prayers caused the cloud to descend. Darker and darker turned the cloud as it came lower and lower. Just when it was a few meters from the ground, Theeng created a hailstorm with just a clap of his hands. Hailstones started pelting down into the dry crater. With an ominous roar and mighty clatter, it kept pelting down till there was no sign of the cloud and the lake was now overflowing with hailstones.

It was Pakhring's turn. He brought a big bronze plate with him and set it on the ground. People were already afraid of what they had seen and he decided not to scare them anymore. He muttered a prayer to his gods and stared at the plate. In a few minutes, there was a loud clatter as the bronze plate shattered into a thousand little pieces.

Up jumped Goley and walked swiftly around the field, muttering incantations, and lo and behold, the midday sun slowly darkened, and people could see the stars slowly twinkling one by one till all the stars blazed in their cold splendor and the bejeweled sky convinced everyone it was really very late and they ought to be at home and in bed.

Just as they thought of leaving, Gaiba, the next commander, snapped his fingers very loudly thrice and the entire starry sky was covered in a thick murky, fog. People felt lost and couldn't see where their friends and family were. Shouts of terror rose from the crowd.

Syangden hurried forward and with a wave of his hands created fire that raged all around them and quickly dispelled the thick, dark haze. Higher and higher the flames rose, and the fire roared with the wind. It was getting hotter and hotter.

Before the fire went out of control, Syangden nodded towards the calm and composed Theeng who walked completely unafraid to where the fire burnt the brightest and hottest and gently caused rain to fall and extinguish the fire. He coaxed the rain to fall with a little vigor when the flames were dangerously high and then cajoled it to fall gently on the smoldering embers. After a while, people could see the sun shining merrily and the sky looked bluer. There were still two commanders left.

Mikchan moved forward and picked up a stick. He tapped the stick on the ground a few times, and the stick had now turned into a very poisonous snake. It slithered among the grass, growing bigger and bigger by the minute. It hissed angrily and reared up as if looking for something to attack.

The youngest of all the horsemen, Bozu smiled cheerfully and whistled into the wind. Still whistling and clicking gently, he created a vulture out of thin air. The vulture flapped its wings picked up the snake in its talons, and swallowed it to the relief of great many people in the crowd.

After this display of prowess, the twelve horsemen had no trouble finding friends or family in the new land. Powerful families vied with one another to have alliances with them and cheerfully gave their daughters and large dowries as gifts.

The twelve horsemen called themselves and their clansmen the Tamangs, roughly translated to horse-borne warriors, and settled in their own lands called Kipat. There were 12 kipats in Chatara, and Dhadhing districts of central Nepal. The kipats were named after the 12 commanders themselves. Moktan Kipat, Bal Kipat, Gishing Kipat, Goley Kipat, Theeng Kipat, Gaiba Kipat, Syangden kipat, Pakhring Kipat, Yonzon Kipat, Bomzan Kipat, Mikchan Kipat and Bozu Kipat.

The sons and daughters of these gallant heroes lived in peace and prosperity in their lands for many years. That is until 1768AD, when winds of change came sweeping across the tribal lands and Hindupati King Prithivi Narayan Shah decided to unify the lands into one unified country called Nepal.

12. CHARI BHUTLAE OR THE BIRD FEATHERED CLAN

There was a time when people still lived in forests, and houses were unheard of. Humans lived solely on whatever they could find or hunt in the dense jungles. Among the many of the nomadic tribes that lived in the foothills of the Himalayas. There was a very clever tribe. They lived together and had learnt to help each other and avoided fighting among themselves or with other tribes.

Every day the men and women went in small groups to different parts of the forest to gather food. They hunted or trapped game while the women collected fruits and edible leaves. In the evening, the whole tribe would gather in a certain place and share the day's finds. This way they ensured that the ones who were not so lucky at finding food for the day did not remain hungry.

Many more years passed, and the tribe grew larger. It became difficult to find food for all. The fact that some of the lazy ones did no hunting at all and did not help either! Slowly but surely, disharmony set in. The elders decided that it was time for the tribe to be split up into groups. The tribe was then divided into smaller tribes. Each tribe moved away and started to fend for themselves.

One of the tribes that moved away from the jungles reached another forest higher up in the hills and decided to stay there. The forest was a pleasant place with fruit trees and snow-fed streams. The tribe found that there was enough game to feed the whole tribe with ease. The tribe settled down and once again, peace and harmony set in.

Then came winter — a very bitter winter it was.

The fruit trees were bare, the forest was silent, and the streams were friendly no more. Not having experienced such bitter cold before, the tribe suffered and thought longingly of the warm plains they had left behind. Food was hard to find, and night fell very quickly. The dark and cold nights stretched for many hours before it was light. That winter, the tribe lost half their numbers to starvation and sickness.

The frost retreated, and the sun warmed the hills. Winter was gone. The tribe crept out of their rude shelters and warmed their thin bodies in the sun. They had learnt a bitter lesson. They wanted to leave the forest in search of better land, but many did not agree. They pointed out that though the winter had been rough, the forest was undoubtedly the most beautiful and bountiful place during the summer and the spring. Realizing what most of them said was true, the tribe decided to stay and battle the winter. That was how their wanderings came to an end.

The preparations for winter started early that year. Men and women worked together to plant edible roots, and store seeds after drying them in the sun. The animals they trapped were kept in captivity inside deep pits, so that the tribe could eat when game was scarce. They collected and dried sweet grass to feed the trapped animals as well as for their winter bedding. They dug a huge pit and lined it with a thick bed of grass and put the green vegetables and fruit there. Then they covered the food with a thick blanket of dried grass and covered the pit up with mud.

While all this was going on, one tribesman was busy thinking about how the tribe could keep warm. He realized that unless the tribe found a way to keep warm, they would surely die, even though they had enough food to eat. He thought deeply about the matter and felt that he had to find a way to clothe the tribe suitably for the winter.

He started experimenting with different types of leaves only to find that the result was not as good as he had expected. Upon meeting with failure at every step, the man gave up and began to despair. "All the animals have a form of protection from the cold," he brooded. "Even the little birds survive." There he stopped and laughed. He had found a solution to his problem. He knew that his tribe would survive.

Calling all his tribesmen together, he asked them to gather every single feather they could find. He also advised them not to throw away the feathers of the birds they killed. As months passed, the heap of feathers grew larger and larger, but the man did not stop. His friends, who had at first obliged his rather strange request, now began to think that he was mad. But the man did not stop. Throughout the summer and autumn months, he collected feathers.

Sometime later, the migration of the birds and the cold nights heralded the coming of another winter. The man went out one morning and collected tree sap in many dried gourd shells. Coming back to where his tribe was, he gathered his people together and let them into his secret. "All these months you have thought me mad," he said, "but now I am going to teach you how to keep warm when the cold winter months begin."

Leading them to the feather heap, the man proceeded to apply the sticky sap all over his body, while his fellowmen watched half amused. Once he had covered himself thoroughly with sap, he started to stick the feathers all over. When he had finished, he looked rather strange, but the tribe saw his point, and everyone followed suit.

That winter the tribe survived, and they were able to move around even in the bitterest cold, thanks to the coat of feathers.

The other tribes slowly got used to this rather strangely apparelled group. They promptly christened them as the CHARI BHUTLAE, literally meaning "Bird-feathered." This started the practice of dressing in feathers and furs, though the furs became more popular. This was because it took much trouble to collect enough feathers to clothe an entire tribe.

The Chari Bhutlae, however, did not opt for furs. They simply stuck more feathers on their feather-coated bodies, and this tribe was later known as the WAKCHALIS (meaning the same as Chari Bhutlae in the local dialect). That is how the Wakchalis got their name. In these modern times, they are called the SAMPANGS, who form one of the many sects of the Khamboos/ Rais.

It is said this gentle tribe of the Kirati Rais is blessed with the second sight and has a larger number of Dhaami/Maangpa (shamans) from their tribe than shamans and healers from other tribes. People also refer to them as the Dhaami/Maangpa Jaat (shaman tribe).

13. THE SWALLOWS NEST

Long years ago, when the hills were young, the Creator had been in a particularly good mood and had taken the trouble to create many beautiful big birds and a great many little birds. He filled them with music and colours and joy and beauty. Once they swooped, swirled and glided into this world, the earth became a better place for many.

These birds were loved by one and all, and various trees spirits, river spirits and animals befriended them. Everyone wanted them to live near them. So, the birds did. Some learnt the ways of the river and lived among the murmuring waters.

Some learnt the ways of the earth and lived close to its warmth. Some learnt the ways of the icy rocks and lived in the stark beauty of the snowclad lands.

Others learnt the ways of the trees, and yet others learnt the ways of animals and learnt to hunt and eat the flesh of other prey.

The little creatures brought melody to the hills, and welcomed the morning and the spring. The wind carried their songs far and wide.

It was springtime and all the little creatures felt wonderfully happy and free after the long, cold winter. Of course, the trees, the rocks and the rivers had sheltered them but winter had been hard to bear for most of the songsters.

This was because none of them had learnt to make their own homes. The trees had tried protecting them with their branches and the river had asked the reeds to block out the winds, but it had always been so cold.

"We must all learn how to build a home for ourselves first." Said the birds.. "We cannot expect others to look after us always," said the woodpecker.

"You are right," "we can ride the wind in the spring and summer but in the winter the same wind becomes our enemy."

"Besides, its too much trouble trying to raise our young without a house," observed the Drongo.

After some time, all the birds agreed that they all needed a home and all of them needed to learn how to make one.

"I think I already know how I am going to build my house," said the wood pecker, "I keep boring holes in the trees to help them get rid of the worms. Perhaps it would be best if I just lived in one of the bigger holes I hollow."

Everyone thought this was a wonderful idea and congratulated the woodpecker for being so smart.

"My friend the bear lives in a den," remarked the weaver bird. "It is warm because it has only one small opening, of course it does become a bit smelly, but I think I can make my house just like it. All I have to do is weave some grass and shape my house like a den, a narrow passage to go in and a big chamber inside, and still thinking aloud the weaver bird who always put his thoughts into action, flew away.

"There he goes," said the dove. "One can be pretty sure he will make it work. He is the most determined amongst us all don't you think?" And all the birds agreed.

"I have been thinking," said the owl suddenly. "Why don't we all try and find our friends and see how we could all learn from them and build our homes similarly?"

"That makes sense," said the Kalij Pheasant who had befriended the deer and ran to where her friend the Deer sat in the grass below the big ferny hill.

The rest of the birds too thought it was a great idea and went to where their friends were. The owl was the squirrel's friend; he too decided to make tree hollows his home. The Bat was the cicada's friend, so he decided to just hang from trees in the warm weather and then find a warm cave in the colder months.

The Quail decided the ground was as good a place as any home one could wish for and made her home there like the rabbits and like the pangolin.

This was how all birds went their different ways trying to learn to build their homes. All, except the swallow.

The swallow had befriended the wind before the eagles and kites had. She had always taken great delight in floating in the wind and smiling up at the clouds. All that had changed when the eagles and kites had taken to riding the wind.

The wind found it great fun to roar and whistle with his new found brothers. The eagles screamed and the kites whistled as they rode the wind up into the clouds and then hurled themselves earthwards at breakneck speed only to swoop up just in time and gently brush the tips of the tall pines with their wings.

The swallow had watched in jealousy and refused to be friends with the wind thereafter. He was a swift flier too but did not want to share the fun with the eagle and the kite.

She decided to build her home by herself. The eagles and the kites learnt to build their nest from the wind. Just as they had seen the wind tear away small twigs and take them swirling over the trees. They plucked dry twigs and swirled over the clouds to finally put them together among the very tall hill tops and tree tops. The swallow did try to copy them in secret but she was not strong enough to break off the dry twigs. Being a proud and haughty bird, she refused to ask for help.

Her valiant efforts to break away a twig almost as big as herself had not escaped the sharp-eyed eagle. The kite too had observed how the little swallow had watched them and then tried to imitate them.

Feeling sorry for the little bird, the eagle sent a message to the sparrow asking him to help the swallow.

The wind carried this message to the sparrow, who promptly twittered his apologies to the Great Eagle and said he had to get to the warmer plains where grain was being harvested, and he was already a little late due to all the nest building.

With that he, launched himself into the air, and away he went flapping his little wings very hard, still twittering out his apologies. Besides, he didn't exactly care much for the haughty swallow or the eagle.

The Kite sent a message to the very clever crows to help the swallow but the crows only laughed and laughed and sent back a very impudent message to the Kite that included some very rude bits like pecking his eyes out and plucking out his brown feathers. The crows thought the eagle and the kites had no business telling them what to do.

The Kite was furious.

The wind thought of a plan and asked the two friends to leave the problem to him. He glided gently over the green grass and went to the wasp and promising to lead the way to the sweetest flowers and fruits. The wind tried to coax the wasp into helping the swallow.

"I don't know why you ask me to help her. I really don't really like her much," snapped the wasp waspishly. "It's only because of my stinger she hasn't eaten me up, and now I'm supposed to help her with her house."

The wind was patient and hummed a soothing tune and sang to the wasp about sweet nectar and sweeter fruits and by and by the wasp, who had a sweet tooth, agreed.

He flew buzzing contentedly thinking about sweet nectar and came to the swallow.

"I have come to help you with your house," the wasp said. "Do you want my help or not?"

The swallow, who was feeling rather sorry for herself, was only too glad that someone had come to help her out.

She meekly followed the wasp to the riverside and watched him scoop out a bit of wet mud from the riverbank and fly over to a big rock and carefully lay the foundations for the nest. Following his example, she scooped out a bit of mud and carried it across and bit by bit the nest started to take shape.

"Not there."

"We have to think this through."

"Hold on, I don't think that much mud would be enough there"

"A little less wet mud, please"

"Don't be so impatient. You have to let it dry for a bit." The swallow was getting heartily sick of the wasp's instruction.

"If you don't check to see how the sides are."

"I know. I know. I know."snapped the swallow. What makes you think you know it all?" She trailed off as the wasp buzzed angrily.

"Well then make your nest yourself. This is what happens when we try to meddle in affairs that are of no concern to us." With that and another angry buzz the wasp flew off in a huff.

The swallow looked at the half-built nest and decided she would build it on her own. Away she flew to the riverbank scooped some mud out and rolled it into a pellet and back she flew to the rock, to and fro, to and fro. Alas! she did not quite know how to complete the nest.

Tired and exhausted at the end of the day, all she was left with was a half built cuplike nest stuck to the side of the rock. She decided it was just as nice as any other nest and made it her home. Tired and exhausted, she settled in for the night. Well, it was a lot warmer than sleeping in the open and if she made the cup a little deeper, she would be really comfortable. "If she could stick the mud under a rocky outcrop well. She would have a roof," drowsily thinking such thoughts she fell asleep.

The wind thought the wasp had done enough. The next morning, as promised, the wind led the wasp to the sweetest nectar and fruits. The wasp and its sweet tooth were happy.

The eagle was satisfied the little bird had a safe place for itself.

The Kite never forgot the rude message from the crows and started a feud with them. The crows were more than happy to take it further still.

The swallow decided she didn't like anyone much, especially the wasp and decided to live near Man who also didn't like the wasp.

This is why the swallow lives in a cuplike nest, and we often find swallows building their nest in our homes.

14. A TALE ABOUT THE MANGAR LANGUAGE

Dedicated to the memory of my dear brother, **Mahendra Reshmi Thapa Mangar.**

Once upon a time in the hills far away there lived a young lad and his mother. They lived in a small village tucked away somewhere among the foothills of the snowy peaks. The village people herded sheep and had a few heads of cows as well. Life was hard, but the people were used to it and did not think much of it.

The old lady was not happy. She had grown up in a house full of many siblings and had always wanted a large family. This was not to be. Her husband had died many years ago and left her with her only child. Her son had now grown into a young, strong lad of 21, and to her disgust, he showed no signs of bringing home a daughter-in-law for her.

She thought about the times she had tried to cajole the village belles for her son. Though the girls had accepted her gifts and shown they were more than willing to marry her son. The lad displayed no interest in the matter to her dismay. All the nice girls were married one by one.

It was no surprise therefore to have her grumble every day and berate her son for being a wicked and selfish fellow for not bringing home a wife to help his 'old mother who was going to die in a few days'.

The son, on the other hand, was extremely good-natured and had a big heart. He did not want to get married because he had seen how marriage changed his friends. He had seen all his friends fall in love and get married. In the beginning, it was all about how beautiful, and nice the girl was and after marriage, it was all about how difficult it was to keep their wives happy and things got worse as the children grew.

He had seen many of his happy-go-lucky friends forget how to laugh and slave away from dawn to dusk for their many children. He felt with so much responsibility to shoulder, they no longer had any fun. He valued his freedom too much and carefully avoided all the young ladies in the village like the plague. He felt he could never love any girl that much.

One evening he sat down to dinner and patiently listened to his mothers, usual complaints about how old and weak she had become and how unfortunate she was because the girl she had hoped her only son would bring home as his bride was now married to someone and how she was sure that someone would prosper greatly with his clever bride.

The lad laughed good-naturedly and teased his mother by saying she had forgotten to add how the girl she had chosen for him three years ago and had even given her a golden ring was now married to a very successful wool trader and had borne him a healthy daughter who was as beautiful as the moon.

The old woman got angry and grumbled that all the other village women of her age were so lucky. They had two, three or even five daughter-in-law to complain about whenever they met, but here she was all alone without a daughter-in-law to complain about.

"And I don't think I will be lucky enough to see any grandchildren before I die. I am really most unfortunate," she sighed deeply and was quiet for a while.

Seizing this break in her monologue, the lad told her he would be going into the hills for some salt and herbs.

"I will be gone for three or four days, don't worry about the sheep; I have asked my friend to come and take care of them for a few days." His mother said "She would come and keep you company every evening."" "She just wants to come over to brag about how her three hardworking daughters in law don't let her lift a finger and how one is an excellent cook, another is so skilled at weaving and the third daughter in law is so strong that she tends to the farmlands all by herself."

"You forgot about the vain, one and the foolish one," her son teased; "You could ask her if she would give them to you. That way you could have the ones to complain about and both of you would be happy."

"Any way," he continued. "You have me to complain about, so the two of you should be fine."

"I have already boiled and set the sheep wool to dry. You can sit in the sun and discuss the next girl you have selected for me while carding and spinning and before you know it, I will be back. Who knows I may meet a beautiful sheep in the forest and bring her home to you."

Leaving his mother grumbling about his stupidity, he turned in for the night.

Early next morning, after completing the chores around the house and making sure there was enough dry firewood for his mother, he packed the things he needed and left.

He walked to the river and headed up stream. After he had walked a fair bit, he stopped and tasted the water; he could taste a faint trace of salt and kept walking. He knew there was nothing to be afraid of as there were no dangerous animals around. He camped for the night and the next morning he set off again. By noon, he found a spot where the water ran through a bit of salty rock and decided to halt. He collected the salty water in a container and lit a small fire. As the water bubbled away, he kept adding more.

He enjoyed his time alone. He collected the herbs he needed and spread them out on a rock to dry. He kept adding dry wood to the fire and more salty water to the container. Bit by bit, he had a small amount of salt he had harvested from the water. The short happy days flew by and it was time for him to return.

When he woke up in the morning, the last stars were still fading. As he silently collected his belongings, he thought he heard someone singing. Not knowing what to expect, he swiftly drew his khukuri from its sheath and crept silently from rock to rock towards the song.

The last star glimmered faintly and dawn broke. Seated on a rock and singing softly to herself, sat a beautiful woman. The first golden rays of the sun bathed her in its golden light.

The young lad had heard many stories of river sprites and nymphs; he silently approached and grabbed her by the hand. The frightened nymph did all she could to slide back into the water but the lad held fast.

"Please calm down," he said. "I mean you no disrespect or harm, please just talk to me. I am letting go of your hand now; please do not run away, I just want to talk to you."

The nymph calmed down and nodded. Time stood still as the mortal and the fairy spoke and by the time the stars came out, the two were in love and had decided to wed.

The nymph agreed to marry the lad as she saw he had a pure heart. She had only one condition. He had to tell the world that she was dumb because when she spoke, she could speak only the truth, and if humans found out she was a fairy, they would fear her and avoid the lad and his mother. The nymph was aware of the evil that lurked in the hearts of humans.

They would ask her to fulfil their wishes, ask her to predict their future or worse, they could blame her for anything that went wrong in their lives. It was best for all that she never spoke to anyone except the boy and let the world think she was unable to speak. The day people found out she could speak, she would return to her home and never live with him as his wife. She made him promise he would not stop her.

The lad who had fallen head over heels in love with her agreed readily. He would have agreed to anything to have her as his bride.

The old lady finally had a daughter-in-law she could complain about to her friends. She was pleasantly surprised to see how skilled her daughter-in-law was at carding, spinning and weaving. It wasn't long before the local traders flocked to her home for blankets, wool and cloth. Soon the old lady could confidently brag about how her daughter-in-law spun the softest wool and wove the finest blankets in the land. Her happiness was complete when she was presented with a grandson.

As for the young man, he found great happiness with his wife and child and realized his fears about marriage and children were not true and he believed he was truly blessed.

The husband and wife spoke when no one was around and slowly the husband learnt to speak her language. As their child grew, the mother taught her son he was never to let the others know she could speak. The son too learnt his mother's language and did not question why his parents let people think his mother could not speak.

Six happy years flew by and the old lady moved on to the next world. The child now played with his friends and grew stronger each day. Sometimes his friends would tease him about his mother being dumb, but he said nothing. As he grew older, he started getting annoyed with people whenever they referred to his mother as the dumb one.

Children can sometimes be cruel; one unfortunate day the teasing went a little too far and he lost his temper. He shouted at his friends; his mother was not dumb; he said she was a whole lot smarter than all their mothers put together. Amidst laughter and jeers from his friends, the child went home in tears and it took a very long time for his mother to calm him down.

It wasn't long before a similar thing happened and soon the village was talking about how the little boy found it difficult to accept his mother was dumb. This led to more and more teasing from people and one sad day the young child had enough. He hit out blindly in anger.

Later in the evening, the angry mother and her brothers and sisters came to the child's home and demanded to know why the father and mother did not control their son. The Nymph watched with growing unease as her husband tried to placate the people and asked his son to apologize. The son said he would not apologize for hitting someone who insulted his mother. One thing led to another, and it wasn't long before her son was demanding she speak to prove his claim. She shook her head and tried to plead with him silently with her eyes but her son was not going to listen.

"Speak," he cried, shaking with rage. "Speak and show them you are not dumb. I am tired of being called a liar. Speak out, Mother." The pitying glances of the people only infuriated the little boy. "My mother is not dumb, you fool," he raged and turning to his mother, he demanded her to speak to prove he was telling the truth. In the end the Nymph, unable to bear her son's distress, spoke.

She told the people why she had chosen to stay silent for so many years. She told them who she was and where she came from and just as she had known, they looked uneasy and mumbling something or the other, they hastily went away.

The next morning, she was gone. No one had seen her go. She had simply vanished. The devastated husband went to the river and begged her to come back but, he never saw her again.

The father and son found it hard to live in the same place and decided to move away. Determined to keep her memory alive, the father and son started speaking the language she had taught. When the son married, he taught it to his children, and they taught it to their children. This is how the Mangar language is said to have originated.

They honoured her memory by weaving soft wool blankets made of sheep wool called Raari and Burkasaan and spun fine sheep wool for warm clothes and called it Luk Uni (literally translated to sheep wool).

Even today, when people celebrate an auspicious occasion, it is customary to sit on a sheep wool blanket called Raari.

It is very important to note the Burkasaan is spun of finer wool and is used as a blanket.

The Raari is used like a mattress.

It is considered very inauspicious if the Raari is used as a blanket to cover oneself. Some Kirati clans cover themselves with it during the prescribed days of mourning a dead parent.

The practice of gifting sheep wool blankets as a mark of respect and love was very common among the Kirati tribes till my grandparents' times. This practice slowly died out as modern machine-made soft blankets replaced the coarse traditional Raaris and Burkaasans.

It is interesting to note there is mention of it even in the Mahabharata (The glorious ancient Indian Epic), the Kirata kings are said to have offered gifts of blankets to Yudhistira when he was crowned the emperor in Indraprastha.

This would explain why even today one of the most common presents to the newlyweds are .... you guessed it.... Blankets.

15. THE HALAESO, DHANASE AND KHOCHEELEPA

Many years ago, in the land of Khambuwan, an old couple lived in the shadows of the Water-Giving stone mountain Chuwalungma, now known as Mt Everest.

Their twin daughters Tayamma and Khyiamma gave them much joy and later the gods blessed them with a special gift, a son the old man found in a rocky hollow. He christened him Khopchelipa meaning someone found in a hollow.

One day, the old couple died in their sleep, and the three children were left all alone. Tyamma could not bear to live there after their deaths and asked the Khyiamma and Khocheelepa to accompany her to another place far away. According to one legend, the sisters turned into birds the elder one into a Hornbill (Dhanesh) and the younger twin into a wood pigeon (Halaeso).

The Dhanese however, could not leave the bodies of the couple behind. She buried them and carried their parent's gravestones on her head. It can still be seen today as the bony protuberance on the hornbill's head.

The three of them made their way to a far-off land and lived there. The two birds gleaned the fields and fed little Khocheelepa who was growing up into a young and strong boy. A few years had passed when the land was struck by famine. There was no food to be found. The fields and granaries remained empty and silent. The sisters flew far and wide in search of food but could not find food. Khocheelepa cried with hunger, and the desperate birds flew further away in search of food to feed their brother. After searching for a long time, they managed to gather a small amount of grain.

They flew back to where Khocheelepa was and began to cook the grain in a pot. The birds, in their hurry to cook the food, placed long pieces of branches in the fire and fanned it with their wings. When he saw the food, the boy danced about in glee. Alas, he came too close and tripped upon the long firewood and upset the pot. The fire died out and the rice lay in the dust. Seeing what he had done, the boy started to weep. The sisters consoled the boy and flew off in search of more food. When they returned tired and unsuccessful, they found Khocheelepa lying on the ground. The boy had fainted from hunger. The birds tried to wake him up. Khocheelepa remained silent. Giving their brother up for dead, the birds cried and beat their wings in the dust. After a while, they covered the boy with leaves and sadly flew away.

Later, much later, Khocheelepa revived and found himself all alone. He called out to his sisters but received no reply. He set out towards a big forest in the distance to look for them. There he found some wild fruit and berries and ate them. While he was eating the fruit, a witch saw him and captured him. She took him to her house and called out to her daughter, "Boil some water and prepare for guests; I have brought Shikar (meat)." She locked Khocheelapa in her cellar and went away to call her friends for dinner.

The witch's daughter, curious about the shikar, opened the cellar and saw Khocheelepa. She felt sorry for him. She caught a boar and cooked it instead, and decided to let the boy go. She led him out and showed him the way out of the forest. Khocheelepa made his way out of the forest and found himself in a small village. The people took pity on him and let him live there.

Many years passed, and Khocheelepa grew into a young man. He was never able to find his way back to the witch's house, though he had tried often. He had, within these years, bought cattle, built a house, and was living a comfortable life. Soon he began to get offers for marriage from eager parents. Looking for a suitable match, he agreed to marry the daughter of one of the village's headmen.

There was a great deal of bustle and laughter as the preparations for the wedding began. Khopcheelepa called the pig to him and asked him to go and look for his sisters and invite them to his wedding feast.

The pig searched everywhere and finally located the sisters. He went to them and said, "Khopcheelepa, your brother, has asked you to attend his wedding feast." The Dhanase replied, "Go away and do not tease us. Our brother died many years ago, and we still mourn his death." "He is not dead, he wants you to attend his marriage feast," squealed the pig. The Dhanase got angry and pecked the pig, and chased him away. The pig went back to Khocheelepa and told him what had passed.

Khocheelepa then sent the rooster, who met with the same fate. The two sisters pecked the rooster and chased him away. When the rooster went back to Khocheelepa, he realized that he had to resort to trickery to bring his sisters there. He sent for the cicada and whispered instructions. The cicada flew to where the two birds were and began to sing a song about how his two sisters Halaeso and Dhanese had brought up Khocheelapa. Hearing the song, the two birds followed the cicada who continued singing and led them to the wedding.

The birds looked down and saw Khocheelepa waving at them. They felt ashamed of themselves for deserting their brother and leaving him for dead when he had been alive all the time. They circled the feast but did not come down despite Khocheelepa's pleadings. Finally, Khocheelepa asked the people to bring a long bamboo pole and placing some fruit on it, he raised the pole above their heads. The two sisters ate the fruit from the top of the pole and called out to their brother, "We have attended your wedding feast, o brother! May you live in happiness." Having said this, the birds flew away, never to be seen in Khocheelepa's village again. As for Khochleepa, he lived to a ripe old age in peace and plenty.

However, the story lives on, and it is a common practice to tie bhakimlo (a sour wild fruit) in a Baalaam (a bamboo pole) during a marriage feast. When the Baagdaata (the giving away of the bride) is conducted, people jump and try to get at the bhakimlo without using their hands. (Now a days, it is not uncommon to see them use their hands.) Only after the fruit is eaten the ceremony is said to be complete. Thus, the hornbill, the wood pigeon and Khocheelepa are remembered even today.

16. GARUDA MEETH OR THE EAGLE BROTHER

Many years ago in the hills, a boy was looking for firewood in the forest when he suddenly heard a scream of anguish. Leaving his load behind, the boy ran swiftly towards the noise. When he reached the spot, he stopped and saw a magnificent eagle struggling frantically in a trap.

He was about to run and free the bird when a look at the razor-sharp talons and beak stopped him. The eagle glared at the boy and said, "O son of man, the Creator has given you enough skills to hunt, fish, and raise crops to feed yourselves. Must you now resort to treachery and set traps for the citizens of the air as well?"

"Be calm, my friend," said the boy. "It is not I who set the trap, nor have I come to harm you. I heard your cries for help, and I am here to help you. Sit still, I'll set you free." Saying this, he walked up to the bird and gently eased him out of the trap. Smoothing the eagle's feathers, the boy let him go.

The eagle spread his wings and slowly soared into the clouds above. As he flew away, he screamed, "Remember your Garuda Meeth (Eagle Brother) if ever you are in trouble, call out my name and I'll come to your aid." The boy laughed good humouredly and called back to the receding speck in the sky. "Thank you, my brother. I'll remember." "Remember Garuda Meeth. Remember!" came the answer and the eagle was gone.

The boy carefully dismantled the trap and threw it away. Turning back, he went to the place where his load of firewood was. By the time he reached home, he had forgotten all about his newfound eagle brother. Many days passed, but the boy never met with any trouble and did not have to call upon his Garuda Meeth. Not surprisingly, he completely forgot his eagle brother.

One sunny morning, the boy decided to go fishing. He walked along the hill until he reached the river. He looked for a comfortable stone and sat down to fish. The first catch was offered to the forest spirits on three leaves, and after that, luck seemed to favor him.

Excited with his luck and his ears filled with the music of the swollen river, the boy did not notice a very hungry python slither up to his rock and wrapped its coils around his legs. The boy realized his danger too late and was unable to free himself. Pretending to be unafraid, he said, "Well now, I never thought I'd have shoes made of a real live snake."

The Python looked up at the boy and softly hissed, "I'm very hungry. I haven't eaten for many months, but you will fill me up very nicely."

"I don't think you'd like my taste," said the boy politely. "I think you'd feel much better if you went after a nice, tasty deer and had him for your meal."

"A good idea," said the Python, "but first let me feed on you!" Saying this, the python started wrapping his coils all around the boy.

"I've not only got snake skin shoes, but even snake skin trousers," said the boy, still pretending to be unafraid. The Python wrapped some more coils around the boy. "A shirt made out of a real live snake! I didn't know it would feel so cool," gasped the boy because the Python was slowly starting to squeeze him to death.

The Python raised his head over the boy and said, "I'm going to eat you now, but I'm not as bad as you think I am. You can make a wish before you die, and I'll grant that." "I was hoping you'd say that," said the boy who had suddenly remembered his Garuda Meeth.

"Well, alright, this won't take long. You see, when I used to collect firewood in the forest, I would shout aloud and hear the echoes reply. Will you let me shout a few times and listen to the echoes reply, because I'll never hear them again?"

"You may, but please hurry up and let me satisfy my hunger soon."

"Alright," said the boy, "this won't take long. Could you please loosen your coils a bit so that I can get some air in?" And filling his lungs with air, the boy cried out loud, "Garuda Meeth!" Far away, the echoes answered. The boy called out again, "Garuda Meeth!"

High up in the sky, the eagle heard the cry. Looking below, he saw his brother in the coils of a huge Python. "Garuda Meeth!" called out the boy desperately.

Straight as an arrow, the eagle dived, the clouds parted, and the leaves on the tree fluttered. The Python opened his mouth to swallow the boy.

Whoosh! The eagle hit his mark, and the Python lost an eye. Before he could recover from the pain and surprise, the eagle struck again and blinded the python completely.

Wild with anger and pain the Python set the boy free and lashed out blindly at the enemy he could not see. The eagle swooped, dove and pecked. The sharp talons ripped and slashed. It wasn't long before the python lay dead, stretched out on the rock.

The eagle cleaned his beak and claws, and said, "Any time you need me Meeth (brother), I'll be there." He then soared towards the sky and was lost among the clouds.

Realizing that the boy had had a narrow escape, the eagle started a personal war against the snakes and taught his sons to do the same. Even today in the hills, the eagle hunts and kills snakes to protect the Sons of Man. As for the sons of man, they stopped trapping eagles for many years. Though the practice of hunting birds still prevail in some very remote villages, no one hunts the Eagle.

There is an interesting story of Garuda the Eagle in Hindu mythology as well. The story goes that Garuda and the snakes were half-brothers who became sworn enemies after the snake brothers and their mother tricked Garuda and his mother into slavery by winning a bet unfairly.

To redeem his mother and himself from slavery, Garuda was asked to steal the Amrit (Nectar of Immortality) from the Devas (Gods), which he did after many an adventure.

The snake brothers released the mother and son from their slavery, and took the pot of Amrit with them. Before partaking of the nectar, they went to the river to bathe themselves. The pot lay unguarded on the bank of the river and Indra, the king of Gods, seized the pot and took it back to heaven.

The snake brothers blamed Garuda and a fight ensued where the Eagle God destroyed every one of them. After this, Garuda became the vehicle of Lord Vishnu (The Protector) and the sworn enemy of all snakes.

17. PILLAR OF POTS

This story is about the hills when the world was no longer young. Man had forgotten the languages of the animals, birds and trees. They had now started living in groups called tribes and had learnt to till the land, make clothes, and make pots and pans. The Creator had been happy and had let the people continue to live in peace.

In a certain village, there lived a tribe of simple people called the Lapcheys. They hunted and fished and grew crops to feed themselves and were very gentle and good people. Their whole existence was a simple one.

Among them lived a simple man who sometimes wondered why the sun shone, why the leaves were green, and why fire burnt. One day, he happened to look up at the sky and saw the clouds sailing by. He stood and started for many hours and thought to himself, "I wonder what is beyond that great big sky." This thought kept him occupied for some more time, until at last, he decided to find out.

Calling all his fellow men he said, "Brothers, do any of you know what lies beyond the sky." "No! Can you tell us?" Asked the villagers.

"I've thought about it for a long time now, brothers, and with your help we can find out."

"How?" They asked.

"Let us make pots, a great many pots, and place them on top of each other. This way we can construct a pillar of pots, climb on it and rip open the sky with an ankusae (a stick shaped like a shepherd's crook)."

"A capital idea," agreed everyone, and they went home and began to make pots. After many days, they decided that they had enough and gathered in a meadow to build the pillar. Every man, woman and child were present.

The man stepped forward and showed the village how the pillar was to be built. He picked up a pot and placed it on the ground, then picking up a second pot, placed it on top of the first. He then climbed on to the first pot with a third pot in his hand and placed it on top of the second. The people got the idea, and the pillar started growing rapidly. How excited the people were! They laughed and talked and sang, as the pillar grew taller and taller.

The women helped pass the pots. The men formed a long chain along the pillar and kept passing the pots, one after the other to the person above, who in turn passed it to another, till it reached the man on top. This way he kept climbing higher and higher, and the pillar grew taller and taller, while the chain of men clinging precariously to the pots became longer and longer.

After a while, the man thought the pillar was high enough. It was then, when he realized that he had left the ankusae behind. "Ankusae Dye," he yelled to the man below. What he meant was, "Give me the stick." The message was passed down the pillar, but somewhere along the line, the message was wrongly heard. The message that finally reached the people below was, "Bhatkai dye," meaning destroy it.

The villagers were aghast, "What? Destroy all our hard work?" they asked. "No, we won't." This was the message sent up to the man. When he received the message, the man got angry and said, "Tell them to do what I say!" This message was passed down to the crowd. "No!" they shouted together. Their answer was brought up once more. "What?" exclaimed the man and shook his fist at the crowd.

"Just tell them to follow my orders," he cried.

Once more, the message was passed down. The people looked at one another and sadly shook their heads. They could see the man hanging on to the topmost pot shaking his fist at them.

"Let us do it before he gets angry, suggested someone." The simpletons picked up their cudgels and started smashing the pots.

The pillar swayed and came crashing down in a cloud of dust and men. Needless to say, many were severely injured, and several died. The man who had thought of this idea also died, and thereafter the people never tried to reach the sky and try to see beyond it.

18. THE BIRCH AND THE RHODODENDRON

Once upon a time in the high hills, lived two trees, a Birch and a Rhododendron. At the time, the Rhododendron did not have any flowers, while the Birch had a strong and supple trunk and could be found in plenty only over the best lands. The Birch and the Rhododendron tree were very good friends. Every day, they talked about many things: the sky, the clouds, the weather, and the birds that visited them.

Time went on and it was not long before the Rhododendron fell in love with the Birch and thought of asking her to marry him. Mustering up his courage, the Rhododendron asked, "Dear Birch, you look so lovely with your beautiful leaves and straight and slender trunk. I have loved you for a very long time. I have enjoyed your company and our conversations, and I think there is no one as beautiful as you. Will you marry me?"

The birch was quiet for a moment and then laughed. She laughed so hard that the birds resting on her branches were frightened and flew away. Controlling her laughter with a great effort, she said, "O you twisted little thing, did you think that I talked to you because I loved you? How did you ever think that I would marry you? I had nothing to do, and you kept me amused; that is the only reason why I held such long conversations with you. Whoever heard of such nonsense!" She snorted.

The poor Rhododendron was crushed and said humbly, "I am sorry, my friend; I never realized how insignificant I am. Forgive me for my mistake." Saying this, he turned his branches away from the Birch and sadly shed his leaves. The haughty Birch did not even look at him. Looking up at the sky, she preened her branches and said to herself, "How beautiful I am. I'm sure the trees down below look up to me as their queen."

This idea, having entered her head, made the Birch very vain. She gave herself air and fancied herself above the rest of the plants. She would not even let little birds rest upon her. Whenever a bird flew to her to rest, she would rudely shake her branches and angrily say, "Shoo! You ugly creature, don't sit here and dirty my branches. Shoo!" The bird would then fly over to the Rhododendron tree and rest there. The Rhododendron would be glad for the company and would say, "I may not have real flowers but you sure make me look beautiful."

In a few days, the birds learnt to leave the Birch alone and went to the Rhododendron. The tree was happy with his newly found friends and let them build their nests and raise their young. He sheltered them from the wind and the rain, and they told him tales of other trees they had seen in the plains. He heard of the tall and mighty Sal trees, the Silk Cotton tree that burst into flame-coloured blooms in spring and the majestic Banyan with her many limbs.

As for the Birch, she was not interested in hearing of others. She was very happy being left alone with her silly pride.

The Creator, who had been watching, decided it was time the Birch was taught a lesson. Merciful always, he wanted to give her one more chance to mend her ways, hoping the vain tree would change.

He transformed himself into a tiny bird and flew to the Birch. He had only just alighted upon a branch when the Birch shook her branches and said, "Shoo!" The bird kept on sitting there. "Get away you, miserable creature," screamed the angry tree.

"Please, dear tree, let me stay here. I am very tired." Begged the bird.

"No! Go and rest elsewhere, not here. Leave my beautiful branches alone." Saying this, she shook her branches so hard that the little bird nearly tumbled off. The Rhododendron, who had been watching, softly called out, "Little bird, come here and rest. There is plenty of room. Come away. Do not make her angry."

The Birch who heard this as well, screamed, "Yes, go away to him. He can keep you. Go now."

"Very well," said the Creator, throwing off his disguise. "Very well then, you vain and silly creature, you are henceforth to be found in plentiful only in places where you are hidden from the sight of man and beast. May you grow in plenty in wastelands and ravines! May your branches, which I had made very strong, turn brittle and break when a strong wind blows. May you be valued for nothing more than firewood by the sons of Man."

The Birch, upon hearing this, stood speechless with shock. Turning to the Rhododendron, the Creator continued, "You of such little faith, why did you think you were of no importance? You have helped so many, but I forgive you. I bless you with this, when all creatures turn their eyes to the hills, they will all agree that you are the most beautiful tree among the hills forever and ever." Having said this, the Creator left.

The next morning, the Birch woke up to find herself in a deep ravine overgrown with thistles and thorns. There she was all alone and at night, when a strong wind blew, her strong branches snapped off like matchsticks. She was very sorry for herself, but there was nothing she could do. Since then, the Birch can be found in plenty in wastelands, ravines and deep gullies. Having lost her strength, the timber is not valued as it used to be, and the people of the hills used her fallen branches and logs as nothing except firewood.

As for the Rhododendron, he woke up and found his twisted branches covered in a flame of bright red flowers. Since then, all creatures, man, bird, and beast agreed that when they turn their eyes to the hills, the most beautiful sight is that of the Rhododendron tree in bloom.

19. THE TALE OF THE CAT AND THE TIGER

Many years ago, when the hills were young, there lived, in the sunny part of a jungle, a cat. He was a clever and cunning hunter, and lived all by himself in a cave. The Creator had not let man domesticate and master the animals, and therefore all creatures were free. Meanwhile, on the dark side of the same forest, a tigress lived in her cave with her cub. She too was a fearless huntress, though a bit clumsy, because at that time, tigers did not know how to stalk their prey. All they did was look for slow-moving animals, tire them out, then bring them down.

One day, the tigress left her cub and set out to hunt. She warned her cub not to venture out and told him especially to remember that the sunny part of the jungle was full of danger. He was not to go there at all. No sooner had the tigress left the cave, the cub, full of curiosity, bounded merrily towards the sunny part of the jungle. He had never been there and hence found the place very interesting.

He saw the beautiful wild flowers and the golden bees. He chased butterflies and rolled in the soft-smelling grass. A little further, he saw a pool. He went to it and looked down. Imagine his surprise when he saw his face looking back at him. He patted his reflection and laughed when the ripples made it appear all wavy. He liked the sunny side of the jungle. He thought of the dark, murky pool where his mother took him to drink, and he thought of the damp cave where he slept. He did not want to go back. Feeling tired after so much excitement, he lay down by the pool and slept.

When he awoke, night had fallen and the moon had come up. Looking around, the cub saw dark shadows and felt afraid. He was hungry and tired, and most of all, he missed his mother. He got up and ran towards the dark side of the jungle, but in his excitement of the morning, he had forgotten to remember the way. He ran and ran but got hopelessly lost. Feeling hungry, tired and very sorry for himself, he sat on a rock and started to cry.

Luckily for him, the cat who was out hunting found him. "Dear nephew, what are you doing here?" He asked. "I am lost and want to go home," sobbed the cub.

The cat realized what had happened and said kindly, "Dear nephew, the dark side of the jungle is very far away. Even if I know where you lived, I am afraid I cannot help you go home because I cannot go there. We have to keep to our own sides. It is safe for everyone that way."

"But ... I ... want ... to go...home," wailed the cub. "Hush! You'll frighten the animals away," said the cat. "I'll take you home with me, and when you are big enough to find your way back, you can go to your place." The cub agreed, and after some time the two were fast asleep in the cat's cave after a hearty meal of wild rats.

The cat and the cub lived together for some time. Then one day, the cat said, "Nephew, it's time I taught you to hunt. I think it will be easier to find your own food rather than having to grow up on a diet of birds and rats." The cub agreed. He did miss the taste of meat his mother had fed him.

The cat taught the cub to track animals and find his prey by looking for signs and smell. He taught the cub to lie perfectly still near the water hole and look like a part of the forest foliage. He taught the cub to stalk his prey noiselessly and to kill mercilessly. With time and practice, the cub became a skilled hunter, and was able to kill bigger animals to feed himself. He had forgotten the dark side of the forest and his mother, and lived contentedly with his newfound "Uncle." It was not long before he grew into a handsome young tiger with powerful muscles and a glossy coat. (The cat had even taught him to groom himself).

One afternoon, the tiger and the cat were lying on the grass, sunning themselves after a hearty meal. Presently the tiger spoke,

"Uncle, is it true that you are the most cunning and clever hunter in the forest?"

"That is what they say, nephew, but don't listen to such talk. It does no one any good," replied the cat. The tiger was silent for a while and then said, "They also say that I know a lot because I have learnt from you." "That's true, nephew," said the cat affectionately, "you do know a lot."

"Then, if I know a lot, why am I not the best? After all, I'm big and strong now!" "Patience, dear nephew, you will learn more later on. Now, let me sleep." Saying this, the cat turned around and went to sleep.

The tiger could not sleep. He felt restless and unhappy. He could not help but compare his strength, cunning and skill with that of the cat and felt that he was much better than the cat was.

Just then a bird alighted on a nearby tree and burst into a song. The tiger eyed it and idly thought how nice it would be if he could have the bird as a snack. Suddenly he realized that he did not know one thing the cat did and that was how to climb trees.

"Uncle," he shook the cat awake. "What is it, dear nephew?" asked the cat, yawning. "Teach me how to climb trees. You've taught me everything, but you have forgotten to teach me how to climb trees." The cat looked at the tiger silently, then turned towards the forest and said, "Come."

He sped towards the edge of the forest, followed by the eager tiger, and stopped when he reached the border of the dark side. Turning to the tiger he said, "Remember nephew, how you got lost long ago and came to me? The dark side was your home, and you left your mother there. Now the time has come for you to go back and find her." "Yes," said the tiger, "I remember." He looked at the dark side as memories came flooding back.

The cat suddenly leapt up onto the branches of a nearby tree, and looking down at the surprised tiger, he continued, "Dear nephew, I have taught you many things and now I ask you to go in peace.

As for climbing trees, forget it, because that is something I am NOT going to teach."

"Why? You have taught me everything I know. Why will you not teach me how to climb?" Asked the tiger, but the cat sat silently and did not answer. In vain did the tiger plead; after a while, he started to get angry and roared at the cat to get down. The cat, perched high up among the branches, went to sleep. Wild with anger, the tiger clawed the tree and tried to jump up to hurl the cat off its perch. He could only jump and claw at the trunk and roar with rage.

He jumped and roared and clawed and demanded the cat come down at once, but it was no use. The Cat finally opened its eyes and lazily stretched. He yawned and climbed higher into the tree and sat there washing his face. The Tiger had another fit and howled and roared and clawed the tree clean of its bark, but he could not get to the Cat. Finally, he gave up and lay down under the tree and sulked.

Finaly the Cat opened his eyes and said, "Dear nephew, I have only one last thing to say. That is, however close you maybe with anyone, remember not to let him know the secret of your survival. Had I not remembered this adage and taught you to climb? And someday if you decided to harm me, I would have been at your mercy. Here we are today, even though you are really angry with me, I can sit here safely and laugh at you."

The tiger realized it was futile to try to catch the cat and that he had been too stupid to think he was smarter than the Cat.

He got up and shouted out to the Cat, "Dear uncle, I am going into the dark side from today, but be warned, should our paths ever cross again, I'll do my best to hunt you down mercilessly, that I promise you!"

Saying this, the tiger turned and ran towards the dark side. The cat could hear him crashing in the undergrowth. He jumped down from his perch and went home. Being a crafty old cat, he knew that as long as he lived in his cave, he would be in danger. So, he exchanged his cave for another and lived there. He also remembered how he had taught the tiger to stalk his prey by looking for fresh tracks and droppings and was very careful thereafter to bury his excreta in case the tiger found it and tracked him down.

This went on for many years, and the two never forgot this. The tiger told his sons this story, and the cat told his sons this story, which explains why they are still sworn enemies. Even though man, later let the cat stay with him, the cat did not forget the tiger, and that is why the cat still buries its excreta. As for the tiger, he still hunts for the cat in the jungles but has not managed to find him so far.

20. THE STORY OF THE BEAN

Long ago, when the world was young, there were three friends; a lump of coal, a straw, and a young bean. They had become friends as soon as they had found themselves in a kitchen.

One day, the farmer's wife placed the coal, along with the others, into the hearth and started a fire. Looking around her kitchen, she said, "Bean soup it'll have to be, for there is nothing else, and I'm far too busy to go the market." Just then the farmer called out to his wife, who went out grumbling.

The bean, who had heard every word, softly called out, "Dear friend coal, did you hear what she said? She is going to make soup out of me!" "Yes," said the coal, glowing bright red. "Imagine having to provide the fire to cook your best friend; I have had enough of this. I think I'll go out into the world and find myself a better job." "I'll come with you," said the bean. "What about you?" asked the coal, to the straw. "I guess anything is better than being thrown into the fire," said the straw.

The coal rolled out of the hearth, the bean jumped out of the bowl, and the straw stalked out of his corner. Together, the three friends stepped out of the kitchen and into the farmer's garden.

"How beautiful the world is," said the coal.

"Yes, how wonderful it feels to see the green grass and the blue sky," said the bean.

"Just wait until you come to the fields; there you will see the bright sun and the yellow corn, and then you will know how beautiful the world really is!" Added the straw.

The straw had been in the fields before, because that was where he came from. But the bean, who had been raised in the kitchen garden, had not seen the fields, and neither had the coal. "What are we waiting for?" Said the coal. "Let's go!"

The three friends walked to the edge of the garden and then stopped in dismay. There before them, they lay on an open drain. "How are we going to get across this?" Said the bean. "Just when we were about to set out upon a wonderful adventure, grumbled the straw." "Wait," said the coal. "I remember when I was brought to the market, we crossed a big river over a bridge."

"What's a bridge?" Asked the bean. "It's a big piece of wood that lets you walk across the river." "Let's make one," said the straw. "There is no need," said the coal. "I've already thought about it." Turning to the straw, he continued, "All you have to do, my friend, is to lie flat on your back, and we will walk across you and cross the drain." "A wonderful idea," said the straw and promptly lay down across the drain. The coal, burning bright red with excitement, importantly stepped on to the straw's back.

"Wait!" Cried the straw, "I'll get burnt, you silly." But the coal had already hopped on to the straw's back.

"Stop wriggling," said the coal sternly. "It's undignified." But by then the poor straw was ablaze. Puff! The straw was reduced to a heap of ashes. "What's happening." Plop! Fizzzsss! The coal fell into the drain and was swept away.

The bean who had been watching all this found the whole thing very funny and he started to laugh. He laughed and laughed. Tears poured down his green face, but he could not stop laughing. He laughed so hard that his stomach burst open and the seeds spilled out. He stopped laughing, took a good look at his stomach and then burst into tears. "I have been punished for laughing at my friends," he sobbed. He sat on the grass and wept bitterly.

A busy little tailorbird came flying into the garden, looking for worms. "Hello, little friend, what's wrong?" She asked. "Oh, dear bird," wept the bean. "I laughed at my friends and didn't help them when they were in trouble, and now my belly has burst open."

"There, there now, don't worry," said the bird. "I'll help you." Saying this, she picked up a long piece of grass in her beak and placing the seeds back into the bean, she deftly sewed up the little bean's belly. When she had finished, the bean was as good as new. "But mind you, don't laugh too much now, otherwise, the stitches will not hold," she warned. "Thank you, thank you so much," cried the bean, and turning around, he walked back towards the kitchen. He thought that he had enough adventure for the day and decided never to go out in the world in search of more.

That is why, dear readers, you can find a thin thread that runs through the length of the French bean. This is what holds the bean together even today, thanks to the tailor-bird.

Mountain Ballads (Part One): Nepali Folk Tales

21. A STRANGE TALE OF LITTLE MEN

The day was bright and sunny, and the blue sky stretched over the green hills as a few flecks of clouds lazily drifted towards the horizon, sheep grazed contentedly, and the fat cows dreamily chewed on the sweet grass. The shepherd smiled and settled down under the tree. He was feeling a little tired after all the morning chores and with the brisk walk uphill to get the sheep and cows there. He decided to take a nap.

He had hardly shut his eyes for about a minute when he heard a rustling sound among the grass. He lifted his head and peered towards the ground above him; there was nothing to be seen. He shut his eyes again. Something rustled among the grass again, and he heard a voice mumbling something in a sing-song voice. He decided to ignore it. He knew his friends usually played such pranks on him; they were always trying to scare him with stupid stories of how the forest was haunted or how a leopard could attack them and how a bear could maul him and other silly pranks.

He pretended to be fast asleep and tried to ignore the whole thing; however, the sing song chanting continued louder and louder till he felt someone was actually speaking really close to his ear. He got up suddenly, determined to smack his friend in the head. As he opened his eyes, he could hear someone scramble in the bracken. He gave chase, and he ran swiftly up along the forest path determined to see who had been teasing him.

As he turned around the corner, he saw his cousin sitting on a rock by the side of the path and laughing merrily. He stopped panting for breath and then burst out laughing as well. The two lads were more than just cousins. They had grown up together under the watchful care of the shepherd boy's maternal aunt. The boy's parents had died within months of each other, and his maternal uncle had taken in the orphan. His wife was a cheerful, kind-hearted woman; she took good care of the orphan and treated him as her own.

"Want a chestnut?" the cousin offered some to the shepherd who didn't particularly care for chestnuts. He shook his head.

"I've got to look for a certain creeper and collect its leaves for my father," said the cousin. "I thought it would be more fun if the two of us went." The pair set off into the forest, leaving the sheep and the cows grazing contentedly. Very soon they were deep in conversation about the different birds and their nests and beautifully coloured eggs.

The narrow forest path meant they had to walk one behind the other. The shepherd lad who was walking a little ahead, asked his cousin if they should stop and start looking for the plant. His cousin said they would go a little deeper into the forest, as he wanted to show him the unexplored part of the forest.

They walked on for some more time and sure enough the shepherd realized he had not come to this bit of the forest. He luckily espied the said creeper on a tree and asked if they should collect it and head back home. Upon getting no answer he turned around to ask…

Imagine his horror and shock when he found a tiny old man standing there instead of his cousin

He froze in his tracks; he knew who the little man was. He had heard of him often enough around the village fires. The little man standing in front of him was the "Ban Jhyakri" (literally translated, it meant Forest Shaman).

It was said that the Forest Shaman was a little man, about two feet tall. He was known to have a lot of magical powers; shapeshifting was one of them. The young shepherd had heard plenty about how the Forest shaman used his skill as a shapeshifter and lured people deep into the woods to take them with him. The young lad had no intention of being taken prisoner without a fight. He tried to reach out and grab the little man by the throat and found he could not move. Fear gave way to anger, rapidly and he yelled at the little man to let him go. To his horror, he found he had lost his voice. He struggled and tried his best to free himself from the invisible bonds that held him immobile. He could not move or speak.

The Ban Jhyakri watched him for a while, and finally, when the shepherd decided it was useless for him to struggle, the shaman spoke. "Do not be afraid of me, I have come to help you achieve your destiny."

"You have been chosen to carry forward the knowledge that is here. Come it is getting late." With that the little man led the way through a small half-hidden path. The reluctant young man, who had a million questions but couldn't speak, was half dragged by his own feet, which suddenly seemed to have developed a mind of their own. Cursing freely in his mind, he stumbled after the little man who was now walking so swiftly that the shepherd's legs had a hard time keeping up. Had he been in control of his limbs, he would have gladly run away in the opposite direction but this was not to be.

Just like he had heard around so many village fires before, the young lad was taken to a tiny cave deep in the woods. The little man carefully led him inside and sat him down. He looked at him carefully and spoke again in his sing song voice, "Listen very carefully, O Son of Man. I am not going to harm you. You have been brought here for a purpose. I promise I will send you home after twenty days. For those twenty days, you will be here in the forest while I teach you all that I know about herbs and healing. Once you have learnt, you can go back to the village. The people will have a guide and a healer with them."

"You have been chosen to learn things that will help your people. I will teach you, but remember not to run away or wander around too freely as my demon wife has a deep-rooted craving for human flesh. As long as you stay hidden from sight and not leave the cave, you will be perfectly safe."

The lad had heard of the Ban Jhyakri wife, the "Lam Lammaey" rumoured to be a terrifying witch who was said to actually eat humans. She was said to have a wild mane of hair, bloodshot eyes and a mouth full of fangs. People said her feet faced backward and her breasts hung down to her knees.

The village folk always warned their young men and women, that if ever they came across very large footprints in the mud or sand, they should immediately run in the same direction as the foot prints thereby escaping the witch, who had trapped and eaten many people stupid enough to run in the opposite direction of the footprints and thus running straight towards her.

It was also advisable to run downhill if ever one was chased by this demon as she would keep tripping over her own breasts while running downhill. Whereas, if one was stupid enough to run uphill, she would hoist her breasts over her shoulders and run like the wind uphill and eat the unfortunate victim.

Sitting around the village fire and listening to such wild stories generally caused great laughter among the young; however, the young shepherd did not find much to laugh about in the given situation.

He had never believed in the stories about the 'Ban Jhyakri', well here he was a prisoner of one. What if the stories of the 'Lam Lammey' were true? He wished he had not made fun of the old village shaman who claimed he had been taken away by the "Ban Jhyakri" when he was a young lad. He also wished he had paid more attention when the village healer had narrated how she had managed to escape the Ban Jhyakri's wife. She too claimed that she had been abducted at the age of ten and had lived in the Ban Jhayakri's cave for about a year.

He remembered laughing at her description of the Lamm Lammey and asking her to tell him the story each time he met her just so he could mock the old lady.

He also remembered her always warning him not to go wandering around alone in the forest. He wished he had listened to her.

Life in the forest with the Ban Jhyakri was not very easy for the lad. To begin with, he was always confused about the time; he sometimes felt he had been there for a couple of days and then sometimes he felt he had been there for months or years. Even though he drew small lines in the cave wall to mark the days, they mysteriously vanished, leaving him even more confused.

Food was something he didn't exactly remember eating very regularly. Sometimes he thought the "Ban Jhyakri" gave him proper human food, then again at other times he felt the little man gave him only earthworms to eat.

Thankfully, there was one thing he did remember from the stories around the village fire. The old healer claimed when she had been offered earthworms to eat, she had held out her hand with the palms facing the ground. The earthworm had been served up on her knuckles, and as she pretended to eat them, they thankfully fell off on to the cave floor. He did the same and though he was hungry sometimes, he didn't have to eat earthworms.

The strange thing was that he could keep track of every shrub, herb, vine, root, bark, flower or fruit he was shown. The little man would lead him in the woods and show him how he could make medicines out of the various plants and minerals.

Then one morning, the "Ban Jhyakri" came to him with a steaming bowl of delicious food. Once he was full, he collected the various bark bags and they set off as usual. After walking for what seemed like a longer time than usual the Forest Shaman asked the shepherd if he knew the way back home. The shepherd said he didn't.

Without another word, the little man led the way through many trails and soon enough the shepherd found himself standing near the rock where he had seen his cousin. He looked all around and felt relieved he could finally figure out where he was. Strangely, the Forest Shaman was nowhere to be seen.

He hurried forward to see if his sheep were okay; the pasture was empty. He walked briskly towards the village and with loud cheers the village folk welcomed him back.

He learnt he had been missing for the past two days, and the men folk had scoured the entire length and breadth of the forest looking for him. They were finally convinced that he had either been carried off by a leopard or had run away.

The shepherd was happy to be back and did not want the people to know that he had seen the forest shaman. He went back to his old life, but strangely he found out, that he knew exactly what to do whenever one of his friends got hurt or fell ill. It didn't take people long to realise that he had been abducted by the "Ban Jhyakri" and had been taught to become a healer.

People started treating him with respect and reverence, and finally he had to tell them all about his meeting with the Forest Shaman.

It is a widespread belief in the hills that people do get taken once in a while by the "Ban Jhyakri" and return in a day or two but are themselves confused about the number of days they had spent with the Forest Shaman.

The strangest thing they say is that these people who had no knowledge about herbs and medicines suddenly have vast knowledge of hundreds of plants and herbs and are able to heal many ailments.

The funny thing about the existence of the "Ban Jhyakri" is, although I cannot say I have seen one, I cannot say I believe they don't exist.

I have met many people who actually believe they exist even today; some tell me they have seen him fleetingly; others swear they have heard him beating his drums deep in the woods; one of them is an internationally recognised member of the Mountaineering fraternity. He told me he didn't "believe" little people exist in the forests. He said he knew they did.

"We have seen tiny bundles of firewood lying in the forests during our treks in the Himalayas. Yes, Ban Jhyakris do exist."

I have loved and respected this gentleman as a child, and the Indian Government has showered him with much honour. I choose to believe him.

22. HOW THE BEAR LOST ITS TAIL

Long, long ago, among the tall pines lived a big black bear. He was a huge creature and was said to have a terrible temper. Whenever he came down from the hills to the grasslands below, the animals would all move aside to let him pass. They were all afraid because they had all heard about his hot temper. This was actually not true, because the bear was a gentle creature who liked nothing better than to amble through the jungle path and look for honey and roots. He had a comfortable den where he slept when it was cold, or rainy nights forced him indoors. His days were spent peacefully sleeping, looking for food, and lying in the sun.

In the same forest lived a cunning little fox. He was a tiny red creature, and was universally detested in the forest, because he was a mean animal. He would play tricks on the unsuspecting animals, frighten their babies, carry tales and create trouble wherever he went. When the fox realized the forest could be a dangerous place for him with so many animals in it, he decided to make friends with the bear and seek his protection. The clever fox, unlike the rest of the animals, knew the gentle bear was not as dangerous as everyone thought him to be.

He made friends with the bear and when the bear asked him to share his den, he promptly moved in. He was again able to move around unafraid and unmolested. Soon, he was back to his old self, bullying, teasing, and creating trouble for everyone, only this time they did not complain. The fox would boast and say, "My friend the bear will punish anyone who dares harm me." The poor animals began to avoid the fox and some even moved away to another forest just to be rid of the pest.

After some time, the fox became conceited; he started believing in his own greatness and believed the animals were actually afraid of him. He forgot it was because of the bear that the animals had left him alone. The more he thought about it, the more conceited he became. He decided the Bear's presence limited his greatness and growth and decided to trick on his friend and get him out of the way. He didn't think it would be too hard as the Bear was not very smart.

He took the unsuspecting bear to a high cliff where some vines grew, and said he would teach the bear a new game. Selecting a vine that would take his weight, he swung across the cliff face to the projecting ledge.

"Wwwhheeeee this is FFFUUUNNNN," he cried as he swung across.

Throwing the vine back to where the bear was waiting, he called out, "Come along, now it's your turn." The bear took hold of the vine and swung across.

SNAP, the vine broke and the Bear tumbled headlong into the ravine.

The fox watched the Bear fall and laughed to see the big bear go rolling and crashing into the undergrowth. Luckily for the bear, his fall was broken by a few young saplings and landed in a pile of leaves.

He made his way back to the cliff face, where the fox pretended to be very sorry for him. He fussed over the Bear and brushed the leaves away from his fur, and the Bear thought, "What a good friend he is."

The Fox was really angry his plan had failed. The whole exercise had been in vain; he was furious. The fox decided to play another trick on him soon. He was so busy thinking about the next trick that he failed to see where he was going and walked straight into a tree. When he came to his senses, he found himself back in the cave he shared with the bear.

The kind bear gave him his dinner and asked him to go to sleep. He would not let the fox get up the next day and insisted that he rest. He brought back sweet honey that was found only in the high hill and a freshly caught rabbit for the fox, who was by now beginning to enjoy his illness. He pretended to get worse the next day and did not go out to look for food.

It wasn't very long before the bear was doing everything while the cunning fox lay in the sun and pretended to get slightly better, and again suffered a relapse.

Throughout the summer and autumn months, the bear tended the lazy fox that became very fat. The winter months marched in with the cold, and the bear promptly wrapped his paws around himself and went to sleep. The cave shook with the bear's snores, and no amount of prodding or pinching from the fox could wake him up. The lazy fox began to grow hungry and tried to wake the bear up again, but the bear only snored some more and kept on sleeping.

Finally, cursing the bear for going to sleep, he went out to look for food. All the months of sleeping in the sun had made him forget hunting and tracking, and many nights he came home tired and hungry. The days became colder and the forests bare. The fox grew thinner and thinner, while the bear kept on sleeping. The fox grew desperate with hunger and thought longingly of the days when the bear had looked after him. He wished spring would come and waited anxiously for the bear to wake up.

One morning, the fox wandered very far out from the usual hunting grounds and came upon a house. He looked around carefully, for he had heard of the Sons of Man and their dislike towards all foxes. Then he saw the man. He was weaving, a basket of reeds, and every now and then, he would whistle merrily as he worked. The fox crept around the house and came upon a chicken coop. As quick as a flash, he ran forward, seized a chicken, and ran off into the forest, leaving a very angry and surprised man behind. That night the fox ate well and slept well. The next few days the fox did not go to the man's house, but after remaining hungry for another three days he was forced to steal another chicken from the coop. Sometimes the fox would steal eggs, and man got himself a dog to guard the chicken coop. The fox was unable to steal any more chicken and had to scrounge for food in the bare forests.

The days were slowly becoming warmer, though the snow still covered the ground. One day, the fox was looking for food along the path that led to the man's house when he saw the man coming towards the same path carrying a basket. He sniffed the air and caught the scent of fresh fish. Unable to bear the thought that he would not be able to catch fish for himself, he slunk after the man, hoping to fish for himself. He had his wish. The man slipped, and the basket flew out of his hands, and the fish fell out. The fax ran forward, and gathering about half a dozen fish, ran as fast as he could to the cave, where he proceeded to devour them.

The bear, who had been sleeping all this time, woke up and sniffed the air appreciatively. The fox, who did not want to share the fish with him said, "It's a good thing you woke up today; the river is teeming with fish. You will be able to catch plenty today." "How did you manage to catch so many?" Asked the bear, who was feeling very hungry. "Simple, all you have to do is make a hole in the ice and put your tail into the river. The fish will come and cling to your tail, and then you can pull them out at once."

"Sounds very simple," said the bear stroking his long tail. (Those days, the Creator had made the bear with a very long and lovely tail. Though the tail had nothing to do except hang behind the bear, he was very fond of it.)

The hungry bear went to the river, and choosing a spot, he broke the ice and sat down, letting his tail through the hole into the river. The river looked very strange when it was frozen over. The bear sat there, looking all around him. He could feel his tail freezing in the icy water, but the thought of having fish for dinner made him wait. The ice meanwhile had begun to form, and the bear was unaware that his tail was slowly being trapped in the ice.

After a couple of hours had passed, he decided to pull out as many fish that had stuck to his tail and got up. Imagine his surprise when he found he was unable to raise his tail!

That must be a big catch of fish, he thought and pulled. The tail stubbornly stayed stuck. He pulled harder and thought how delighted the fox would be when he walked into the cave with a big catch. "The poor thing has not been eating well," he thought. "It will bring back his spirit if he eats well." The thought of making his friend happy made him pull hard, and he was surprised to find himself sailing along the ice. He landed heavily on his side and picked himself up. To his dismay, he found his lovely long tail gone. Suddenly he heard someone laughing. Looking up, he saw the fox looking at him and laughing until tears ran down his face.

The bear realized he had been tricked and said, "You ungrateful creature, should I ever see you again, I will teach you a lesson you are not likely to forget. Be gone now and remember, I am your friend no longer." Saying this, the bear walked back to his cave, vowing to punish the fox the next time he met him. As for the fox, he slunk away to live in another forest, lest the bear catch and harm him. Since then, the bear and his descendants have always had very shot tails like the ones we see today.

23. MORE ABOUT THE FOX AND THE BEAR

Once upon a time, high up in the hills, lived a bear. He was a bear like any other bear and spent his days snuffling around the dead leaves and the mossy logs. He stayed well away from the village below, for he was also aware of how cruel man could be. He led a relatively uninteresting life. This suited him just fine because this is what all bears do and he thought he was no different from all the other bears that had lived before him.

In the village below, lived many strong men and red-cheeked women with many fat laughing babies and happy old people, who tilled their small plots of land, sang, whistled, looked after their cattle and made merry whenever they could.

They didn't need much and were a happy lot. Once in a while a home would slaughter a pig or a sheep and the village would sit down to the feast and make merry. Their wants were few and life was not too hard.

Somewhere between the Village and the High Hills lived a clever little Fox; he was a disgraceful little creature as all creatures go. He was lazy, cunning, sharp-eyed and ungrateful and would stop at nothing to get what he wanted, even if it meant getting others into trouble.

This fox had developed a craving for chicken from the village. He could think of nothing else but chicken.

Fat red roosters, plump brown hens, yellow fluffy chicken, chicken with bright red wattles and short black chicken. The longer he thought of chicken, the more desperate he got, but there wasn't much he could do as fierce, large black Tibetan mastiffs guarded the village coops.

He hated the bears like mastiffs with their huge paws and deep barks. Most days the fox would be preoccupied thinking how he could make the dogs fear him. He racked his brains night and day, till at last his cunning brain came up with a solution of getting rid of all the dogs that guarded the chicken so vigilantly.

One day, one lucky day, he spied the huge bear bumbling along. He knew the big bear was kind-hearted and not too smart. Instantly an idea hatched in his cunning little brain.

Pretending not to see the bear, he hopped and skipped with his eyes closed with his tail sticking straight up in the air. The surprised bear almost bumped into him. "Hello," said the bear. "Where are you off to? You seem very happy."

The fox, fighting down the urge to run away and hide, looked at the bear squarely in the eye and answered boldly "My friend, I have come looking for you. The forest is a very big place and one could always use a good friend you know." With that began an unusual friendship of the bear and the fox.

They spent many happy times ambling through the juniper and walking all the way down to the wooded areas just above the village. Slowly, the cunning fox took the unsuspecting bear closer and closer to the chicken coops each day. Till finally, when they got a little too near one of the coops, the mastiffs guarding the coop bounded towards them and gave chase, barking loudly.

The other dogs came tearing down to see what the problem was and they all set up a huge clamour. The fox and the bear ran like the wind into the trees up into the high hills where the dogs would not follow. It wasn't long before they scrambled to safety among the fern in the high hills and sat down to rest.

Presently the bear recovered his breath and asked the fox. "What were those?? I have never seen such terrible creatures. They have such a loud voice and they do howl and shout a lot"

The clever fox found out that the bear had never seen dogs, so he pretended to look very wise and said they were all his followers and friends. They were all inviting him to come to the village and help himself to all the chicken but he was a small fellow and he would not have been able to eat all of them.

The bear who was feeling rather hungry said, "You could have told me I could have done the eating for you." The fox pretending to be sorry about the whole thing said that the offer was only for him and him alone. He asked the bear if he would accompany him to the edge of the village and wait there; if he were lucky, he would hide a few chicken for him and get him some.

The bear expressed his doubt about the dogs, and the clever fox showed him a small tree. He asked the bear to run and climb up the small tree if the dogs barked.

The two friends made their way down to the village once again. Sure enough, the bear had hardly reached the village path, one of the dogs saw him and barked and all the dogs arrived and gave chase to the bear. The bear scrambled as fast as he could and shinned up the tree. All the dogs surrounded the tree and kept barking at him. In the meantime, the clever fox entered the chicken coop unhindered and had a feast. He also managed to kill and carry off three more chicken. He worked swiftly and silently, once he was safe among the trees he started howling as loud as he could. The foolish dogs barked and went tearing in the direction of the howls leaving the bear behind. The bear scrambled to safety and went home.

The fox presented his friend with the chicken and the bear also enjoyed his treat. The fox lied about how hospitable everyone had been to him and how he could come up with only three chicken for his friend.

The fox tried a second time but this time he was not so lucky. The village folk were waiting for the chicken thief at the village chicken coop. They caught hold of the furry thief and tied him up.

Although they were angry, still they didn't exactly want to kill the fox. So, one of them suggested that they drag the fox through stones and thorns to teach him a lesson. The clever fox lolled out his tongue and wagged his tail hard as they dragged him through the thorns. He pretended he was enjoying himself thoroughly. The minute they sat down to rest in the grassy meadow, he started yelping in pain.

"Look," the village people shouted. "We have been doing this all wrong; let us drag the thief through the soft grass and that should teach him a lesson."

The fox yelped and whined and put up a good act and thoroughly enjoyed being dragged through the soft grass. The simpletons thought he had been punished enough and let him go. He laughed and laughed as he made his way to his friend the bear.

"Did you see that?" he asked the bear. The bear nodded. "They love me so much that they wished me to stay there forever and eat chicken and be dragged through the grass to drive away the ticks and fleas." I refused and ran away as fast as I could. "How can I leave the jungle and you, my friend?" He added slyly.

The simple bear thought it was very nice of his little friend to say so and took extra care to share his food with his friend and make sure he got the best bits.

After some time, the fox decided the village would have forgotten all about him and the chickens and he decided to go on another raid. He spoke to the Bear about being invited to another feast. The Bear said that was really nice, but he would not accompany the fox like the last time. The fox coaxed, pleaded and tried everything but he was not able to do so. So, he changed track and asked him to accompany him half way. After many hours of pleading, the bear agreed to wait for the fox by the trees above the village and promised him that he would come looking for him if the fox didn't return.

"They love me so much," the Fox said. "They may decide to keep me with them forever."

"Don't worry," the Big Bear said. "I'll make sure you return, I will come and get you."

The fox set off and took his time stealthily creeping on his belly, hiding under bushes and hugging the long evening shadows. All this was of no use. A large net fell on him, and he was captured…again.

The village people decided that they had let the fox off a little too lightly the last time so they would have to think of a harsher punishment.

They dragged the fox up to the tree by the side of the main path and tied him up securely to the tree trunk. They put up a sign and a stout stick that read, "Here he is, the one who steals our chicken and causes so much trouble. Passers-by, please make sure to punish this mischief maker with the stick provided." They decided they would tie him up for two days and then let him go.

The poor fox. There he was tied to the tree and everyone who passed by read the notice and hit him with the stick and went their way. The poor fox was heartily sick of being hit by every passer-by. One would have thought being punished would have taught him to be a nicer fox but that was not to be.

The bear patiently waited and waited and finally, after dark, went into the village looking for his friend. The dogs barked and rushed headlong to attack him but the bear was so worried about his little friend, he just sent them tumbling with a sweep of his paws. A few well-meaning snarls were enough to get the dogs out of his way. He sniffed the ground and picked up his friend's scent. Then he went looking for him. His nose led him to where the sad little fox stood tied to the tree. It was pretty dark, and the bear patted his friend's face and head to find out if he was okay.

"Are you okay?" He asked "I said I'd come looking for you, didn't I? How come your face feels a little puffy? Did you fall down and hurt yourself?"

The Fox laughed and said, "I'm perfectly fine, my friend. It's just that I was trying to run away from them as I cannot eat so many chicken and so they tied me up here with a sign that said everyone passing through has to feed me a whole chicken or else they would be punished with the stick that is there next to the signboard. I'm just so sick of eating chicken. If anyone even feeds me a tiny bit more, I'd probably die of a stomach ache.

"Dear Me," said the bear. "So what do I do now? Do I set you free or would you rather stay here?"

"Of course, I would rather be free." No sooner had he said this and the fox was free. However, instead of being grateful to the one who rescued him, he thought of playing a trick on the bear again.

"You like chicken, as much as I do," he said. "Why don't you take my place and enjoy the treat?" The Bear thanked the fox for his kindness and stood against the tree while the fox took the same rope and tied him up.

"Enjoy yourself," the fox laughed and slunk away in the darkness.

The bear waited patiently and presently he heard voices of two people. It was not yet light and the two were deep in conversation till they came to the signpost. One asked the other what this was, and the other explained how the village had decided to punish the fox. Without much ado, both of them picked up the stick, hit the bear and went their way.

The Bear who had thrown back his head and opened his mouth wide for the treat was puzzled and angry. He waited for the next person to pass by and once again threw back his head, closed his eyes and opened his mouth very wide. The passerby who had read the sign the day before just picked up the stick and hit the bear and moved on.

By then the sun had come up, and a passerby noticed that the fox they had tied up the day before had now miraculously changed into a bear. He was shocked. He ran away as fast as his legs would carry him.

The man decided to rouse his whole village so that they could all take a look. The Bear had other ideas. He decided that he didn't quite like being tied up while people hit him with sticks. With a shrug, he snapped the bonds that held him captive and ambled away towards the high mountain. Deep in his heart, he made up his mind to punish the fox if their paths ever crossed again. By the time the village folk had arrived, he was long gone.

The Bear decided it was too dangerous to live so close to man and moved further away from the High Hills and as for the fox, he thought he had had enough adventure for now and stayed well away from the bear and the village, and everyone was at peace.

24. THE MOON, A COBBLER, AND SOME FLOUR

Many years ago, when the world was no longer young, there lived in the hills a cobbler. He was no ordinary cobbler; he made shoes for all creatures. Of course, now days we don't call them shoes. We call them paws and hooves and claws, but those days, that was what they were called.

Everyone who had trouble with their footwear came to him. The elephant, the tiger, the lion, the horse, and of course, man too. He was a very useful cobbler.

One day, a man came to him and asked him to repair his shoes. The Cobbler obliged and mended them so well that the man was very pleased. To show how pleased he was, the man gave the Cobbler a sack of flour.

Later that night, the Cobbler prepared some rotis (bread) made out of flour. The Moon, shining over the Cobbler's house, watched with great interest as the Cobbler rolled out the perfectly round discs and expertly turned them over as they puffed up slowly. Having watched the Cobbler prepare the rotis, the Moon wanted to taste some. Before he could gather enough courage to ask for the rotis, the Cobbler, who was quite hungry sat down and finished his meal.

The next evening, the moon rose early and shone above the Cobbler's house once again. He watched the cobbler take some flour from the sack and prepare his meal. Just as he was about to eat it, the moon called out, "Wait Cobbler, please let me taste the roti first."

The Cobbler looked up and said, "I'm sorry, my friend Moon; but I have made just enough for me. I can't let you have one. Please take some flour instead and prepare your own rotis." Having said this, the Cobbler gave the Moon a generous amount of flour and sat down to his meal.

The Moon took the flour and made some rotis for himself. He ate them with relish, and wished he had some more. The next evening, the Cobbler found the Moon shining over his house. Once again, the moon called out, "Cobbler, dear Cobbler, please let me borrow some flour; I'm very hungry today. I'll return the flour soon, I promise."

The Cobbler felt sorry for the hungry Moon and gave him some flour again. The Moon took the flour, made some rotis out of it, and ate them. He felt full and satisfied and shone happily over the laughing streams and the silent hills.

Meanwhile, the Cobbler found that his sack of flour had finished and could not make any more rotis. Feeling very hungry, he decided to go to the Moon and ask him to return the flour he had borrowed. He went up, towards the sky, and met the Moon who was resting on a cloud.

"Dear friend," said the Cobbler. "I've come to you because I'm very hungry and I want some flour to make rotis."

The moon laughed and said, "Then why did you come to me? Go to Man, he and his sons have flour, I don't."

"But you had borrowed some flour from me, and I want it back. I'm very hungry. Please don't talk as if you have forgotten all about it," said the Cobbler angrily.

"Did I borrow some flour from you? I must have forgotten. Hmm…" the Moon scratched his head and pretended to think. "You said you'd return it soon, and now you are pretending to have forgotten," the Cobbler shouted.

"Did I say that?" Laughed the moon. "I must have forgotten that as well. Even if I had borrowed some flour from you, dear Cobbler, I'm sorry I cannot return it. I've eaten it all, and you know I can't grow anything in the sky. Go home, and forget the whole thing."

"Very well then, you ungrateful fellow, you brought this upon yourself. If I cannot have my flour, then I will eat you to satisfy my hunger." Saying this, the Cobbler opened his mouth and slowly started swallowing the Moon!

"Let me go!" The Moon struggled, but could not free himself. The Cobbler opened his mouth wider and wider, and with a huge gulp, swallowed the moon whole. Satisfied, he let out a huge burp.

The hills grew dark, and unfriendly. Animals cried out in terror, and there was panic in the villages. Babies cried, dogs barked and the Sons of Man came running out of their house. "O Moon, why have you hidden yourself?" They shouted.

The Cobbler's voice boomed from the sky, "The moon has eaten all my flour. Sons of Man, now he says he cannot return it. I was hungry, so I ate him up instead. Now don't you shout! I want to sleep." Saying this, the Cobbler fell asleep, turning a deaf ear to all the shouts and pleas of the Sons of Man.

The Sons of Man and their wives quickly gathered a little flour from every house. When they had collected enough, they began to beat their drums and pots and pans to get the Cobbler's attention. "Cobbler, Cobbler," they cried out. "Here is your flour, take it back. Take your flour back and set the Moon free," they shouted. The Cobbler, still angry with the Moon, pretended not to hear.

"Chordey Chamaraey Chordey," they chanted meaning, "Let him go O Cobbler, Let him go!"

"Chordey Chamaraey, Chordey," they yelled as they beat the pots and pans and created a din. The Cobbler still pretended not to hear anything. "Here is your flour, let him go!" Screamed the wives and scattered some flour from the bag for the Cobbler to see. "Let him go! Set him free!" Chanted the people on top of their lungs. Dogs howled and babies wailed.

The Cobbler looked down and saw the flour. He decided that the moon had been taught a lesson. Besides, the beating of the pots and pans and drums, the wails, screams and barks had begun to give him a very big headache.

He opened his mouth and slowly, very slowly, let the moon out. The Moon was finally free. The Sons of Man, their wives and children kept on screaming at the Cobbler who decided he had enough. Taking the flour the people had offer, the Cobbler made his way back home.

As for the Moon, he was so happy to be free; he shone twice as bright over the villages and the hills.

The Cobbler and the Moon, became friends, forgetting this incident, and every once in a while, the Moon borrowed flour from the Cobbler, who lets him have it and then the Moon refuses to replace it.

The Cobbler had to swallow the moon to teach him a lesson, and the people once again had to offer flour to the Cobbler to free the Moon.

It is therefore not surprising, on a dark, dark night, to find people in the hills beating their drums and pots and pans, scattering flour and chanting, "Let him go Cobbler! Oh, let him go!" When a lunar eclipse occurs. And when the eclipse had passed, they say that the Cobbler has gone home with the flour and a headache.

25. THE CREATOR SOME MILK AND SOME ALCOHOL

Many years had passed since the Creator had done his work, and created man and his world. Man had learnt many things. Man had learnt to subjugate the earth and his brothers. Man had learnt he was better than the others and that the earth belonged to him alone. The animals had learnt to stay away from man. The birds and the beasts had become wary of one another as well. The rivers were silent, and the trees spoke no more to man or beast.

The Creator had let things be and had not visited the hills for a long time.

One day, however, he felt a strong urge to go and see how the Sons of Man were. Aware that the Sons of Man would no longer be able to behold him in his true form, he changed himself into an old man and made his way to the hills.

He was sad to discover that the hills were no longer free. Man, and his sons had erected bars and fences to keep out the animals, and even his own brothers. Fear walked in the day, and Greed had settled in the heart of man. Sorely troubled by what he saw, he walked on to another village, and there he saw the Sons of Man toiling in the fields. The Creator sadly shook his head when he saw this, because he knew that they were not toiling to raise crops to feed themselves and their families, but to sell them for money.

The Creator's orders about sawing trees, and been disregarded. He had said that the trees were to be left alone. Moreover, even when fire had been given to man, the Creator had instructed them to use only dead branches or trees that had either been uprooted by the wind or struck by lightning. However, man had forgotten all this and had felled living healthy trees. The spirits of the trees and the spirits of the forest had fled. There was no one to greet the Creator as he walked through the torn and mutilated forest.

Sad and angry and very thirsty, the Creator looked around for water, but even the river nymphs and spirits had all fled. The Creator was unable to find a river or spring that had not been polluted in some way or another by Man. He looked around and saw a hut. He walked up to it and called out to the people inside. A son of man and his wife stepped outside.

"Please let me have a drink of water, O son of man," said the Creator. "I am very thirsty and have walked a long way." "No, there isn't any water to spare," said the wife sharply. "I have to walk a great distance to fetch water, and I can't waste it by giving a drink to every wayfarer who passes by."

The Creator, surprised by this, looked around, and saw a pail of milk standing in a corner. "Then please, O son of man, give me some milk, for I'm dying of thirst." "No," said the man. "I cannot do that because I have to take it around the villages and sell it. Without it, we would not be able to earn money. I think you should go now."

The Creator turned away and walked on to another milk seller's hut, where he received the same answer. He was about to drop his disguise and go home when he decided to visit one more hut. He walked on to a hut a little further away and looked inside.

Inside the hut sat a man busily brewing some liquid. The Creator called out, "O son of man, I'm very thirsty. Can you let me have a drink of water?"

"Why would you want to drink water when you can have some Nasi (millet beer)?" Replied the man cheerfully. "Come in and help yourself." The Creator went in and rested his weary feet. The man handed him a large mug of Nasi and said, "Here, if you want more, you can pour it out yourself." The Creator drank the Nasi and refilled his mug. Looking at the generous and cheerful man, he could not help comparing him with the two milkmen. He realized that the man had not become a slave of greed. Setting down his mug, the Creator stood up and said, "You, who have not let greed conquer you yet, have pleased me, unlike your neighbors, the milk sellers."

"From this day I order that all milk sellers shall go from door to door to sell their ware. May the hot sun beat down on them, and may the hail and the sleet freeze them. May the cold wind bite them, and yet, may they have to go out in such weather to earn their bread!"

Turning to the surprised man, the Creator continued gently, "As for you, my son, may you and your sons and their sons be blessed, and have people come to your door to buy your liquor. Let them walk under the hot sun or in the icy rain, but may you never have to leave your house to sell whatever you brew."

With that, the Creator disappeared. From that day all milk men had to carry their wares on their backs and go from door to door to sell milk, while all the makers of Nasi and Raksii (an alcoholic drink), sat at home and always had customers come to them.

26. THE PRINCESS AND THE LEAF

Once upon a time, there lived a prince who was noble and kind. The people of his kingdom were happy and prosperous, and every one of them loved him. The prince managed to lead such a peaceful life that wars and battles, so common in the other kingdoms, were unheard of.

Beyond the prince's land, in the north, lived some wicked Boksies (witches), who had heard about the prince and his peaceful land. The boksies, being mean and wicked by nature, were jealous to hear anything good and peaceful. Sitting down together, they decided to think of a way to harm the prince. Among these boksies were two sisters, who were the meanest and the wickedest of the lot. It wasn't long before one of them, the elder one, stood up and announced that she had thought of a plan.

"It is a simple plan," she said. "One of us shall marry the prince. On the wedding night, she shall cast a spell on the prince, so that when he wakes up the next morning, he will become as wicked and cruel as we wish him to be." The boksies were all satisfied at the plan and began to discuss the wicked plot step by step. It was decided that the one, who was to marry the prince, was to be the sister of the boksie who had thought up the plan. They were so pleased with the idea that they spent a whole month discussing it, just as women would.

Meanwhile, unknown to the witches, the prince had found himself a bride. She was the daughter of another powerful but virtuous king who thought that the prince would be the most suitable husband for his daughter. Thus, while the witches were busy with their plans, the wedding had taken place. The people immediately liked their princess and said that there was none as beautiful as she was. The price gave away a lot of gifts and money in honour of his bride, and the people celebrated the wedding and blessed the couple.

One day the prince decided to go hunting, and taking up his bow and arrows, he set off alone. The prince wandered far into the jungle, and after a long chase, he brought down a deer. Tired and thirsty, he sat down under a tree while his horse cropped grass nearby. It was a hot day and the prince, feeling drowsy, fell asleep. He was fast asleep when suddenly, his horse neighed, and the prince woke up with a start. There before him stood an old woman, who seeing that he was awake, began to speak, "O king, I have come to you because you are known to never refuse anything to anybody. Will you give me leave to speak?" The prince, surprised to hear himself thus answered, "Amaai (mother), it would give me great pleasure if I am able to help you. I give you my word that I will try my best to help you. So don't hesitate, please speak what is on your mind." The old lady, who was in fact the elder boksie, began, "My lord, I am a very poor woman, and I have a beautiful daughter, who has now come of the age. My poverty does not let me find a suitable husband for her and I beg you to marry her." Hearing this, the prince answered respectfully, "Amaai, I will not be able to fulfill this request because I already have a wife." The boksie was surprised to hear this but went on, "O lord of the poor, that has never been a problem with any king in the past. A king can marry more than one wife if he wants to, and I assure you, my daughter will not mind being the second wife. She will be happy to be your wife's slave and serve the two of you faithfully." The prince who loved his princess very much and had no intention of marrying the old woman's daughter, replied politely but firmly, "I do not wish your daughter to lead a life of servile faithfulness, because that's how her life would be if I married her. Being the ruler of this land, it is my duty to see that none of my subjects are unhappy and it would be very wrong on my part to commit such paap (sin). I would not be able to give her anything. My kingdom is promised to the firstborn of my wife, be it a son or a daughter. Even if I did marry your daughter and she was willing to lead such a life, would her sons agree to lead their lives like her? Would they not quarrel with their halfbrothers and sisters? What would happen to a land whose rulers fought amongst themselves? You tell me, Amaai, would I not be a cursed ruler?"

The boksie could not argue against such a sound reasoning and kept quiet. Then, the prince spoke to her kindly, "I know you did what you did out of love for your daughter and I did promise to help you. Take this," he said, removing the costly jewels he had been wearing. "It will help you to find a better husband for your daughter. And remember that a woman is always happier in being the mistress of a poor house than a slave in a rich one. Find her someone worthy, and if the jewels are not enough to pay for the wedding, you can ask for more when I come here next week."

Taking leave of the old lady, the prince rode off, while the boksiee gnashed her teeth in anger. She was frustrated at the failure of her plan, and furious that the spells she had cast over the prince while he was talking were useless. Little did she know, that the prince had been protected by his Dharma (virtue). Screaming out curses, she made her way home, where her sister awaited her. The sister had been expecting the prince but one look at the elder sister's face was enough to let her know that their plan had failed. When the younger boksie heard the story, she smiled to herself because another plan had been taken from her evil mind. She asked her sister where she could meet the prince. "Because I have thought of a way to make the prince marry me," she said.

Back at the palace, the prince narrated the happenings of the day to his wife, who was very much relieved that the prince had refused the old woman's request. However, being a woman, she could not help feeling jealously protective about her husband, and the prince's reassurance about not marrying again did nothing to help her. Not surprisingly, the following week she insisted on accompanying the prince to the forest.

The prince led the way to the place where he had met the old woman. The princess, who at first had half expected to see the old woman and her beautiful daughter waiting for her prince, was soon lost in wonder at the beauty of the forest. The princess begged the prince to show her around, and the prince happily led her through the forest, showing her the places where the rabbits made their burrows and where the tigers came to drink. Presently, they came to a pool. There were huge lilies in the middle of the pool, and the princess asked the prince to get one for her. The prince, who never refused his wife anything, agreed. Looking at his wife, the prince noticed that she was tired, and pointing to a clearing not far off said, "You rest there while I wade into the pool to get your flowers."

The prince watched his wife walk towards the clearing and then turned to his task. The younger boksie who had been searching for the prince saw him in the pool collecting lilies.

Knowing that all her wiles were useless as long as the princess remained with the prince, she decided to kidnap the princess and leave her in a forest where no mortal could survive. So, she crept stealthily towards the princess, who was now fast asleep among the wild daisies. As the boksie came nearer and nearer, she suddenly felt very dizzy and felt her evil powers draining away. She realized quickly that the virtue of the princess made her stronger than her.

Meanwhile, the prince, unaware of the danger stalking his beloved princess, had gathered a whole bunch of lilies for her. He turned back and walked to the clearing. The boksie heard the approaching footsteps of the prince and tried to make herself invisible, but found her spells had suddenly lost their full power.

She looked around wildly for an escape and suddenly saw a couple of black crows sitting on a branch above the princess's head. "Ha," she thought. "That gives me an idea." Saying this, she transformed herself into a likeness of the princess and lay down a little away from her. Imagine the prince's surprise when he reached the clearing to find two princesses who looked exactly like each other! As he stood there perplexed, the two woke up and each addressed him as their lord. When the real princess saw the impostor, she realized that they were up against some very evil powers. Desperately trying to keep calm, she prayed for help, and turning to her prince, she said, "My lord, do not look so troubled I am the real princess." To the boksie she said gently, "Dear lady, to covet another wealth is sin. Therefore, do not fall into this trap that leads to disaster. Leave my husband to me. I realize that you are no ordinary mortal, and I cannot guess what you are, but I pray to you to let me keep what is mine." Hearing this, the boksie laughed merrily, and addressing the prince said, "My Lord, this must be the daughter of the old lady. She was right. Her daughter is indeed beautiful and very clever, but also very greedy. Realizing that you would never accept another in my stead, she has come to trick us. But my lord, do not be deceived by this sorceress. Come, let us go home, for I do not like such treachery." The poor prince stood there not knowing what to do. Each looked exactly as his wife, and each had the same soft voice. Not knowing how to react, he gave a dejected cry and said, "My princess, save us both from this plight, for I fail to recognize you, and I realize that I would never be the same without you. Save your prince. With that, he fell down on the grass, weeping brokenly, and the lilies lay scattered on the ground.

Seeing her prince in such a state, the princess once again appealed to the witch and begged her to leave them in peace. But the witch only laughed and asked the real princess to go away instead. Looking around in desperation, the princess sought some assistance but in vain. There was no one around. Suddenly she spotted some long, sharp bladed leaves of the Amliso (or the broom plant, as it is commonly called). Snatching up a sharp and long blade, she held it up and said, "Sister, since you insist that I am the sorceress, let us undergo a test. Holding up the sharp leaves, she continued, "Whoever amongst us two is able to swallow this leaf is the real princess, and the one who fails will have to leave."

The witch agreed, knowing well enough that her magic would help her overcome anything. "How easy it is going to be, she thought. The princess prayed fervently, asked the forest gods to help her, and swallowed the leaf. The witch watched the princess swallow the leaf, and not to be outdone, she picked up a larger one and popped it in. The princess, protected by her virtue, was unharmed, but the witch, on the other hand, fared badly. The leaf refused to obey her magic and go down her throat smoothly. Instead, it tickled her, it scratched her, it twisted in the most annoying manner in her throat, and it made the witch cough violently. The prince and the princess were meanwhile watching the witch intently. In another violent fit of coughing, the witch dropped her disguise, and her hideous visage was clearly seen by the prince. In a desperate effort to keep the leaf in her mouth, the witch bit the leaf as it was leaving her mouth, but the harm had been done.

Turning to the witch, the prince said severely, "You have caused undue grief and anxiety to both of us. If I ever see you or any of your kind near my domain, I will destroy each and every one of you." The witch gnashed her teeth, tore her hair, and screamed out curses at the couple, but it was of no use. Finally, she had to slink away in shame.

The young princess and her prince rode back their kingdom, having leant to treasure one another and to think clearly in times of trouble. The witch, on the other hand, had to hide with the bats in a dirty cave for fear of being laughed at by her sisters and being outwitted by a human.

As for the leaf that helped the princess, it still carries to this day the teeth marks of the witch, when she bit it in a desperate attempt to keep it from leaving her mouth.

27. BHADRAYO: THE VOICE OF MAN.

Many years ago, when the creator still walked the earth and took great delight in seeing his work.

The hills were still young, and the birds and animals and rivers and trees and stones and sky and the wind all understood and spoke the same language.

They never stopped speaking to one another. Sometimes the trees stretched out their branches to the sky as their roots burrowed deep into the heart of the earth where thoughts and hopes and warmth of mother earth travelled up to the surface through the roots to the tree to the leaves and the winds carried their tales to mingle with the laughter of the skies above.

Rain brought a message of new beginnings to the rivers and trees and to the earth.

The hills adorned themselves with wild blooms and young green shoots during the day. The sky took pleasure in their beauty and arrayed itself in magnificent, jeweled stars that shone through the crisp night air.

Sometimes the pale moon would be its only adornment, and the skies and the earth never looked more beautiful in the light of that one single jewel.

There was joy in being and in existing. The creator was delighted in his creation, so delighted, that he created Man, his Sons and Daughters, so that they could enjoy his creation.

In the beginning, everything was good.

Man lived and loved his brothers. He spoke with the wind, laughed with the rivers and loved with the warmth of the earth. There was beauty in him and the Spirit of Goodness chose to live in him. The

Creator loved him above all and was kind to his sons and daughters. Man grew in strength and numbers and in thought.

Gradually Man grew proud and haughty. He let Greed settle in his heart. He fought with his sons and daughters, who in turn fought among themselves. He claimed the earth as his own, and the spirit of goodness left him. By degrees, he forgot the language of the skies and of the earth.

The Rivers fell silent, and the whistling winds made no sense anymore. The forest spirits all avoided him. The animals were no more his brothers. Man grew ambitious, and man wanted to tame the earth, the sky, and his brothers.

The creator watched in silence amused and interested at the puny being's audacity. Maybe in his heart the Creator did feel a little too proud of his creation, like the doting father of an intelligent but wayward child. So, he did nothing. Man set out to claim the earth first. He cleared forests, mercilessly cutting and burning the forests down. The forest spirits fled, and Man could neither see nor hear them anymore.

He turned to water next and turned the course of small streams so that they would irrigate his lands and provide his food crops with water.

He fenced in his lands and kept out his brothers and sons. He then went on to conquer his brothers and turn them into his slaves. The creator still watched and held his peace. Thus, man went on to make life easier for himself and his tribe.

Then man turned upon man. They started living in groups and started speaking in ways that other groups would not understand them. They grew ugly and cruel.

They started making war with each other. They fought and quarreled and took sides and became sick in their hearts. They grew more food and turned it into wine and beer and drank it to become intoxicated and violent. They hunted no longer for food alone but for sport. The animals hid from them and Man turned his sport to the birds.

The Creator was particularly fond of the birds because he had made them for beauty and beauty alone. Their songs had warmed the hearts of many rivers and trees. The forests had looked beautiful with their brilliant colours flashing in the sun. Just as the colourful fish that swam the seas and the rivers, the creator had decided these beautiful creatures would swirl and float and soar in the air.

Man hunted and killed these beautiful little creatures for sport and this made the Creator furious.

He felt he had tolerated enough evils of Man. He had watched his creation suffer in the vain hope that Man The best of his creation would ultimately seek and find the balance that held the whole of his creation together.

But here was Man, the same Man he had created with so much love and effort, trusted, loved and forgiven, here he was, destroying beauty. The same man whom he had created with a pure heart, who now held much evil in it. This was unforgivable.

He first wanted to destroy them completely but held himself back. After all, he did love them. He thought it over for a bit and then came to realize that if Man was unable to speak, then more than half the evils that he held in his heart would be unable to spread. The creator thought it over some more. Man was able to spread evil by infecting others. Trouble was caused by them speaking to each other, infecting each other with their ideas, ideas that spread destruction and sorrow.

Man had learnt to speak in various different ways so that not many could understand his secret thoughts. He had also learnt to form groups based on the various tongues he had made. This had led to division of tribes and tribal rivalries.

The Creator knew that very soon, using the same excuse that they were different and each tribe spoke a different language, they would select their own leaders who would then teach them to turn upon one another and destroy what the other had built.

It would be a pity to take away their songs but the creator was left with no choice. He had to do what he had to do.

From that day Man and his Sons and his Daughters were struck dumb. They could not utter a single word or produce a single sound. All they could do was weep, silent tears and wonder what happened to them.

Life without any speech was terrible for Man. The daughters of Man were unable to sit in groups and tell each other the little everyday things of their lives. The Sons of Man found it impossible to speak of glorious victories and of new conquests. The younger lot found it impossible to lie and scold. Live was quite hard.

Slowly, as the years slipped by quietly. Man found he was able to live in peace with his brothers and sons. There were no words to injure the other with. With this new-found peace and silence there came to earth a quiet kind of calm.

The years slipped by quietly and smoothly. In the quiet, Man and his sons and daughters slowly found themselves listening to the voices of his brothers, the trees, the rivers, the animals, the birds, the earth, the sky, the rain, the wind, the thunder and hail.

As anger, jealousy and hate slowly slipped away from their hearts, the sounds grew clearer. The clear sounds lead them through long forgotten memories where lay buried the simplicity of thought and love for all beings. Of the oneness of creation and of the cycle of living and dying and being born again, ever alive, ever changing, ever living, always a part of each other. The earth always a part of Man and Man always a part of the earth. Ever changing yet the same, inseparable and harmonious .

Each day Man and his Sons and Daughters heard the songs of the earth and remembered a little more. Till one day they remembered everything. Of wind and hail, grass and of sky, the earth and their brothers. They also remembered how they had mercilessly cleared forests and slaughtered the animals and persecuted the birds.

They soon realized what they had done and understood they were being punished for their crimes. They realized what they had done and what they had lost. They were thoroughly ashamed of themselves and wept for their crimes

Man wept soundlessly and helplessly. The Creator did feel a little sorry for him but did nothing. As he actually liked this newer version of the soundless man.

Thus, life went on for many more years and Man became as he was. His brothers, the animals and the birds started feeling sorry for him. Especially when the little children of Man were in distress and could not cry out in pain or fear or for help.

But there was nothing they could do for them.

Until one day, a tiny little bird, the Bhadrayo decided to approach the Creator.

Hopping awkwardly on one foot and then the other, the tiny little bird asked the creator if he would ever return Man's voice to him. Smiling gently at the little bird's anxiety and marveling at the great love that he bore for his brother Man The creator answered that it was not within his power to return speech to mankind.

The little bird felt very sorry for Man and his children and asked if there was something that could be done to help them get their speech back. The creator looked grave and said, "Only if someone decides to give them his voice, will Man and his sons ever speak again."

The Bhadrayo was stunned, who would ever want to give up his speech to Man and his sons and be dumb for the rest of his years?

He flew off in silence and sat on a tree next to a man's house. The Daughter of Man had had a baby two winters ago, and the chubby infant was sitting in the sun waving its fat fists in the air. A bee flew past and landed on the grass next to the child. The child curiously put out her hand and caught hold of it. The angry bee stung the child.

The child opened its mouth in distress and wailed soundlessly. The Daughter of Man could not hear her baby wailing and continued winnowing the grains she had collected.

The kind-hearted Bhadrayo felt very sorry for the child and made up its mind. He flew straight back to the Creator and offered his voice to the Creator to distribute to Man and Sons of Man. The creator amazed at the sacrifice of the little bird and created another sound from the whistling winds and gave it to the Bhadrayo.

"I cannot and will not let someone as brave and generous as you, go without sound," he said. "Little bird, the Man, the Sons and Daughters of man shall forever be in your debt." Saying this the Creator gave the Bhadrayo's voice to Man, his Sons, and Daughters.

Of course, this was not a very good thing to do because before long, Man was back to his old and evil ways. They quarrelled and fought and made war with each other. They sharpened their skills in the art of persuasion to spread their poisonous ideas which later led to many social ills.

As for Man's gratitude to the Bhadrayo. Man told his sons, who told their sons that the Bhadrayo was responsible for them regaining their lost speech.

Man being Man decided he would prevent his children from losing their speech at any cost.

So, he and his sons hunted the little birds and ripped out their tongues to use them as spoons to feed the first solid meals to their children with the hope that those children, who ate their first solid food with the tongue of a Bhadrayo would learn speech early and be good in the art of oration and persuasion.

This cruel practice remained with the sons of Man in the hills for a very long time till the hills no longer woke to the song of the Bhadrayo.

Man had finally managed to silence the one voice that had pleaded his case with the Creator.

Now that the Bhadrayo is no longer seen, Man feds his child its first solid food with a silver coin or a silver spoon. This seems to be working just fine.

I only wish Man had thought of this before.

28. BREAD OF HUSKS (*Or Bhoos Ko Roti*)

(Like many folk tales the story of Bread of Husks has more than one ending. The Reader please decide which ending you would like)

Many years ago, when the hills were no longer free, there lived a young boy and his step mother. They had a house on a hill and a patch of land to grow their food and two cows that gave them milk, a few chickens to give them eggs and a few orange trees that gave them fruit.

Life was simple and their wants were few. Life would have been good.... very good.

If only the step mother did not hate the young man so much. She hated him because she had married his father who had been a fairly rich man. The father lost all his money trying to help the poor. She hated him because his father had died without giving her a child. She hated him because he was always happy.

As for the young boy, he tried very hard to be happy because he knew if the spirit of his father saw him, the spirit would feel sad. He always had a song on his lips, and a merry laugh, lest people discover his step mother hated him and pity him.

He tried very hard to keep his mother happy (he never thought of her as his step mother). He fetched the firewood and the water, looked after the cows and the fields. He hunted and brought home rabbits and wild fowl. He searched for berries and looked for honey and brought home something or the other for her, hoping against hope that one day her heart would thaw and he would have a mother.

The step mother on the other hand, hated him even more because all his actions did was to make her wonder what it would have been like to have her own son do the things that her step son did for her.

So that was how things stood for a very long time.

One day, the young boy thought of going to the river to fish. He asked his step mother to pack him some food for the day.

"I'll bring home the finest fish the river holds," he told her. 'Don't you worry mother, I will be back before the sun sets, and you will have fresh fish for dinner. I know you grow tired of the wild fowl I bring home."

Without saying anything, the step mother set down the boy's morning meal in front of him and went into the kitchen.

There she saw the paddy husks she had separated from the grain in the morning. Taking some water, she kneaded the husks and made three dry rotis (flat bread). She rolled them up and wrapped them in a banana leaf and gave it to the boy.

The boy took the package and placed it in his basket. Taking his fishing rod, he set off. The narrow path snaked down into the valley below, and he could hear the river.

Upon reaching the river, he made his way to a spot where he knew he would find plenty of fishes. Muttering a prayer to the River Spirit, he cast his rod.

The first catch he offered on three leaves to the forest spirits.

It was the forest spirits who gave so much to Man. He knew the law. He would never dream of cheating the forest spirits of their share. While hunting, he would always offer the heart and a piece of flesh each on three leaves for the forest gods.

It was said that the forest spirits kept count of all the birds and animals in the forest and after dusk they would come and count them.

If they found someone missing, they would look far and wide for them but if they found the offering of flesh and the heart, they would understand that Man had needed food, and he had taken the missing animal.

Of course, the spirits understood if one left only the heart and a few tail feathers of the jungle fowl there wasn't much to share. But when it came to bigger game like the boar and the deer. Then the portion included a bit of liver, the heart and one whole ear of the game. This made sense as the portion was large enough to make a good meal for a hungry fox or weasel. After all the forest spirits never wanted the leopard or the fox to go hungry.

The boy patiently waited, listening to the gurgle of the river, and before noon he had caught two big fish and decided it was enough.

He knew if one took more than what one needed, ill luck would follow and he would not be so lucky the next time he fished.

Carefully keeping his basket on a large flat rock, he decided to look for Thotney, a sour wild plant that his mother loved to eat. After having gathered a large bunch, he decided to collect the dry bits of wood and take it home. He whistled as he worked and made a large bundle of fire wood.

Tired and hungry he decided to have his meal and rest a bit before making his way uphill with his load of firewood and fish. He merrily hummed as he sat down on the rock to have his meal. Carefully opening the banana leaf package, he broke three pieces off his husk bread and offered it on three leaves to the forest spirits.

The bread was hard to swallow but the river supplied the young man with plenty of water. Looking down into the water, the young man saw tiny fish gleaming in the sun and broke off a small bit of his bread and threw it in the water for them.

The little fish swarmed all over the bits, and the young man felt happy to see the tiny creatures enjoy themselves. He threw in a bigger bit of bread and piece by piece he shared his lunch with the little folk of the river.

After his meal he stretched his arms and decided to take a nap. Lying on the rock, he slowly drifted to sleep wondering if the ache he felt inside was his half empty stomach or his heart that craved his mother's love.

Now the scraps of bread that he had thrown down for the fish had been carried downstream by the river.

There a snake had come across the and eaten it. Having found the morsels strangely nice, he went on ahead to look for some more. Collecting a few small bits, he had taken it to his mate who had not been speaking to him for two days because she was angry with him. The snake loved his mate dearly and had been miserable when she refused to speak to him. They were no ordinary snakes.

The peace offering worked and the female snake forgave her mate and all was well again. The snakes felt they had to thank the person who had given them the bread and their peace. The two of them swiftly swam upstream looking for the boy. Slithering up the flat rock, the two snakes looked at the sleeping boy.

Through their powers, they could see into the boy's heart. They saw his tale. They saw the love he bore for his mother. They understood the step mother's hate for the boy.

They understood her rage against the world because of her being childless and poverty-stricken. They understood how she had poured out her venom on the boy, who had somehow thought he would win her over one day and all would be well.

The female turned to her mate and asked, "Can we give this pure soul what he needs?" The male nodded. "Reward him for bringing us together, give him what he needs the most."

The male snake looked at the blazing sun above and the clear blue sky and said, "As you wish. Your happiness is what matters to me." Then in one swift and smooth motion, he buried his fangs deeply into the sleeping boy's neck. The boy twitched in his sleep and floated into the dreamless sleep of eternity.

The female was shocked, "I asked you to help repay our debt of gratitude. What have you done?"

The male snake calmly replied, "You asked me to give him what he needs. I did just that. This pure soul would have felt a lot more pain and sorrow while he spent the rest of his years here trying to do what was right. The woman he calls mother, would never be happy as long as he lived. He would have ended up feeling guilty for not having tried hard enough and she would have just been more embittered and more demanding. His merry song would fade and his pure heart would wither in the fire of her hate."

"Would you have him live like that for the rest of his life? So, I gave him what he needed most....... freedom from this world."

The female bowed her head to this piece of wisdom, and the two slithered down the rock and slipped into the stream leaving behind the lifeless body of the young man.

"Please do so. I would be happy if you could give him what he needs."

The snake looked at the blazing sun above and lowered his head. The wish fulfilling jewel, he carried on his head winked in the sun light.

The boy woke with a start to see two snakes slowly slithering down the rock and into the stream. The afternoon sunlight blazed in the jewel the snake had left on the rock.

The boy knew what it was. He had heard enough stories from his people about the wish fulfilling jewel that adorned the heads of some special snakes.

Seizing the jewel, he ran all the way home to his mother. He knew at last he would be able to keep her truly happy.

He used the jewel to get all the comforts his mother wished for, built her a beautiful home and filled her house with everything she had ever wanted.

He wished for great wealth for himself as well, and married a beautiful young lady.

After he had used the jewel to wish for great wealth, he did go back to the river to return the jewel to its rightful owner.

He lived in peace and happiness in his beautiful house with his mother and wife and children.

29. SEERING AND LHARING

The name Darjeeling means the "Land of the Thunderbolt."

It is said that a Tibetian monk from Sikkim came and established monasteries in Darjeeling. One of the oldest monasteries he founded is said to be in present day Rishihat Tea estate which was formerly known as Seering. The neighbouring hill, known as Relling today, used to be called Lharing.

Seering and Lharing (meaning Thunderbolt and Electric current in the Limbu/Subba language,) used to be humans in their previous life. This is a sad tale of two cursed siblings, this is a story from erstwhile Limbuwan that would actually explain the origin of the name "Land of the Thunderbolt."

Once upon a time in the ancient world, there lived a brother Suhempheba and sister Lahadongna. They had been orphaned at a very young age and lived in a house a little away from a tiny hamlet where the rest of the people lived.

When their parents had died, the only living creature in the house had been a dog. The dog looked after them and served them faithfully. Later, when the two children grew up, they committed a terrible sin and started living together as man and wife. The dog did not like it but held her peace and kept on serving the two faithfully as she loved them very much.

Between the two, they soon had many children and there was more to do, and the dog found herself very busy indeed. She did not complain. Lahadongna on the other hand, grew exceedingly ill-tempered and began to be irritable and angry. She started venting out her anger and frustration at the dog. She would complain about the dog to Suhemphaba, who would scold her harshly, and later as time went by, she started throwing things at the poor creature and the dog always had to slink about the house with her tail between her legs.

The Dog often went to bed hungry but still did not complain. She tried to help Lahadongna as much as she could. One day, one of the elder children upset the cooking pot and the fire went out with a great big hiss and ashes flew all around the room. The rice spilled all over the floor. Three of the younger children, who were very hungry, began to cry.

Lahadongna in a fit of rage, kicked the dog very hard, and threw her out of the house saying it was all her fault for not having watched over the children properly.

The dog was old, hungry, sad and tired of the ill treatment meted out to her every day by the wicked woman. She decided to go to the spirits and ask for justice. She walked for many days till she came to the place where the eight spirits of the eight directions met. She called out to them and they answered her.

The dog who was feeling very sad and hurt, asked the eight spirits if she could meet the Great Spirit and ask for justice.

The spirits asked her why she thought injustice was being done to her, and she narrated her tale of woe.

The eight spirits listened to what the Dog had to say and then asked. The dog to be patient. Man and his son consoled her and sent her back to live with the humans and said if the woman illtreated her again, then she should come back and tell the Great Spirit her problems. The Dog agreed and went back.

When she reached home, she found Lahadongna sitting near the fire with all her children. She quietly walked into the house, and Lahadongna started scolding her for having left without a word and how she had to do everything herself. Silently, the dog fetched the broom and started sweeping the house. The woman kept on scolding the Dog, and demanded to know where she had been. The dog finally told her that she had gone to meet the eight spirits to help her meet Tagera Ningwaphuma, the Great Spirit, and complain about her ill treatment at the hands of humans.

Lahadongna flew into a rage, and snatching the broom from the dog, she started hitting her with the broom. She kept on hitting the dog till she ran out of the house again. This time she went straight to where the Great Spirit lived and demanded justice.

She asked the Spirit why she had been ill-treated when all she did was help them even when they had committed the gravest of sins and lived as man and wife. She asked the Great Spirit why Suhempheba and Lahadongna had gone scot-free for such a long time even though they had committed such sin. She also mentioned that she thought that they were becoming bolder and becoming more sinful because they were certain they would not be punished by anyone.

The Great Spirit smiled and said that it was time Man learnt how he was going to solve such problems on his own because then all creatures would have to keep making the journey to where he lived, and that would be very difficult for most of them.

The Great Spirit asked the dog to remain loyal to humans as there was much good in them still. He advised the dog to go back to the village, and collect the pious and elderly men of the village and form a council and ask for justice.

The dog went back to the village and gathered the people together. She told them what the Great Spirit had told her. The village people helped select the eight most worthy men to form the first council. They were to represent the eight spirits of the eight directions. The people decided these eight men had to be men who were courageous in battle and also very spiritually enlightened men. They decided to choose the following.

Nawara Samba,

Sumona Samba,

Samsingbung Samba,

Yengaso Samba,

Tappaeso Samba,

Chonuso Samba,

Muktubung Samba,

Khesewa Samba.

These men were all called Sambas which meant they were well versed in the six mundhums(the songs of creation) and had led pious and righteous lives. Sambas were blessed with divine power of speech, and what they said would always come true. The sun and the moon both shone brightly on the council to show the people that the Great Spirit was happy with their choice of council.

The meeting began. The council asked the dog to put forward her grievances in front of them. The dog did so and finally ask the same questions. "Why do Suhempheba and Lahadongna who are living in sin, themselves, punish me and ill treat me every day?"

"Why do Suhempheba and Lahadongna scold me and throw things at me when I look after their many children they have had through sin? Although these two have very many children, this is a sinful thing because these are blood brother and blood sister."

"Is it because these two have never been punished for their misdeeds that they think the Great Spirit doesn't exist?"

They decreed it was a grave sin for people related by blood to live together as man and wife, and Suhempheba and Lahadongna could no longer continue to do so. It was also decided that to keep such incidents from repeating, no Kirat was allowed to wed into his blood line for seven generations.

The children were divided between the two and each was asked to go in different directions and settle far away. The eight councilors felt sorry for the children who had to stay away from either their mother or father and each other through no fault of their own, and blessed the children. The descendants of Suhempheba would be known for famous Priests and the descendents of Lahadongna would be known for famous kings.

Suhempheba took his children and moved towards the mountains, and Lahadongna moved towards the plains with her children.

When they died, Suhempheba's soul turned into a thunderbolt (Seri) and Lahadongna's turned into electric current (Lharin). It was just as the Sambas had decreed. It is said that people who do not adhere to these rules will be punished by Seri and Lharing.

(With the exceptions of some tribes whose sons are allowed to marry their mother's brother's daughters. But Sister's daughter and the Brother's son were not allowed to wed.)

As for the faithful Dog, she was satisfied with the punishment and lived with the sons of man till her time came to move on into the next world. The Great Spirit rewarded her loyalty by letting her guard the doorway to the next world, and she was given the right to refuse entry to any soul who had committed crimes, especially ill-treating helpless animals.

Thus, in Kirati homes the dog is worshiped once a year (see the story of Bhailo and Deusurey Chapter). Needless to say, there is a very strict rule in most Kirati houses that says women are not to kick or hit any dog especially with a broom.

As for the men and boys, if they treat the dog badly, they are told the dog will refuse to let them enter the next world and their souls will wander the corners of the earth forever. That generally works as an incentive to all to be kind to their dogs.

Source: The History and Culture of the Kirati People by Shri Iman Singh Chemjong. First published in in 1948 in Kalimpong. Second edition published in 1952 in Darjeeling.

30. THE TALE OF THE MILLIPEDE AND THE GODSON

Long, long ago, when the world was young, there lived a millipede. He lived all by himself in the dark shadows of the jungle and lived a solitary life, scuttling on his hundred legs among the damp ferns and mosses. Maybe it was because he led such a lonely life; he would always be in a mean temper. Of course, the fact that he had a hundred legs must have been the reason he lived apart, afraid that the others would make fun of him.

The reason why the Creator had created the millipede was probably that he (the Creator) had been in an exceptionally good frame of mind or that he wanted to satisfy his fancy. Whatever might have been the reason behind the creation of the millipede, he was not very happy about his hundred legs.

One day a son of man who was very dear to the Creator, came to him with his new-born son. The Creator was delighted to see the little child and blessed him. Being very pleased at the man for having come to him, he said, "From this day onwards, this child shall be my favourite son. Let no one harm him. For if anyone dares to do so, he shall feel my displeasure. He shall walk on land and sea unafraid, and shall become a great person when he grows up." Thus, he blessed the little child.

The man, pleased with the blessing, went back home. From that day, the little child remained unmolested by all beasts.

The parents left him among the sweet-smelling grass when they went to look for food, and he chuckled and gurgled happily waving his chubby fists in the air.

Time went on, and the little one learnt to crawl. He would gleefully crawl to an ant's nest and watch the little creatures run about busily. Since no creature harmed him, the little child was unafraid of anything. Snakes lazily basked in the sun close by, and wasps hummed by without harming him. Deer came to the pool to drink, and watched the little boy playing by the water. Tigers watched him with their glowing amber eyes and growled their approval.

Even the angry nettles and thorns moved aside to let the little one toddle past. They were afraid to try the Creator's displeasure. This was how the animals and plants kept the Creator's command. All except the millipede, who had been asleep among some moss deep in the ground when the Creator had passed his command. No one thought to inform him about the command, and in fact, some of the creatures did not even know that he existed.

The millipede, however, did not have to worry, because no one ever came to where he lived, he did not venture out too far, and he never ever saw the child.

One day, however, the boy's parents left him by some trees and went far into the woods looking for edible roots. The little one was playing happily as usual, when suddenly the skies turned black and a steady rain began to fall. Never having seen the skies pour down thus, the child unsteadily walked towards some trees and tumbled down among some ferns. He sat there for some time and made his way towards the line of trees.

The millipede, who had been far away from his ferns, had taken shelter among the lower trunks of the pine trees. The child now came to where the millipede was resting and rested under the same tree. Tired and wet, the child fell asleep among the damp grass. The millipede, which had been looking at the child, crept lower and lower to get a better look, and fell on the sleeping child who brushed it away in his sleep.

The millipede felt highly insulted and angry at the way he had been swept off the child's face and thought the child did not respect him enough. He scurried up the tree and once again landed on the child's face. The boy woke up. Having never known anything to have hurt him, the child reached out and picked up the strange creature with so many legs and laughed. The angry millipede immediately bit the little child, who dropped him in surprise. The ill-tempered creature bit the child very hard again and ran into the grass.

The parents, meanwhile, worried that the child might not have found shelter, hurried to where they had left him, and to their dismay found their baby badly bitten and bleeding. The father decided to go to the Creator and ask for justice. The Creator was furious when he saw his godson hurt. "Who has done this to you?" he thundered. It did not take him very long to find out the culprit who was by now hiding among the pines. CRACK! The great tree fell with a great crash. The millipede moved away quickly onto the next tree, his hundred legs carrying him away swiftly. Crack! Another forest giant was downed. The Creator's anger was terrible to behold. Tree after tree fell before his wrath, and the millipede wisely chose to creep amongst the ferns once more. After some time, the Creator calmed down, and turning to the child, gave him some herbs that would cure him.

The Creator never forgave the millipede for disobeying him, and on rainy days, he is reminded of the millipede even more. Then he hurls his thunderbolt among the pine trees again in the hope of destroying the creature that dared disobey him. That is why people are warned not to stand under trees, especially pine trees during thunderstorms. Who knows, the Creator just might decide to hurl his bolt that way!

As for the millipede, he still hides himself and hardly ventures outside for fears that the Creator might see him and punish him. That is why he comes out in the evenings and runs away as soon as he hears anything suspicious.

This is only a story, and the readers have to keep in mind that the millipede does not bite. Nor does it sting. It is a harmless little creature that looks frightful so that the other animals will leave it alone. As for not standing under pine trees during a thunderstorm, we all know why, don't we?

As I have mentioned many times in this book folk tales tend to have different versions so does this tale.

It is said that a brother and a sister decided to live together as man and wife and that displeased the Creator greatly (please read the story of Seri and Lahring).

It was decreed thereafter that no man or woman could wed anyone from his/her family for seven generations, if they did their children would turn into Millipedes and the Creator who had turned the two siblings into Thunder and Lightning had given them strict orders to destroy them. Therefore the millipede is actually an offspring of siblings that dared defy the Creator and it keeps hiding amongst ferns and pines to escape the wrath of the Creator.

31. PLANTING SALT

Long time ago in a small village, there lived a Limbu and his son. They were not very rich nor too poor, but managed to live a simple and comfortable life. Their possessions consisted of two buffalo, a goat and a fairly large plot of land. In those days, salt was brought all the way from a far-off land. Otherwise, they had to settle for the coarse and gritty rock salt that they could find, often with great difficulty, from the hills.

The Limbu and his son used this coarse salt to flavour their simple meal and thought they saved some amount by their thrift. One evening the son was preparing the evening meal when he realized that they had run out of salt. The father decided to borrow some from his rich neighbour, the Chettri.

Now the Chettri was a miser, and hated giving anything away when he could sell it. But he could not ask the Limbu to pay for a tiny amount of salt and so grudgingly he measured it out. That night the Limbu and his son ate well, because the Chettri's salt, having been bought from the salt traders, was not coarse and full of grit like the local salt. The Limbu and his son liked the white salt very much and decided to borrow salt from the Chettri more often. Slowly, the Limbu started borrowing salt almost every day.

The Chettri soon began to get thoroughly fed up of the Limbu, and thought of a plan to get the Limbu stop borrowing any more of his expensive salt. That evening, the Limbu turned up once again to ask for some salt. The Chettri put on a very sad face and greeted the Limbu. "Brother," he said. "I know you have come to ask for some salt but unfortunately, I cannot give you some from today. A great sage has told me to stop giving any salt to anyone from today." The Limbu, like all simple villagers, was a superstitious person and readily believed what the Chettri said. As he turned to leave, the crafty Chettri thought of another plan as how to make a profit out of the Limbu's simplicity. "Brother, since I will no longer be able to give you salt, I think it's time you grew some of your own," he suggested. "Grow salt?" The Limbu asked. "Yes," said the Chettri, "If you are interested, I will teach you how it is done." The Limbu readily agreed and asked the Chettri to come to his house the following day.

The next day the Chettri turned up and took the Limbu and his son to their field. He told them to uproot all the corn and to dig the field so that the land was smooth and clear. The foolish Limbu did as he was told, and the father and son spent the whole day clearing their field of the young corn that had taken many days of toil to plant.

While the Limbu and his son were thus engaged, the Chettri went to the nearby forest with his sons and told them to catch as many grasshoppers as they could. He warned them not to let the Limbu or his son know anything about it. The sons did what their father had ordered them, and by the evening, they had captured more than a hundred grasshoppers. The Chettri was pleased, and praising his sons, he stored the dead grasshoppers in a theki (a container with a lid, made of either wood or clay).

The next day, the Chettri went to the Limbu's house and asked him if the field was ready. The Limbu said it was. The Chettri then asked the Limbu if he had any of the "salt seeds" that were needed. "That, you see," the Chettri said "Is the most important thing you need, for without that, how do you expect the salt plants to come up?" The Limbu thought it to be very sound reasoning and asked where he could get the salt seeds.

As they were discussing this problem, the Chettri saw two salt traders coming towards them. Pointing to the traders, he said, "Brother, your problem is solved. Go and buy a sack of salt from those traders, and you will have enough salt seeds to sow." Taking out his savings, the simple Limbu bought a sack full of salt from the traders. Coming back to where the Chettri was, he asked what he had to do next.

The Chettri asked the Limbu if he could get an armful of banana leaves. No sooner were the words out of his mouth, the father and son ran to their banana grove (actually, this banana grove consisted of only four to five banana plants) and stripped the plants clean of their leaves. Hurrying back to where the Chettri was, they threw down the leaves, asking if it was enough.

The Chettri said it was and then showed them how to plat salt. He tore a small section of the banana leaf, and putting a good handful of salt in it, he proceeded to bind the packet tightly. "So that the salt does not fall out," he explained. Next, he dug a hole in the ground and put the packet inside. "That's all there is to it," he said, covering the packet with mud and making a small mound over it. The Limbu and his son got the idea and did what the Chettri had shown them. By the end of the day, the salt was all planted. Satisfied with the day's work, the father and son went home after thanking the Chettri for his help.

The sunset and night began to steal in. The sky was clear and the stars were just beginning to show. The moon silently rose and illuminated the land below to show the Chettri and his sons stealthily approaching Limbu's field. Silently and swiftly, the father and his sons dug up a mound, and opening the salt packet, they poured out the contents into a sack. They replaced the salt with a dead grasshopper, buried the packet and made a mound over it. One by one, they emptied all the salt packets and finally hoisting their now heavy sack on one of the brother's backs, they silently left the field. Early next morning, the Limbu eagerly looked out towards the field, half expecting to see salt plants climbing out of the soil. When he saw that there was no sign of the plants, he decided that it would take a whole week before the seeds sprouted. Comforted with the thought, he went about his daily work with a light heart and a dreamt of being rich at last.

Two days passed, and the Limbu began to get impatient. Going to the Chettri's house, he asked him, "Brother, you showed us how to plant salt, but you did not mention when the plants would come up. Nor did you tell us what we were to do next. Do we water them, or do we leave them as they are? Please be kind enough to tell us what to do next." Secure with the knowledge that the man suspected nothing, the Chettri feigned surprise and exclaimed, "What? Haven't the plants sprouted yet? They should have come up the very next day." Then asking the Limbu to follow him and making a show of great haste, he hurried to the Limbu field.

Reaching the fist mound, the Chettri started muttering something about evil spirits and the evil eye. The master of the field too lent a hand, and they soon had the salt seed, or rather the leaf packet, in their hands. The Limbu hastily unwrapped the packet, and to his dismay, found the salt gone and a dead grasshopper instead. The Chettri cried out, "How did you expect your salt to grow when it had already been eaten by the grasshoppers?" Pretending to be very sad, he continued, "Alas! It is all my fault. I should have warned you about those grasshoppers; they come at night and creep into the leaf packets and eat all the salt. But the only happy thing about this is that they die because their greedy bellies burst." The Limbu listened to all this in silence and said, "Do not blame yourself, my brother, it is not your fault. Anyway, only one seed has been destroyed. We still have the rest." Having said this, the Limbu started digging up another mound to make sure if the seed was all right. The reader can well imagine the man's dismay when he discovered a dead grasshopper in this place. It wasn't long before the master of the field stood over a pile of dead grasshoppers and empty leaf packets. The Chettri pretended to be very sorry and kept cursing the insects, while the Limbu and his son sadly looked at the remains of their hard work.

After some time, the Chettri left, outwardly sympathetic about the incident but inwardly chuckling with glee at the success of his plan. When he was safely out of hearing distance, he started roaring with laughter at the simplicity of the father and son. He was still laughing when he reached home.

Back in the field, the father and son had begun discussing the problem. "Let's grow more salt," the son suggested. "No," said the Limbu, quite fiercely, because as with all Limbus, it had taken him all this time to get really angry about the incident. "No. We can grow more salt and maybe we will have enough to sell and make up for our loss." The son argued. "No," said the Limbu even more fiercely, because he had now worked himself up into a furious rage. With that, he turned abruptly and started walking back to the house. The son followed him, hoping to make his father see the value of planting salt.

By the time the son reached the house, the father was already striding out with a bow and a quiver full of his best arrows. Seeing his son coming up to the house the father asked him to come along. "Where to?" asked the son. The father replied, "As long as those grasshoppers are alive, we have no hope of growing rich. If just a few grasshoppers can eat up all the salt we planted in just two nights, you can imagine the damage a swarm of grasshoppers can do. We will never be rich as long as there are grasshoppers alive. We will hunt them down, and soon there will be no grasshopper left to plague us." Hearing these fine words, the son too was inspired, and soon the two of them were well into the forest looking for their enemy.

The forest was a pleasant place where birds and animals moved around contentedly, while bees hummed busily and butterflies fluttered in the air. The two hunters searched everywhere but could not find a single grasshopper. Dusk was approaching, and the father and son started back. They were both disgruntled at not being able to shoot even one grasshopper. The forest path was narrow, and they walked in a single file, the son a little ahead of the father. Just then, a single wandering grasshopper landed on a rock in front of the father who promptly fitted an arrow in his bow to shoot at it. As he took aim, the insect jumped and landed squarely on his chest. Seeing that he was unable to shoot the pest, the man decided to let his son do it.

Hardly daring to breathe, he gave a low whistle. The son heard it and turned to see his father frantically gesticulating. Looking closely at the spot his father was pointing to; he saw the insect resting on his father chest. The father, through excited signs, asked the son to shoot. The son, fitting his best arrow on his bow, took careful aim and let it fly. The grasshopper jumped to safety, and the father fell to the ground badly wounded. It was only then the two of them realized their foolishness, and decided to hunt grasshoppers no more. Instead, they decided to plant mustard and potatoes and did that so well, that after some years they became quite rich.

As for the Ricochet, he was so happy at the success of his plan, he tried it once again on another farmer. Unfortunately, this farmer was not simple like the Limbu and his son and decided to play along. That night as the Ricochet and his sons were was creeping into the farmer's field, they were rudely surprised by the farmer and his three grown up sons. The Chettri and his sons were soundly thrashed.

As they lay there groaning, the Chettri decided it was safer to sell salt than trick others into planting salt. As a result, he started a salt trade, and soon became very rich. But having learnt his lesson, never again did he try to trick others to get what he wanted, but like all decent folk he bought it and paid for it as well.

32. MUKKUBUNG

The Sakaela drums throbbed and thrummed out the beat of Life and change. White Khastos (shawls) shimmered in the sun against the black blouses, and black swirling skirts of the dancing girls. The Lopamis (yak tail whisks) swished in a flurry of a black and white cloud. As the bare feet of the dancers moved in unison to the throbbing music, a single silver anklet gleamed on each of the dancing girl's foot. It was a time to celebrate life.

The men held the Silimis, originally a long blade punctuated with tiny holes all along its sides to hold small metal rings. It was to be shaken in time to the drums like a tambourine. An instrument of war turned into an instrument of peace, a musical blade if you will.

The Sakela festival celebrated the harmony of opposites in nature. Towering in the horizon, the pristine white snows shimmered against the black rocks of Mount Chuwa Loongma, the hardness of the rock and the softness of the snow from where the life giving waters of the Dudh Koshi flowed. It was the time to celebrate the harmony of the earth with both male and female dancers, old and young all holding green leaves in their hands and moving in perfect unison under the tree where an alter had been made to honour the Earth.

The drums united them all in the pulsating rhythm of the heartbeat of the ancient land of the Khamboos. The white waters of the Dudh Koshi hummed through the land singing through the blood that flowed in the veins of all creatures and the life-giving sap in the trees.

The harvest was done, and the peach blossoms bloomed as the hills thrummed with life and laughter.

Like so many before, there started a story of a girl and a boy, Mukkubung and Khamsoso. Two simple souls from neighbouring villages who decided they liked each other enough to fall in love.

Like any other couple, they would have married and lived in peace, had it not been for Mukkubung's seven older brothers.

Khamsoso was an orphan who had been brought to the village many years ago by an old man who had found him wandering from village to village. When he heard the boy speak the same language, he had brought him along to his house. War and disease sometimes left young children like Khamsoso to live thus. It was nothing new for a tribesman to adopt such orphans.

The old warrior conducted the prescribed rituals before the tribe and Khamsoso was inducted into the tribe as his son. They lived in peace for many years, and one day the old man moved on to the other world leaving Khamsoso his little hut, few heads of cattle and a tiny path of land. Khamsoso conducted the death rites of the old man and completed his duties of a son. The tribesmen were satisfied and said he was a good lad.

Mukkubung's seven brothers made it very clear to their sister, that they would not let her wed Khamsoso and warned her with dire consequences if she dared defy them. They said they would never let a boy whose lineage was unknown marry their sister. They said they would become the laughing stock of the whole village. Mukkubung knew all this was a lie.

The boy had been inducted into the tribe with the proper rites and ceremony, so that was not the problem. The real reason was that they did not want their sister to marry anyone. The whole village knew the seven brothers were in fact complete wastrels. It was Mukkubung who kept the house going.

She managed the household and the fields, while they just looked after their cattle. Each brother had his own sheep and cows. Each of them looked after his own herd. They spent their earnings however they liked. They would each just toss a few coins every once in a while, for house hold expenses. She would somehow manage to keep the house and farm together.

She looked after the chickens, the vegetable patch and the rice fields. She would do all the cleaning, the cooking and the mending.

She would also take some time out to work in the fields of the village folk, who in turn came and helped her out with her own fields. Why would the brothers even let her go? Who would do all the work?

Khamsoso understood this very well. He decided to speak to the brothers any way. Of course, he could not speak with them directly, so he went to an old neighbour who was distantly related to his foster father.

He carried two bottles of Rakshi (country made liquor placing these on a bronze plate) before the old man; he made his offering. He folded his hands, and respectfully told the old man that he had decided it was time for him to take a bride and that his heart was set on Mukkubung.

He also informed the old man that he had been successful in winning her heart and she too wished to marry him. He said since he was an orphan and had no one else, could he make the request to the old man and ask him to speak to the brothers on his behalf. The neighbour agreed and assured Khamsoso he would speak to them.

In a day or two, the old neighbour took two other men from the village and went to Mukkubung village. Khamsoso had provided them with two bottles of local liquor, fruits and the prescribed gifts. It was evening and the brothers were all at home that day. The old man placed his offerings and gifts on a bronze plate. The brothers pretended they did not see the plate and didn't ask anything, nor did they even ask why they had come. They just pretended the old men had just dropped by and didn't even offer the customary glass of water to them. They pretended to be busy with their chores and three of the eldest sat down and spoke to them about the weather.

The old man just continued with the small talk and praised their home, farm and Mukkubung. After a while, he gently asked the brother if it was alright with them, they would come formally and represent Khamsoso and ask for Mukkubung's hand.

If they were agreeable, they would be more than happy to find out an auspicious day and come again.

The brothers laughed and didn't bother replying. They went on with their conversation as if nothing out of the ordinary had happened. Conversation flowed easily, and after some time the old neighbour again brought up the subject and said he wouldn't mind representing Khamsoso and asking for their sister's hand, because the two of them would make a good couple and both were hardworking and cheerful.

One of the brothers just said that she was a little too young to be married. The old neighbour laughed and said all her friends were married and had become happy mothers.

Conversation continued for another half an hour or so, and finally the old neighbour said that it was getting late and they had to go home. He asked the eldest brother directly that he had come to find out if it was okay for them to come formally as representatives from Khamsoso and ask for Mukkubung's hand.

The eldest brother flatly said he would never ever let Khamsoso wed his sister as none of the brothers were willing to be the laughing stock of the village because Khamsoso was not of the tribe. The old neighbour reminded them that Khamsoso had been inducted into the tribe as a child in the presence of ten representatives of the many clans that made up their tribe.

Anyone questioning this would mean they were questioning the representatives (and thereby the clans) who had witnessed the induction.

The old neighbour continued that he himself was one of the witnesses and the talk of Khamsoso not being one of them was not exactly in keeping with the tribal law. Seeing himself cornered the

Eldest brother fell silent. The second brother, who had been listening, quickly spoke up.

He said that they had only used the argument for argument's sake and nothing else but the real reason they were reluctant to give their sister to Khamsoso was that they were afraid Khamsoso would not be able to keep their sister in comfort that she was used to.

The third brother boasted, they had a much larger house and fields and cattle while Khamsoso only had a small hut a tiny plot of land and a few heads of cattle. Our sister lacks for nothing here in this house. What can he give her? It is our duty to at least think about her comfort and future he said.

"Not only that, what about the bride price?" Asked the fourth brother. "Would he be able to give Mukkubung's bride price?" Of course, the custom was that the bride price was just a token that would in most cases be returned to the bride herself, but it was considered a great honour if the bride price was good. The family would consider their daughter was prized by the groom's family and hence it was a matter of pride to say that the groom's side had given a worthy bride price as per the custom.

The fifth continued there was no bride price good enough for their only sister and Khamsoso should forget all about Mukkubung.

"He will never be able to offer her the bride price we ask. So, there is no point in coming to ask for her hand is there," the eldest brother said.

One of the old men half-jokingly asked the brothers what they expected as their sisters Bride Price.

The brother laughed and said first of all the man marrying her would have to be able to give the bride a large amount of gold ornaments.

Another laughed and said the man who wanted to wed her would have to pay for his fault in marrying the youngest sibling, when all those older than her were not married. This was the custom.

Then another continued, they would ask for a huge amount of liquor, meat and food which they would use to feed the whole village for the wedding feast.

The man who wanted to wed their sister would have to be wealthy enough to present them all this along with a stack of seven Brass containers as well as token presents to both Mukkubung maternal and paternal uncles and aunts. This was what custom demanded.

The old neighbour said though the custom stated that the gifts could be asked from the groom, no one actually asked for so much as people would rather sort things out amicably.

One of the brothers glibly commented their sister was prized to them, and they would rather not be compared to those who gave their daughters away cheaply because they were worried about settling some part of the family property on her should she remain unmarried.

He also added they would not be keeping the gold and the presents as custom also demanded that those who received gifts from the groom were expected to present the couple with something more valuable than what was received, so what they were doing was all for their sister's comfort.

He said their sister was prized by all the brothers, and they would agree to give her away only to someone who valued her as much as they did.

The eldest brother added slyly that they could all come again to ask Mukkubung's hand when Khamsoso had enough wealth to have a nice house and was able to gift the value of Mukkubung. The brothers unanimously agreed, knowing very well that the orphan lad would never be able to fulfil all their expectations. Then they all went back to talking about the weather.

The old neighbour and his friends collected the unaccepted offerings, took their leave went back to Khamsoso's house and told him about all that had transpired. They advised him to forget the girl and marry someone else instead.

They tried to make the young man understand the brothers would never ever let Mukkubung go. They also said they were afraid the seven brothers would actually harm Khamsoso, to get their sister back. They knew there was no way the seven selfish brothers would ever let her go. Or they would have advised him to elope with the girl and never ever come back to the village.

Khamsoso patiently heard all that the three men had to say and was furious with the brothers' words and intent. He decided to go out into the world, make his fortune and come back to wed Mukkubung.

He took a few days to prepare for his journey. He sold his cattle and asked his neighbours to keep an eye on his little hut and field. At the crack of dawn, he carried his small bundle and walked to the spring just above Mukkubung's house and waited for her as he knew she would come there to fill her water pot.

He didn't have to wait for long. He told her he was going away to earn his fortune and would be back in three years. He said if the Gods were kind to him, he would be back in two, but could she wait for him for so long? Three years was a long time. Mukkubung assured him that she could wait for him for as long as it took, and that he should not worry too much about her. With that the two lovers parted with tears and a farewell.

The seven brothers heaved a sigh of relief.

Our hero travelled far and wide and tried to earn as much wealth as he could. He worked like a man possessed and made a little money, but he knew it was not enough for him to satisfy the greedy brothers.

One hot afternoon, found him travelling all alone and on foot along the jungle footpath that led to a town said to be rich and prosperous. The only trouble was that it would take him ten days walk to get there through such terrain. The forest was hot, humid and dense, and the young man felt a little afraid but marched on boldly.

Presently, he stopped at a clearing and sat down to rest under a tree. He moved a big stone out of the way to make things a little more comfortable. Imagine, his surprise when he found a small bag full of gold!

He was rich. He could go back and ask for Mukkubung's hand, he could now and he could give her a good life, better than the one she had led at her own home. He could not believe that it had taken him less than a year to make his dreams come true, laughing and thanking the gods, Khamsoso headed home.

The last of the rains lashed the hills and Mukkubung took shelter under the trees with her load of grass. Her lazy brothers would not bother feeding the cows properly when it rained. So, she had taken the trouble to come out and cut a big bundle of fodder for her cattle. She knew, she would be late but she didn't care too much. Too bad their dinner would be late.

Khamsoso on the other hand, in his eagerness to meet with his beloved, forgot everything else and hurried to his beloved's home. He found the eldest sitting idly in the porch watching the rain. Khamsoso briskly walked into the porch and cheerfully greeted the lazy brother.

The eldest brother saw how relaxed and confident Khamsoso looked and knew the lad had made enough to fulfil their demands. He had never thought the lad would actually come back!

He realized he would have to get rid of the boy for good. He put on a sad face, and inquired after Khamsoso's heath as he invited him inside the kitchen. Pretending to be very hospitable, he offered Khamsoso a stool and asked him to sit close to the fire to dry of his damp clothes.

Khamsoso sat down and politely answered the brother's questions about his health and journey, wondering where Mukkubung was. It was impolite to ask about an unmarried lady so he kept talking to the brothers hoping they would tell him on their own.

The other brothers crowded around Khamsoso, and waited for the eldest to speak.

The eldest brother informed Khamsoso that his beloved had sickened and become very weak after he had left. She refused to eat and looked very sad all the time. She never spoke a word about Khamsoso, and always kept herself busy.

One day, she looked quite pale and sick yet, she insisted on fetching the firewood from the jungle, and as she tried to hoist the heavy load on to her back, she lost her balance and fell down the steep cliff instantly breaking her neck.

The eldest brother looked away and wiped his eyes, "I wish we had agreed to let you wed her, my poor little sister." the brothers all pretended to look very sad. "It took us three days to fix ropes to get her body out of the ravine," he continued, "We gave her a grand funeral....."

Khamsoso was dumbstruck and could not speak. Blood drained from his face and he felt dizzy and faint. He barely heard what the brothers were saying. In his grief and anguish, it never occurred to him the brothers were lying.

Like all hill people, Khamsoso believed if you spoke of a living person as dead, that person's life span would be shortened considerably. It never occurred to him that the brothers would be lying to him. Without a word he left the house, and walked determinedly through the rain towards the cliff that the brother had spoken of.

Night had fallen and the narrow path was slippery. The young lover stumbled in the dark a few times, but he was like a man possessed. He determinedly kept walking to the steep cliff. He did not feel the rain or notice anyone following him in the dark.

The rising sun saw Khamsoso lifeless body lying in the heap in the undergrowth at the bottom of the cliff. No one knows what happened to the unfortunate lover in the dark, and rainy night on the slippery slope of the steep cliff. No one came looking for his body either.

The forest spirits took pity on the broken body of Khamsoso and slowly the earth covered the body with her green veil. A tiny green plant pushed its way up into the warm air the following spring, and Khamsoso was forgotten.

When Mukkubung returned home in the evening, the brothers did not tell her that Khamsoso had come by and that they had all lied to him about her death. The blissfully unaware Mukkubung waited and waited some more, two years passed and she still waited. Her brothers, safe in the knowledge Khamsoso was never coming back, became lazier still.

It was a bitterly cold night and the snow lay thick in the ground while the wind relentlessly blew through the juniper.

The red fire blazed, crackled in the hearth and Mukkubung made dinner for her family. She asked the brothers to get more dried kindling from the wood pile outside. No one wanted to go out in the cold. Irritated at their laziness, she asked them what they would do after she was gone.

She also told them that they should learn to take care of themselves as Khamsoso would arrive in the spring, and she would marry him whether they liked it or not. The eldest brother flew into a rage and slapped her, to her horror the second brother laughingly narrated how Khamsoso had arrived two years ago during the rains, and how they had tricked him into thinking she was dead.

"He hadn't been seen ever since, had he?" It would be best for all if she could just stop imagining things that was never going to come true. As she stood rooted to the spot in shock and horror, her brothers derisively laughed, and told her to stop daydreaming and to fetch the kindling herself.

Without a word, she silently went outside. The wind picked up and wailed through the night as Mukkubung walked in the blizzard trying to make sense of what she had just heard. Where was

Khamsoso then? Had he left her never to return? Was he already married to someone else? A lot could have happened in two years.

She walked and walked and walked till she fell down in an unconscious heap in the snow. That night, the blizzard spent its fury and the morning light saw the juniper clad hills turn completely white as the January snows shimmered and sparkled in a cold haze.

Buried under the snow, drift Mukkubung lay undiscovered and at peace forever. Her brothers looked for her high and low but were not able to find her. The winter winds heaped more and more snow on the snow drift as she lay in her final sleep undisturbed, and untouched at peace at last.

The green shrub that had grown where Khamsoso lay stretched its waxy leaves to the skies and the Spirits could see the streaks of gold among the leaves. It was almost as if Khamsoso himself was asking the heavens, why he was denied his bride, even though he had brought enough gold for her bride price.

The forest gods took pity on the two star crossed lovers.

The gentle wind blew away some of the snow that covered Mukkubung, and carried it all the way to deposit it at the foot of the strange plant, as if to say they could be together in death if not in life. The snow that melted and ran down into the earth as the roots of the shrub, eagerly absorbed it into its veins.

The snows melted and spring came to the hills. There at the foot of the steep cliff, among the undergrowth, the strange green plant flowered. It was an exquisite snow-white blossom with an enchanting fragrance. Mukkubung and Khamsoso had been united at last.

This flower is commonly called the Indra Kamal (Gardenia Jasminoides).

If you look closely, you can see faint traces of the gold that Khamsoso found among the leaves and even in the flower. It is common belief among the hill people that great misfortune befalls anyone who finds gold. Many modern hill people today, still believe this and if at all they find a piece of gold anywhere, they are advised to get rid of it as soon as they can, as holding on to the gold will only increase the misfortune.

Despite its beauty and fragrance, the Indra Kamal is not used as offerings to the gods. This beautiful plant is generally planted by graves of loved ones. Many people do not grow this plant at home, the very few that do plant this flower at home; they take care to keep it a safe distance from the house as they consider it to be a flower for the graves.

Like so many folk tales, the tale of Mukkubung also has another version. It is a similar tale of two star crossed lovers. Mukkubung and her lover part in a marshy place (called seem in the local language), and she waits faithfully for his return.

The lover travels far and wide and falls to his death. The faithful Mukkubung waits and waits till the gods take pity on her, and turn her into a white flower called Mukkubung.

The flower spreads its fragrance in the evening just like the Indra Kamal, and people are advised not to linger around marshy places as the spirit of Mukkubung still waits for her lover.

I have unfortunately not been able to identify the flower Mukkubung. All I have been told is that it is white, has a beautiful fragrance and is not to be planted near homes. This brings me to believe that the Indra Kamal and Mukkubung could be the same flower or that the original story of Mukkubung was retold, and the original flower being unavailable, was replaced by the Indra Kamal.

33. STORY OF THE LAST SOKPA

It was time for the herd to return. The cowherd stood atop a hillock and called. Dotted along the misty hillside were his cows and yaks grazing contentedly. Hearing his call, the herd slowly lumbered up, their bells tinkling.

The sun had already set and the night was promising to be a cold one. The herd walked on, filling the evening with the music of their bells. The boy rushed down to meet them and hurried them towards the cowshed. Occasionally flicking a switch lightly on a slow animal, "Hoy!" he cried, as the black yak turned right to chew at a juicy clump of grass. "Hoy! Move on!" After he reached the cowshed, the boy made sure the animals were comfortably stalled, and then milked the brown cow, the one horned yak and the black cow with a white star. He lit a fire in the hearth and set the milk to boil. With it he would make hard cheese called Churpi, and butter. After the milk had boiled he set it aside and cooked his simple meal of Dhero (flour porridge) and Gundruk (soup of fermented and dried radish tops), and sat down to eat it.

Outside the mist had risen and the night was silent. The moon hung coldly over the mountains silhouetted against a bare sky. Inside the cowshed the animals shifted comfortably and dozed. Far away below the hills the village fires twinkled and then died out one by one. Everything settled down for the night.

The boy, huddled in a corner, manned the butter churn. The "whirr – whirr" of the butter churn lulled him into a dreamy state and made him think and dream of his home and friends. "Whirr – whirr" went the churn, and a thick yellow mass began to form. Suddenly the night was pierced with an unearthly cry, "Yyiieeee!" The boy, started out of his dream, listened. Fear crawled down his spine, and he glanced around the shed. The cows moved closer together uneasily. The black yak snorted and stamped his hooves angrily.

Then he remembered … The village people had warned him about the Sokpa (Yeti) and how it came down to the hills to hunt. They had told him about the creature who would carry off people to his cave and make them work for him. He had smiled and shrugged off their warning. "You'll see," they had said. He also remembered being told not to make any noise, should any cry be heard at night. As he remembered he smiled and thought the village boys had come up to the hills to frighten him.

"Well, let us see who gets the last laugh," he muttered. Taking a deep breath he let out loud cry, "Yyiiieeee!" Pleased with the result, he called out once more and laughed softly. Whoever had come to frighten him would now be running down the hill mistaking his cry to be that of a real Sokpa. He settled down once more and went on with his churn, "Whirr - whirr."

High up in the hills, the Sokpa had heard the cry. He was the last Sokpa of the hills. He did not remember where the others had gone. All he knew was that he was lonely and that he wished he could meet a friend. Taking the cry to be that of another of his kin, he quickly made his way towards the cowshed. He ran silently and swiftly, his strides covering above five feet at a time.

Silently he pushed the door open and stepped into the shed. The cows mooed, the black yak snorted furiously, the one horned yak rolled its eyes and stamped angrily, the cowherd froze and turned white with fear. The Sokpa walked in and squatted next to the fire, looking curiously at the boy. In its mind the Sokpa took the boy to be another type of yeti. One he had never seen before.

Thinking quickly the boy said, "Hush! Hush!" And the herd, soothed by their master's voice, quietened down. Frantically searching his mind about Sokpas, the boy remembered that they were strong and swift but not very bright.

From beneath the shaggy eyebrows the furry ape-man watched the boy carefully. Flight was useless, and silently praying for a way out, the boy wiped his perspiring brow. The yeti did the same, though his brow was definitely not perspiring. Puzzled, the boy pretended to scratch his head and Sokpa did the same. The boy smiled and decided he could get rid of the Sokpa with a little cunning.

He put his hand into the churn and took out some butter and proceeded to rub it thoroughly over his body, liberally smearing it over his face as well. The ape-man did the same. Soon his shaggy fur was covered with butter. The boy then took out his tin of paraffin and proceeded to rub that as well. The Sokpa, thinking it was some ritual, did the same. Once the boy was sure that the Sokpa's fur was thoroughly soaked with paraffin, he reached forward and picked up a dry twig, and brought it close to his arm. The ape-man, fascinated, did the same and then carefully looked at to boy to see what he would do next.

Praying fervently, the cowherd muttered, "I just hope this works, or I am done for." He picked up a fiercely blazing branch from the fire and held it close to his body, making sure that the fire was well away from his clothes.

The Sokpa gleefully grabbed another burning branch and held it close to his body. Before he realized it, his fur caught fire and started to burn. Soon the Sokpa was on fire. The quiet of the night shattered as he howled and screamed, and he tried to beat out the flames with his hands. Still howling, he ran out of the shed and into the hills, never to be seen again.

As for the cowherd, he learnt his lesson and would no longer shrug and look unconcerned when given advice. To guard himself further he adopted two of the village mastiffs to watch over the cows and yaks with him.

And should you, dear reader, ever go to the hills, be warned. Answer no strange cries at night. You might not be so lucky, especially with a badly burnt Sokpa lurking in the shadow of the mountains.

34. HENKEBUNG AND THE TIGER BROTHER

According to the Mudhums, there is an age called the Maang period, the time where there were only female shamans and female heros and leaders.

Children took their mother's name and the father's name was not needed, which is why this story, the father is only referred to as a "Hochha" or a young man.

This later gave way to the samai period where both female and male heros and shamans and leaders existed.

Much later, this gave way to the "pachha" period where chronicles were developed only from the males, mostly male shamans and male leaders started to emerge. However, there were always the exceptions and Mangamas (lady shamans) and female healers, huntress and leaders did step up whenever the need arose.

This tale is from the maang period:

Sikurima, the huntress threw back her blue-black hair in anger. She was out of breath and angry. Her quarry had taken her on a merry run and unlike most days her arrow and her skill failed to bring down the buck.

She had only managed to injure it. Surefooted, she swiftly followed the tiny blood spots on the ground as she closed in on her quarry.

She espied the buck to her right among the trees. She placed an arrow on her bow string with a hiss, and drew the string back. Before she was able to let fly the arrow, another bowstring twanged, and the buck lay dead, its legs flailing and a feathered arrow lodged in its heart.

With a snarl of impatience and frustration, Sikurima jumped into the clearing and drew her skinning knife. She wanted to see who it was that had robbed her of her quarry that she had spent almost the whole day stalking.

She heard footsteps running and turned. A young Hochha walked up to the deer. He was not very tall but walked with an easy confidence and held up his hands by way of greeting Sikurima and knelt down in front of the dead animal. As the hochha placed his hand on the deer, Sikurima placed her right foot on the carcass and said, "I claim this deer as my hunt for the day."

The minute she said this, the Hochha removed both his hands from the deer and backed away. He smiled at Sikurima and said, "you are right, he had been injured by your arrow first before mine brought him down."

"This is your kill"

Sikurima was happy to see the hochha was a fair person. So, she offered to share the hunt.

The two of them quickly offered their prayers to the forest gods for taking a life and left behind, the heart, a whole ear, some hair and a generous bit of liver, along with a bit of flesh from the nose on a leaf, and left it on a nearby stone as an offering to the gods.

This was how the Kirats paid for taking a life.

The heart and bits of liver and ear would be enough as a whole meal for a small animal like a fox, a jackal or a martin or a hungry otter.

Once the animal had eaten its full, he wouldn't hunt that night, so a kalij fowl, a rabbit, a river crab or maybe a fish would be spared from being hunted that night. As an exchange for taking a life in the forest, the hunters placed the offering on a leaf and left it out for the forest gods to decide which fox or martin would find the food and which jungle fowl or rabbit got to live that night.

It was also commonly believed that the gods of the forest creatures would count all the animals each night, and if he found anyone missing, he would come looking for it into the very home of the person who killed it.

The offering was also to let the forest deity know that some human had taken the animal and had paid for another life. Of course, when one hunted jungle fowl, there wasn't much meat to leave out, so hunters were expected to leave a few big feathers stuck on the ground to let the deity know that a fowl had been taken by man.

"A LIFE FOR A LIFE," that was vital for the forest dweller to understand that he or she had to live in harmony with land.

Sikurima skinned the deer with ease, then she cut off a huge hunk of meat and pushed it towards the Hochha who accepted his share with a smile, and proceeded to cut the meat into thin strips.

Sikurima asked him why he did this, and he explained it was to make sure the meat dried out well. He would take the meat and smoke it, dry it out completely to make sure he had a stock of good meat whenever he needed it. He told her how much the dried meat helped during the rains and the cold winter months.

The hochha was from the foothills and had come up to the higher meadows to look for herbs. He found the huntress beautiful, skilful and clever, he lost his heart to her. Somehow, he cleverly won her heart and managed to convince her to wed him and build a home with him.

She agreed to go with him and build a home with him as long as he was kind and cheerful as he seemed. She warned him that she would leave him the minute he turned angry or surly or ill tempered.

The young hochha, smitten by the beautiful Sikurima agreed he vowed to always love her and to be kind to her.

He vowed never to lose his temper and agreed that Sikurima could leave him if he was ever unkind to her.

The happy couple then made their way home down the mountains and into the valley below where after about a week of walking down winding pathways they arrived at the hochhas homestead.

He had a fairly big flock of sheep, many cows, chickens and a large piece of farmland where he grew grain and vegetables.

The huntress used to a free forest life found this way a little strange and didn't like it so much. The hochha however, kept her happy. He was always cheerful, laughed, sang for her and treated her with kindness.

Slowly, the days passed into months and the months into three years. The hochha began to look a little less cheerful and seemed to be lost in thoughts often. When Sikurima tried to ask him what bothered him, he would smile a little to brightly and answer a little too quickly that he was okay and nothing was bothering him.

The day came when Sikurima knew she was going to be a mother; she was very happy and couldn't wait to share the news with the Hochha.

She decided to go and pluck a few sweet berries she liked, and then tell her husband when he came home in the evening.

It was a beautiful day and she got busy plucking the sweet berries, she sat on a small hillock and ate them.

She did not want to go back home just yet. She walked around a bit, plucked some wild flowers and lay on the soft grass where she fell fast asleep.

When she awoke, it was late and dusk was approaching. She walked a little faster wondering if her husband had come home. He had come home tired and thirsty to find no one at home. The chicken had not been fed the house was in a mess and the hearth was cold with no fire.

He had called out to his wife over and over again and was worried if something had happened to her.

When he saw her walking in, he lost his temper and asked her where she had been. She told him how she had gone berry picking and how she had taken a nap on the hillock. She laughed and asked him if he had been a little worried about her.

He turned around angrily muttering under his breath about how the house was neglected and not looked after and how the fire had died out in the hearth.

Sikurima tried to tell him that it was only today, the house was in a mess. She had always kept everything in neat and orderly way.

This only made the matter worse. One thing led to another and in a matter of minutes the couple were arguing.

Each wanting to prove the other wrong.

In the end, the Hochha yelled, "You can't even give me child, yet I say nothing to you about, I am sure you can at least take care of the house, you stupid woman," and he slapped her in a fit of rage.

Sikurima was shocked. She, an independent woodland person who never needed anyone. She had given up everything to come and live with the hochha. Three years and now it had come to this.

The hochha was also equally shocked at his behaviour. He fell on the ground and held Sikurima's feet asking her to forgive him.

He said he had no excuse for what he had done. He begged her to forgive him losing his temper. He held her close and asked her to forget what had happened. He promised over and over again, he would never bring up the subject of children.

Sikurima remained silent. It was a rude shock to realize that the hochha had just disrespected her. She couldn't understand how he could have done what he did. She said nothing.

Her husband spent an uneasy night and got up at the crack of dawn. He prepared the morning meal and left for the fields hoping his wife would have cooled down by the time he came home in the evening. He loved her dearly, and could not imagine a life without her. He bitterly regretted letting his temper get the better of him.

After her husband left the house Sikurima got up and collected her things and taking a final look at the house, she slung her bow and arrow on her back, collected her skinning knife and left home.

She had decided that she was going back home. Home, where she had been free and had to listen to no one.

She had taken the short cut to avoid being seen from the fields. By the time, the noon day sun shone brightly into the valley, she was well on her way leading to the mountains.

The sun was hot and she was thirsty. She had forgotten to pack any food or water for herself. She was not too worried because she knew a spring that wasn't too far away. She quickened her steps and walked and walked and walked, but there was no spring to be found. She had lost her way.

Tired, hungry and sad, she sat on a rock and looked around. Her throat was parched and dry, and she looked around for water. Just below where she sat was a yellowish puddle of water that had collected in the rocky hollow.

She plucked a leaf and rolled it up to make a straw and drank the water.

The water was rancid but she swallowed it anyway. Suddenly, she felt dizzy. The Earth started to swim and she fell down in a faint.

It was evening when the hochha came home, he found his wife gone. He looked for her everywhere, .but true to her words she had left him for good. He called out to her in the dusk like a mad man. He begged her to forgive him and shouted out promises of happiness and kindness always, but she was gone, he knew he would never see her again.

Higher up in the hills Sikurima came to her senses after a while and made her way into the hills where she found a place she liked. She found herself a cave and a spring nearby. Over the weeks and months, she slowly prepared the cave into a safe warm home and stocked it with dried meat, roots and warm soft skins for the baby.

When the time came, she gave birth to a beautiful baby boy. She christened him Henkebung. He was a happy healthy baby, and Sikurima loved him dearly.

A month later, to her surprise she gave birth to another child, this child was not human, he was a tiger cub. She realized the water she drank from the rock hollow had been mixed with tiger urine and that explained birth of the baby tiger. She promptly christened him Khopchelipa (khopche meaning "hollow").

She raised the two boys together and soon she was back to living her old life. She blocked up the entrance of the cave each time she left out to hunt and fish. The two brothers slept warmly on the soft skins, and grew plump and happy. Sikurima was happy, she doted on her two sons. She took pride in watching them grow strong and swift. She taught them to track and hunt and fish and dig for roots. She taught them all that she knew.

Henkenbung, being a human could understand and learn from and help his mother a lot more than Khopchelipa who didn't have hands. Henkenbung was able to learn to use the knife and bow and arrow and it wasn't long before he had learnt to make his own weapons. Khopchelipa would dearly have loved to do the same but he had paws that didn't do much when it came to weaving baskets or cutting or peeling things.

Although Sikurima loved both her sons dearly, she could see jealousy and anger grow in Khopchelipa's heart. She could feel the cold jealousy her younger son carried in his soul.

Her tiger son resented his mother and brother merrily talking about weapons and tools. It did not help that Henkenbung did things better than him.

Khopchelipa also did not like that Henkenbung and Sikurima looked the same while he did not. He kept wondering why he looked so different. He wanted so much to look like them.

The wise Sikruima kept the peace for as long as she was able. Then one day she fell sick. Her sons tried their best to make her comfortable, she knew her time had come. One day, she sent her tiger son to fetch an old log for the firewood and used the time she had alone to speak to Henkenbung. While they were alone, she spoke to him about how he was a human and what he was to do to protect himself from his tiger brother should the need arise.

She warned him of his brother's beast nature. She asked him to take care of him but she also made Henkenbung promise to take care of himself first.

She spoke to him one more time when Khopchelipa had gone to hunt a jungle fowl for Sikurima was worried about both of them but told Henkenbung if in the end if ever the brothers had to part ways then they should. She also said if it came to protecting himself from his brother, he had the moral right to do what he had to. In a day or two, Sikurima breathed her last. Till the very end, the worried mother asked the two brothers to live in peace.

They promised her they would and after her death, they covered the cave entrance with stones and boulders leaving, Sikurima's body resting inside.

They moved on to another part of the mountains and found another cave which they made their new home and lived in peace for a while Time went by and the brothers grew into a fine young man and animal.

Though Henkenbung always tried his best to live in peace but Khopchelipa could not control his animal instincts all the time and they started having difference that generally turned into violent physical fights.

Henkenbung always backed down first and tried to pacify his younger brother. This only served to make him think that Henkenbung was afraid of him, and he started attacking his brother even more savagely.

Henkenbung sadly thought of what his mother had taught him in secret, began to build a platform on a nearby tree.

He carefully hid his spare bow, his sharpest arrows and his long spear there. He made sure the arrows and spears stayed sharp and the bowstring was always in good condition. All the time praying he would never have to use them.

One day, as the brothers sat outside their cave, the tiger brother challenged Henkenbung to wrestle him. Henkenbung refused. He knew his brother would play rough and get really angry if he lost. Khopchelipa on the other hand, kept on insisting and it wasn't long before the two brothers were grappling each other.

The match grew rough and more rough. Henkenbung loosened his grip and called out that it was over.

"That's enough," he gasped when he saw the bloodshot eyes of Khopchelipa.

"Enough is it brother?" He snarled. "Enough because you say so?"

His tail was twitching furiously.

"Enough about you, a weakling, telling me what to do. Enough of you, because of whom my mother never cared about me."

Khopchelipa eyes grew more bloodshot and his snarl becoming a menacing roar, "How I have hated you!"

"Die," he roared.

Khopchelipa leaped at Henkenbung hoping to sink his fangs into his neck and kill him.

Henkenbung was faster.

In a quick fluid motion, he had jumped up and run up to the tree and was sitting on the platform that was very high.

"Come down you coward" screamed Khopchelipa. "Come down and die."

He leapt at the tree trying vainly to climb up. Thankfully, he was not successful.

Henkenbung looked down sadly at his brother and said, "It doesn't have to be this way. You go your way and I will go mine. Go away, brother. I have no wish to fight you."

"Remember what mother said," he continued. "I have no wish to fight. Do it for her sake. Go away, and leave me alone and I promise to do the same."

There was no reply. Peering down from among the leaves, Henkenbung saw the tiger trying to crawl up the tree trunk with murder in his eyes.

He pleaded with his brother to go but the bloodlust was upon Khopchelipa, and he didn't listen. All he wanted was to see Henkenbung dead. The beast in him roared and demanded his brothers blood.

Henkenbung realised Khopchelipa was not going to give up.

He called out, "I know you will not change your mind, but you can't come up here either, so I have decided to come down to you. Open your mouth wide so that I can jump straight into your mouth."

Khopchelipa, believing that Henkenbung had given up because he had no way out of that situation agreed. He wasn't very clever either.

"Okay," he snarled, "jump in and hurry. I have waited for so long for this."

He opened his mouth wide open and threw back his head. Henkenbung quickly grabbed his bow and shot three arrows in quick succession down the tiger's throat, Khopchelipa died in an instant.

Henkenbung climbed down and with great sorrow, placed Khopchelipa's body in the cave and blocked the entrance with boulders and stones, so that none could disturb his younger brother's eternal sleep. Shedding many tears, he collected his weapons and his mother's skinning knife and made his way down the path his mother had told him.

He knew he had to go and find his own people to live with.

Sure, enough after many days of walking, he came upon the house his mother had described.

The hoccha was there, an old man now. "I am Henkenbung,Sikurima's son," he introduced himself to his father.

Henkenbung lived a long and fruitful life and is also known as the first man of some clans of the Kirati Khamboo/Rai people.

He went on to have five sons, the eldest, he named Khopchelipa to honour the memory of his dead brother.

The others were called Jerong (Jerohang), Bhorung (Bhoruhang), Sakabali and Nabali.

The five sons grew up and had their own adventures and founded their own clans later. Thus, starting the era of "paccha," where children were now identified by the father's name, this practice brought about the end of Maang period(according to Shri Rahul Sanskrityana, The Kiratis[10050 BC]) had a matriarchal society that slowly changed into a patriarchal one later.

The new age of Samai came where male and females both took part in leading their tribes in religious, political and social issues but this did not last for long and the era of Paccha caught up, and brought patriarchy into the Kirati society where it stayed for good. This is why many consider Henkenbung to be responsible for ending the Maang period.

35. SEEBAY - MY MYSTERY BIRD

The lamps had been lit and the cows milked. The cowherds had lit the charcoal brazier, and grandmother had placed grandfather's tongba (millet beer in a bamboo container with a drinking straw of thin bamboo reed) in front of him. The day's work had been discussed early that evening, and now we had gathered around grandfather to hear one of his stories. Grandfather looked at all of us and then looked into the fire, as was his habit when he was thinking about a story to tell.

After some time, he brightened up and said, "Listen, can you hear anything?" We all listened to the sounds outside and nodded. "Well?" he asked. Actually, all I could hear was the soft patter of drizzle on the leaves, and the sound of Kalaey, the black Tibetan Mastiff giving himself a thorough scratch. Grandfather smiled and said, "Listen carefully to the night. Far away, you can hear a bird." We listened again, and true enough, the wind carried the mournful cry of the night bird to our ears. "That is the Seebay Chara (bird)," said grandfather, "Listen and I'll tell you, her tale."

"Long time ago," began grandfather, "there lived a widow and her young son. They were very poor and had to work very hard to earn their bread. The mother worked hard in the fields that belonged to other rich neighbors, while the son helped in the house by collecting fodder for the cow they possessed, and doing the chores of the house. Though their lives were hard, the mother and the son were very happy. Seebay, the son, was always cheerful and a happy person, and loved his mother dearly. The mother, lucky to have a dutiful son like Seebay, was content and at peace with the world."

"One day the son decided to go to the forest in search of firewood. The search led him deeper and deeper into the forest, and then the sun began to set. Seeing that it was late, Seebay lifted the heavy load on his back and made his way back home. He had only walked a few steps when "PLOP,' a big raindrop fell on his nose. He looked up to the sky and found that he would not reach home before it got dark. Seebay hurried on. On the way to his village lay a river, and he knew that it would be difficult to ford it because the waters would have risen with the rain. Sure enough, when he came to the river, he found the water level had risen considerably. He turned and made his way to where a row of boulders stood across the river, and decided to make his way by stepping on them. He had done it many times and knew it was safe. The rain was beginning to pour down thick and fast. Seebay stepped onto the first boulder and jumped across to the next and the next, and suddenly… slipped on some loose stone. The load made him lose his balance, and he fell down, hitting his head on a sharp rock. There was a gentle splash as the body fell into the river."

By the light of an oil lamp, the woman waited for her son. The evening meal had been cooked and yet her son had not come. Anxiously, she searched the darkness for the familiar sight of her son. The wind had risen and now blew around the tiny hut angrily. Thunder crashed in the next valley, and lightning cracked. A deep sense of foreboding clutched her heart and her fear rose. "Seebay, my son!" she called out into the darkness. Unable to control her fear, she ran into the darkness, calling out loud. The wind howled and the rain poured down in torrents. That night the storm surpassed itself, and the river roared. The boom of the thunder reverberated in the valley; the wind tore through the hills and brought with it stinging sheets of icy rain."

"By the next morning, the storm had spent its fury and the sun came out. The village never saw Seebay or his mother again. Legend has it that the mother was transformed into a bird that very night, and she flies by the river in search of her son."

"During the summer seasons, when the water is calm and clear, it is said that she can see her son's body lying on the river bed. Then she sits on her rock, looking at him. Then, when the monsoon torrents come down, and the swift current muddies the river the little bird cannot see her son. So, she flies frantically from rock to rock, calling his name."

Grandfather finished his story, took the bamboo straw into his mouth, and stared into the fire once more. The rain had begun to fall heavily now, and somewhere, far away, we could hear the shrill cry of the bird calling from her lonely rock.

I have to admit that I have never seen the bird, because my grandfather died before he could show it to me. Just like the different versions of these tales, I have had many different birds pointed out to me. Now I don't want to know. But it is enough that this story comes to mind whenever I hear the little bird cry.

It is interesting to note that when this story was told to me by a lady, the son was not a young boy but an infant, and that the mother incurred the jealousy of the other village ladies whose infants were not as beautiful as Seebay. They took the mother to the river, and said they would all play with their babies by floating them down the river.

The mother saw the other women float their babies downstream and did the same, not realizing that other women had floated bundles of rags instead of their babies. When the baby did not come floating downstream where she was waiting, the unfortunate woman realized that she had been tricked and died of grief.

People also believe that if the Seebay bird calls for many days, the sheds in their granary will rot. This is probably because an extended period of rainfall is likely to bring in the damp into the granaries.

36. HANSULAE AND PURULAE

Many years ago there lived a hunter; he was lean and strong. He could run as swiftly as the wind and swim across a raging river with ease. His coal-black eyes rarely missed much, and his swift and deadly arrow always found its mark.

He was blessed by the Gods with skill at understanding herbs and had great knowledge about healing. He was even known among some of the old healers as one of the best among them.

Slowly his fame grew, and many a fair maiden wanted to marry the young hunter. He was quite a good-looking man with long blue-black hair, piercing black eyes, and a bronzed and lean physique, but he chose to live all by himself as he did not want a wife nor the responsibilities of a family man or that of a healer.

He wanted nothing to do with things that would keep him away from his beloved forest and the free life he had chosen for himself. He took great care to avoid the company of women, and later, when he realized there was no way he could avoid them all the time, he decided to build his hut near the steep cliff on the next hill.

The hunter had thought he was going to be left alone on the next hill, but he was mistaken. His fame had spread all over and many eager young men came looking for him, hoping to learn about herbs and healing from him. He couldn't be bothered with any of them.

Things got worse when a few young village maids came to wash their clothes in the spring nearby in the hope of accidentally bumping into the handsome hunter, and soon there would be groups and groups of giggling maidens all over the hill.

He tried very hard to be nice to the young lads and the young maids, but after a while it became a little too much to bear, so he got himself a pair of mastiff puppies and took them with him wherever he went, he called them Hasule and Purelae.

The two pups soon grew up into huge, fully grown mastiffs, and it wasn't long before the hunter started seeing a lot less of young lads and young maids. His two dogs became his closest friends, and he could have never been happier. Husulae and Purulae loved the hunter and the life the trio led. The three arose at the crack of down and moved into the jungle to hunt.

With the help of his two loyal companions, the hunter was able to get bigger game soon he started hunting for pleasure rather than for food. He dove down waterfalls and fished for the biggest fish. He gave chase to the fleet footed stag and brought them down when his dogs had tired them out. He even tracked down leopards and bears and the dangerous boar.

It was all about his skill and not about hunger anymore. He had been taught like everyone else he was to hunt only for what he needed, and he was not to touch what had been forbidden by his ancestors.

Like any son of the hills, he had been told how one mammal, one bird and one fish were taboo to him. Like they were to every other tribe. He was aware of how in the distant past, during a few particularly lean years, the hunters of all the tribe had a hard time providing for their clan.

Fights had broken out over kills, and sometimes this had led to unnecessary bloodshed among the tribes that had so far lived in peace.

The heads of all the tribes had gathered on a hill and held council. There each head of the tribe took on an oath to leave off hunting one mammal, one bird, and one fish so that the other tribes would not go hungry.

One by one, the chiefs took a pledge, keeping the sky, the earth, the spirits of the tree and the rivers, that they would no longer hunt the three animals of their choice and also pledged that their descendants would honor the pledge for ever and ever.

This was how the tribes had survived through the ages in peace and harmony, never going hungry, and even in times of hardship and lean days, no one ever fought over the animals they hunted.

Now the hunter of our story, though he was well aware of the pledge, and about how the meat of those particular three was now taboo for him, he still went ahead and hunted them down.

He didn't care if he caught the fish his ancestors had forbidden his clan to hunt.

Most of all, he loved to hunt the boar. He enjoyed pitting his wits and strength against the wily animal. He knew how the boar made its set in a clump of bamboos and how peaceful, solitary male could suddenly explode into a bloodthirsty vicious beast within seconds when threatened.

He had now grown very vain and took so much pride in his skill as an archer that he no longer considered following the practice of just taking what one needed from the forest.

Unfortunately, his ancestors had taken the pledge never to hunt boars or consume any boar meat. The hunter's actions caused much distress to his ancestors unknown to him.

It was only a matter of time before the hunter would have to face the consequences.

One fateful morning, the hunter called out to Hansulae and Purulae and moved deep into the forest.

He decided to go higher than usual and suddenly espied a huge stag standing in the clearing not far away.

He whistled to his two dogs, who tore after the animal barking and howling in excitement. The hunter too broke into a run. The stag ran ducked and bounded in between the trees, and Hansulae and Purulae gave chase, barking loudly in their excitement.

As the stag sometimes disappeared out of sight, the hunter was surprised to see the stag emerge from the trees as a boar and then again and then change back into a stag.

Scarcely believing his eyes, he kept running, determined not to let his quarry get away.

The chase let them all to a grassy clearing; the stag with its majestic antlers swerved and ran faster but Hansulae and Purulae stayed determinedly behind it.

Then suddenly, in a blink of an eye, a red-eyed angry boar stood where the stag stood and turned and charged at the two dogs, who ran away, yelping in fear. The hunter felt fear crawl down his spine, but he wasn't one to turn and run.

Skillfully fitting an arrow into his bow, he moved forward carefully. The boar stomped its hooves and behold then, stood a stag, panting in fear with a foaming mouth.

The hunter crept closer and took aim, the stag snorted and there stood the angry boar whisking its short tail around.

In the distance, the hunter could hear Hansulae and Purulae whine in fear. He stood up straight and let the arrow fly.

The arrow sped towards the boar and in a trice the boar and the arrow both disappeared. A small blaze started where the boar was last seen.

This blaze was unlike any fire the hunter had seen; the flames rose higher and higher and to his horror, the blaze started to spread on both sides.

He whistled for his dogs who came tearing through the undergrowth. The two hounds dropped flat on their bellies and whined in fear, dumbly asking the hunter to save them.

The hunter scrambled as fast he could, but to his horror, he found that he was already surrounded by fire. The flames crackled and roared in his ears.

He could feel the heat creep up as it got hotter and hotter. Hansulae and Purulae whined in terror as falling bits of sparks singed their fur. The hunter desperately looked around for a small break in the fire; there was none.

He saw black smoke roiling up from a burning bush. The black smoke blanketed everything. The two dogs were panting heavily and whining in terror.

Holding his terror stricken companions close to his chest, he tried to get up and run through the flames, he couldn't.

He understood his time had come and that he would not make it this time. He prayed to his ancestors and the spirit of the forest to save his dogs. He prayed for the safety of his faithful companions.

As he prayed for their safety and well-being desperately, he held them close and tried to shield them from the fire with his own body. He prayed to the gods to look after these helpless dogs.

Just as the young man thought that it was all over, the smoke started to clear. A cool breeze blew and the flames started dying down. The black smoke vanished and only a lone flame flickered in front of the trio.

The flame slowly transformed into a ring and from the ring of flames, a bright light emanated. The hunter could not look at the bright light.

Then the drumming started at first it was quite faint but then it became louder and louder. The hunter and his dogs wanted so badly to run and flee but it was almost as their legs were made of lead.

They couldn't move, they kept looking at the small ring of fire in terror and the drumming got louder still, and louder and behold, out stepped a short shaman with a porcupine quill headdress and a white robe.

His torso was crisscrossed with many tiny bells, beads, and bones of the snake. In his hand, he held a wooden drum. The hunter realized he was in the presence of the shaman of the jungle. The keeper of all animals and birds. He was known to have divine knowledge of medicinal herbs and helped heal all injured animals, birds and trees.

He was beating the hand-held drum with a stick and though it seemed like he stepped out of the ring of fire, he seemed to be floating in the air. He looked sternly at the kneeling hunter clasping his cowering dogs.

The drum in his hands disappeared on its own and everything was quiet. Though, the shaman never moved his lips, strangely the hunter could hear him speak . Hansulae and Purulae could also hear and understand every word the shaman spoke.

"O son of the hills," here you are today afraid, angry and unsure of yourself.

Here you are today for dishonoring your ancestor's pledge, and for the indiscriminate killing of innocent animals for your pleasure.

"You have forgotten you may take only what you need and nothing more." "You take extraordinary pride at your skill to hurt and maim and kill."

"You never stopped a moment to think that it was your ancestor's blessing that made you a skilled hunter. Your father took you into the woods and taught you how to track and hunt so that you and your family would never go hungry."

"Your grandfather taught you to shape your arrow and fashion your bow. Your greed and your pride would have caused you to meet a bitter end today."

"An end you so well deserved, but for one thing. Your love for the two creatures that follow you so faithfully. It was your prayer for their safety and well-being when you knew there was no way out that made me see there is still so much good in you."

The shaman spoke to the trio for a long time.

The hunter was ashamed and felt terrible that his deeds had disappointed his ancestors. Hansulae and Purulae who could also understand what the shaman was saying, felt very sorry for all the rabbits, wood fowl and other small creatures they had chased down for fun.

Their beastly nature slowly settled down in their hearts, and the good spirit in them awoke. In the warm glow of the late afternoon sun, the shaman spoke to them of healing. Healing not only of the body but healing of the soul and mind.

Time stood still, and the trio listened as the shaman of the woods explained living and dying and healing and happiness.

The hunter and Hansulae and Purulae did not remember falling asleep, but when they woke up it was morning. They were still at the same place but there was no sign of the shaman or the fire.

It was a glorious morning. The trio made their way home and decided to mend their ways. The hunters offered his prayers to the forest gods and river deities and to his ancestors and promised to never take more than he needed.

Hansulae and Purulae became the gentlest dogs for miles around and the trio grew wise as the years slipped by.

The hunter used his knowledge of herbs to help people, animals and trees around him. Hansulae and Purulae gently brought injured birds and small animals to the hunter to mend their poor broken wings and legs.

His skills had miraculously improved after meeting with the shaman. Although the young maidens no longer came to the hill. Many young men did come looking for the hunter, wanting to learn how to hunt and track.

He never turned them away. He spoke to them about talking only about what we need from the forests and of honoring our ancestors, words that certain tribes would not hunt and eat a certain mammal, a fish or a bird.

He taught them to help heal others with herbs. He taught many about healing the mind and the soul. Having done so much good to all living things, the three friends left their bodies together and travelled to the land of their ancestors.

Though they are no more, their story lived on, and later on the two dogs came to be called Karma and Dharma, that loosely meant good action and righteousness.

This story is from the Tamang tribe of the Nepali/Gorkhali people.

The Tamang community later on embraced Buddhism but kept its shamanistic practices. This is a tale from the days the Tamangs still followed only the Shamanistic practice.

37. PAARO HAANG AND SUMNIMA

Long ago, among the high hills, lived a young man called Paaro Haang. He was a handsome young man and had a golden glow all around him as he held Love, Truth, and Compassion close to his heart and this gave him eternal Happiness. Wherever he went, plants and forest creatures were always drawn to him. He was the Creator's pride and joy.

When Paaro Haang took a nap under a tree in the afternoon, creepers would gently creep towards him and cover him up with their leaves, and trees would move their branches to shield his eyes from the sun. Animals never hid from him as he wandered around the forest, sometimes running swiftly through the trees, swimming in the various forest pools or napping under the shade of a tree.

Paaro Haang was loved by all, but he was alone. One day, as he rested upon the ledge of a steep cliff, he saw a woman near the river. He had never seen anyone so beautiful. She sang sweetly as she washed her coal-black hair in the milky white foam of the river. As she dried her long tresses, the sunbeams danced and shimmered on the waves of black silk.

Paaro Haang watched mesmerized as she sat humming to herself watching the bubbling white crests of foam that made the river look almost white.

Unaware of her admirer, Sumnima left her bamboo comb on the rock to wade out a little further and fill her copper jar.

The comb slid from the rock and was swept away in the stream. Sumnima sadly watched it go. She would have to go all the way to the other side of the forest where the bamboo grew and make another comb. She lifted the water jar on her hip and walked away, swaying gracefully, while her beautiful hair shimmered behind her. Her anklet gleamed in the sun as her feet left wet prints on the smooth round rocks. The cheerful, happy-go-lucky forest sprite lost his heart to her.

Paaro Haang stared long after she could be seen no more and wondered if he would ever meet her. Then a thought struck him as swift as the wind. Paaro Haang scrambled down the cliff and splashed around the water, hoping to retrieve the comb and return it to the girl with the black hair. The comb was nowhere to be found. Long did he scrabble in the water and look for the comb in between the smooth stones but he could not find it.

Somehow, Paaro Hang felt sad that he had lost the only reason he had for seeing and speaking to the girl.

He decided he needed to make one as soon as possible. After all, with what was she going to comb out her tresses?

He moved determinedly along the river bank and made his way towards where the bamboo grew. The silver-winged dragonflies accompanied him eagerly, leading the way through the bank.

Maybe it was the dragonflies who said it, or maybe it was the beetles in the bamboo grove who muttered it to the wind by the time our hero had finished making the comb, the cicadas were merrily singing out loud to the listening hills, their favourite child Paaro Hang was in love and he had even taken the trouble to go to the bamboo groves and make her a comb.

Of course, everyone wanted to see and hear about the one who had stolen his heart. The next day, when Sumnima came to the river with her copper jar, she did not notice much except that there was a beautiful comb on the stone waiting for her. Had she not been so happy about the beautiful comb, she would have noticed there were far too many visitors to the river that day.

Little animals and water beetles and a great number of frogs, toads and birds came to the riverside to take a look at her. Sumnima happily combed out her hair, unaware of the many pairs of golden eyes watching her from behind the trees, under the rocks and even from the skies.

That evening the forest song was all about how beautiful she was and how long her tresses were. The song went on to say how happy Paaro Hang was to have the beautiful lady accept his gift.

Legend grows a bit hazy here, and we are left to imagine how the shy forest sprite and the beautiful Lady Sumnima finally met and fell in love.

Time has passed, and we meet the young couple very much in love and blessed by the gods. Now Lady Sumnima is also much loved by one and all in the hills and she never lacks for company wherever she goes. The years went by, and the couple was blessed with two daughters and two sons.

One rainy season, Lady Sumnima wandered a little further than the familiar places in the forest. There she came upon a tree with a strange vine wrapped around it. The vine had a single fruit on it. She looked at it carefully. It was not a fruit that she had seen before. Like all forest people, she knew it was not wise to eat strange fruits in the forest. The fruit, however, looked tempting. It was not a very big fruit, she told herself.

She felt the creeper wanted her to eat it. After all, there was only one fruit there. Finally, temptation won and without thinking further, she plucked the strange fruit and ate it. Of course it was not very wise of her to do that, but what was done was done.

From that day onwards, Lady Sumnima was unable to tell a lie, not even the smallest one.

It is said that a man soon tires of a very truthful wife. Maybe a little lie here and a tiny lie there would have made life really beautiful for the two, but unfortunately that was not to be. Lady Sumnima's constant truth started to irk Paaro Haang and it wasn't long before he started spending more and more time by himself.

He missed the old days where no one ever expected him to be different or responsible. He missed being alone and not having to worry about anyone else. He didn't like it when Lady Sumnima who had never said anything to hurt him, now started saying things he didn't like hearing. The more time he started spending on his own, the more resentment he felt towards his wife and children.

It was a beautiful sunny day and Lady Sumnima decided to go to the river. It was the very same river, where Paaro Hang had first seen her and had fallen madly in love with her. The white waters of the Dudh Kosi gurgled and foamed and the children screamed and laughed. Paaro Haang sorely missed his freedom. He missed running free among the trees and missed his old life.

Lady Sumnima had given him a talisman to hang around his neck long ago; she had said it would ward off the evil eye. The talisman only served to irritate him further still. He often found himself idly pulling at it, trying to break it off his neck. He felt fenced in and tied to something strange and suffocating. He just wanted to get away from everyone and everything. He yanked it off and threw it away.

The children were tired after their play, and Lady Sumnima decided to take a nap in the sun. After a while, the three of them fell fast asleep. Paaro Haang took a long last look at his wife and children and walked away without looking back.

A few hours later Lady, Sumnima found herself all alone with four children to look after. Long did she wait for her Paaro Haang but he did not come. Grief-stricken the Lady Sumnima decided to wait by the banks of the Dudh Kosi.

Each day she prayed to Rumahang, the God of Truth, Love, Happiness, and Compassion. She knew, as does every Kirat, that the three have to be cleansed thoroughly: the mind, the body and the soul. She bathed every day with the waters of the Dudh Koshi. She held neither anger nor sorrow against Paaro Haang for deserting her. She looked after her four children and kept praying.

As time went by, Lady Sumnima found deeper peace and calm. Her prayers progressed considerably, and she grew wiser and happier. Her austerities led to her eating only a salt less vegetarian diet of only boiled beans and ginger in a Tupla (this is a leaf container made from the very tip of the banana leaf and is used to place offerings during times of loss and grief).

As for Paaro Haang he was happy. He was now finally free of his wife and children. He went back to his old life and enjoyed his new found solitude. He didn't have to bother pleasing anyone he didn't have to be responsible for anyone. He didn't have to worry about anything at all. He was free.

Strangely, this euphoria didn't last long. Somewhere deep inside his heart, he missed something. He tried to brush away the feeling but it did not go away. He tried very hard to ignore the hollow ache inside him and hoped it would go away if he went further; it did not.

He felt empty inside and he was not happy. He missed his wife and his children and wanted to go back to them but was ashamed of himself. After all, he was the one who had deserted them. He wandered around the woods and hills trying to run away from the feeling of guilt and remorse he felt.

His feet took him to the base of Mount Chuwa Loongma (Mt.Everest). He started to climb the mountain. As he kept climbing higher and higher, he found himself becoming calmer. Finally, after reaching the summit, he decided to sit down and meditate.

During his meditations, he was blessed with many visions of the universe and how it worked, and he was also blessed with an understanding of the earth and how it was necessary for one and all to play their parts. How each being was a very important part of the Earth and how the Earth was an integral part of all living beings.

How the earth fed all with her bounty and how each living being was connected with the others. After realizing the truth, he decided it was time for him to return home and fulfil his duty as a husband and a father.

Paaro Haang descended from the mountain and made his way along the Dudh Kosi. The river hopped and skipped skittishly like a fawn and made its way to where Lady Sumnima still waited for her love.

It is said that the Lady Sumnima danced for joy when she was finally reunited with Paaro Haang and the dance steps or pattern (called Sili in Khamboo/Rai language) are still performed today during the Sakewa/Sakenwa/Sime/Bhume/Chandi/Udhauali/Ubhauli/ festival of the Kiratas.

The story of Paaro Haang and Lady Sumnima ends with the worship of Mother Earth, a befitting end to a wonderful story.

After all, when the Male Power and the Female Power of the earth meet, the earth rejoices in bountiful harvests.

It celebrates the idea of love and separation and then reunion of the two protagonists as it explains the journey the Dudh Koshi takes from its source from the base of Mount Chua Loongma (the stone that gives water), Mt Everest and how it jumps and frolics down all the way to what used to be known as Wallo Kirat, the western bit of the glorious Kirati kingdoms that used to exist long ago, now recognised, as Okhuldhunga in Eastern Nepal.

Each year, the waters of the Dudh Koshi, rise as steam and turn into a cloud. Leaving the earth below, it wanders aimlessly and restlessly till it slowly makes its way to the top of the mountains and settles down peacefully as glittering snow.

The land below waits patiently and rejoices when the first snows melt and the Dudh Koshi flows back to the waiting fields far below, bringing with it the gift of Life.

The thirsty earth drinks deeply of the clear, sweet waters of the Chua Loongma and blesses all the people of the ancient Kirati kingdom with their bounty.

This is why many Kiratis believe Lord Paro Haang to be a God and Lady Sumnima a Goddess. Many years later, when the

Hinduisation of the tribals of Nepal started, the learned Brahamins embraced the Idea of opposites from the Kiratas and called it Shiva and Shakti.

Many later preached Hinduism to the tribals and said your Lord Paaro Haang and Lady Sumnima are actually Lord Shiva and Lady Parvati (Hindu Deities). This led to people slowly accepting Hinduism and the practice of the Shaviasm among the people of the hills that is so prevalent even today.

However, since it is a thanksgiving festival many bring a bit of everything that was grown in their fields. The entire village meets in an open space and celebrates the festival of Sakaewa/Chandi with the beating of drums and cymbals. As the celebratory dance continues through the day people come and make offerings of whatever harvest the union of Lord Paaro Haang and Lady Sumnima blessed the earth with. As for the main offering during this festival, it will naturally be salt less boiled beans and ginger in honour of Lady Sumnima and Lord Paro Haang.

38. A TALE OF THE FRIZZLED CHICKEN ......IN THE DAYS OF THE MAHABHARATA

(The Ramayana and the Mahabharata are two of the greatest epics of Ancient India)

Almost every home in the villages has a Rooster that is called *Deuta ko Bhalae in the local language. Literally translated, it means "Rooster that is offered to the Gods." This creature is treated with great respect and no one even shooes it away as it goes about the house and farm doing whatever it wants. When the rooster grows old, it becomes easy prey to the local weasel or fox and people say the Gods have claimed it, and so it 'disappeared'. No one should go looking for it. Another one takes it, place after some time. The practice of offering something to the gods is a natural part of the Kirati existence and here is a tale that explains one such offering of a chicken.*

After clearing the jungles of Khandava, the Pandavas built a beautiful city and called it Indraprastha. When Yudhistira ascended the throne of Indraprastha, he sent his four valiant brothers, each with a mighty army to the four corners of the land to subjugate the kings. Yudhistra wanted to conduct the Rajasuya sacrifice that would place him firmly as the emperor of the realm.

The people of the east were said to be mighty limbed warriors who rode elephants to war and thus the strongest of the brothers, Bhima was sent to the east to subjugate the warlords and tribal kings and conquer the land of Assam.

The Kirati tribes of the eastern Himalayas prepared for battle. Bhima would have to pass through their lands before he reached the land of the elephant warriors.

They had heard of how the Aryan Prince Arjuna, without any warning, had just torched the green jungles of Khandava and ruthlessly slaughtered the peace loving forest tribes as they fled the blaze. Many Kiratas and the Nagas had fled eastwards, leaving the verdant forest behind. Thousands of animals and birds perished along with the many forest tribes that had made Khandava their home.

The news of the destruction of the land with utter disregard for Life had spread far and wide. The Kirati clans had heard enough to make them distrust and dislike the invaders. As Bhima and his army marched through the forests of the East, the Kirati scouts watched the mighty warrior for many days, stealthily following his every move. The Aryan Prince had brought his war to the Eastern lands.

The valiant efforts put up by the various Kirati Chiefs were no match against the Pandava army. One by one, the Kirati Chiefs were conquered. Some fell heroically in battle and others accepted the sovereignty of the Emperor Yudhistira.

Bhima admired the golden-skinned warriors' valor and skill. He grew to like the Kiratis and had respect for their courage and took the warriors to fight his campaign. The Kirati warriors were bound to assist the emperor's forces and accompanied Bhima.

Folklore says the Kiratis noticed Bhima's huge appetite his hot temper and his gentle demeanor towards the weak; they grew to like the mild-mannered hero who could easily erupt into an angry tiger in the face of adversity. Physical strength was prized by all forest tribes and Bhima's amazing physical prowess won him many admirers among the Kiratis.

It is said that Bhima met with very strong resistance further east from a kingdom that fought back bravely. The Pandava forces were nearly annihilated. Bhimsen was urged by his commanders to launch a surprise attack on the enemy at night. The mighty warrior refused to resort to treachery. He also refused to leave without a victory.

The commanders did not know what to do. Finally, a Kirati Chieftain came up with a plan that would ensure the Aryan

Prince's code of war was not broken and yet the surprise attack could be launched.

A little after midnight, the Pandava army silently prepared for battle and took up their positions. The battle code was very clear; battles could take place only from Sun up to sun down. So, what were the Pandava forces up to?

Bhimsen walked silently to the front of the army with his commanders and the Kirati Chief. The Chief stood close to the Pandava with a rooster tucked under his arm. The Prince turned to the east, waiting for dawn to break. Tucked securely under the Chief's arm the rooster dozed away facing west. At three in the morning, the rooster stirred and took a deep breath to welcome the new day with a loud crow.

Bhimsen turned to the Chief and grabbed the crowing rooster's legs and yanked it out from under the chief's arm. He broke its neck with a snap and roared out his command to begin battle. The new day had begun, and Bhimsen's battle code was not broken.

In the other camp, the alarm sounded. Warriors, who were just waking up, swiftly gathered their weapons and shouted out hasty orders. They would not give in so easily. Screaming their defiance to the crisp dawn, they thundered towards the approaching enemy.

The battle was brief and bloody, and though the warriors fought valiantly to defend their home land, they had to finally withdraw and accept the suzerainty of Emperor Yudhistira.

Bhimsen did not forget the Kiratis who had helped him. As he took leave, he promised them his unfailing friendship and blessings in war and in peace. The Kiratis promised him they would never forget him either.

Strangely, after some time, in all the Kirati lands there hatched a strange kind of chicken. The chickens all seemed to have their feathers turned the other way. The Kiratis promptly christened the chicken "Bhimsen's chicken."(A breed of chicken called Frizzle).

They said when Bhimsen yanked the bird out from under the Chief's arm, its feathers must have all turned the other way around.

They believed this was Bhimsen's way of making sure that the rooster that helped win the battle was never forgotten.

Thus started the practice of "Bhimsen Pooja" where a sacrifice of a Frizzled Chicken is offered once a year in honor of the warrior Prince. It is said Bhimsen pooja brings peace and prosperity and victory in battle.

This practice used to be followed in almost all homes long ago. Where once a year the Kiratis honor and remember the Aryan Prince who came to the East as a conqueror and left as a friend.

Of course, this practice too is dying out with the march of time, and some tribes claim this pooja to be specifically their own, but this is not true. Long ago in the hills Bhimsen Pooja used to be conducted in all homes till the practice started dying out.

39. TAYAMMA AND KHIYAMMA

Long ago, when the hills were no longer young, the sons and daughters of men had now given up the old nomadic ways and had settled down in villages and grew crops and herded cattle and sheep. Life had changed a lot from the hunting and gathering days.

Men and women worked in the fields and grew barley, corn, wheat, buck wheat, millet, with milk from the cows they made butter and churpi (cheese). They learnt to press the simple cottage cheese and squeeze out the whey and cut and dried it so that it hardened into very hard cheese called churpi.

These could be stored for a long time without it going bad, they learnt to trade and barter goods for salt and other things they needed from the salt traders who came from across the mountain passes all the way from a land that had no trees where the soil was frozen and barren in most parts, a land they called Toofan (Tibet).

Sheep wool was also something the traders came for the sons and daughters of the hills hadn't learnt to weave and could only make wool. During such times in the hill lived a childless couple. They had a nice little cottage and a fairly large herd of cattle and a very large flock of sheep.

The gods had decided not to bless them with children, so the couple lived quietly and content with their lives, bowing to the will of the spirits and gods. It was a pleasant surprise when the wife one day found out she had been blessed with a child. Imagine their delight when they were blessed with a pair of twin daughters.

The two little children were a source of great joy to the old couple. As the years passed the two small girls were of great help to their parents. The father would see his two little girls help their mother carding wool and would often, good naturedly, say the mother had two little helpers while he had none.

He would often laugh and say if only the spirits would bless them with a son, then he too would have company while tending the sheep or the cows. Perhaps the spirits felt sorry for him or maybe they were pleased with his gratitude towards the gods for his daughters that they decided to grant him his wish.

One afternoon he went looking for a sheep that had strayed into the rocks above. He was surprised to find a baby sleeping in a hollowed-out space on a flat rock.. He picked up the peacefully sleeping infant and thanked the spirit for having heard his prayers.

He walked home swiftly, and it wasn't long before his wife and daughter were fussing over the newest number of their family. The man felt the spirits had left him their gift on a hollow of a rock so he called the child Khopchilipa meaning "one who was found in a hollow."

Three happy years passed by and Khopchilipa grew strong loved by his mother and sisters and most of all his father who doted on him. He would make wooden toys for him carry him on his shoulders whilst tending his sheep and give him everything he wanted. Life in the little cottage was a happy one. One day the spirits decided that the man and his wife had spent their given time on earth. The two gentle souls passed on to the realm of their ancestors in their sleep.

The three children suddenly found themselves orphaned, and Tayamma and Khiyamma decided to do their best and care for their little bother so that he would not miss their parents much. The two sisters prayed to the spirits to look after them and asked them to help them. In their dream, the two sisters were asked to come to a certain hilltop with a basket of wool each. The next morning the two walked up the top of the hill and found a stone bench there.

They sat down and waited; they saw a strange structure made of stone and wood sitting there. The two sisters unconsciously followed their instincts and started to wind the wool around the strange object. Guided by the spirits of the ancestors, within the next two hours the two girls had somehow learnt to weave and understood how a loom worked and what one had to do to weave patterns on the cloth.

Delighted with their new found skill they, went home; thus the two sisters started weaving blankets with sheep wool, and life became a little more comfortable as they were able to barter their blankets for things they needed. Seeing their skills people started to come to them to learn how to weave, they were happy to teach them.

They first asked the people to make the looms and the spindles; however as luck would have it, they could not complete the task they set out to.

The rains failed for two successive years, and the land was dry. This led to severe shortage of food and grains. The village folk started to speak of moving away while they still could. Many scoffed at the ones who left and later saw the wisdom in doing so and followed; taking their animals with them.

The rains still failed. Salt traders arrived from Toofan to go back empty-handed, their salt was no longer valuable to people who had no food. In vain had they made the journey across the treacherous snowy passes. They returned empty-handed to their land and shared news of how the drought had affected other places as well.

More and more people left until there was no one left. The villages soon became empty and silent, and the village springs dried down to a small trickle.

Tayamma and Khayamma refused to leave; they were reluctant to leave behind the graves of their mother and father. They hoped the famine would be over soon. The entire population had moved away except for the three of them. The headman had insisted they move out of the village along with his family and promised to take care of them but they politely refused. Their animals starved and wandered away and it became more and more difficult to find food. The two sisters and their little brother spent the major part of their day foraging for edible grains and roots and mushrooms and moss.

One day the sisters told their now seven-years old brother to stay behind while they went to look for food. Khopchilipa agreed, as the day before had been a very long one and he was still tired. The two sisters went looking for edible roots and shoots and wandered further and further away from home.

Khopcilipa waited impatiently for his sisters to return. He wandered out of house and into the new barren field and decided to dig up some roots for himself. He did not exactly recognize the plant and it was no surprise that once he ate the root, he started retching and vomiting. He had consumed a mildly poisonous root, mistaking it for an edible root his sisters fed him.

He felt nauseous and dizzy. He made his way to his cottage and lost consciousness just as he reached the door. Tayamma and Khayamma came home to see their beloved brother dead. They called out to him, sprinkled water on his face and shook him but he did not wake up. In their tired and frightened minds, he looked dead to them.

The distraught sisters covered up his body with banana leaves and made their way to the hilltop, where the spirit had taught them how to weave. They prayed to the spirit in great sorrow and asked to be changed into birds so that they could leave the place where they had lost all they had loved.

Tayamma was turned into a beautiful, strong hornbill bird. She placed the gravestones of her parents on her head and flew away. Khiyamma was transformed into a wood pigeon and before she left, she made a basket of thin green bamboo strips, placing her beloved brother's body inside and covering the casket with banana leaves the sisters offered their last prayers over their beloved brother's corpse and flew away.

Many hours later, the unconscious Khopchilipa regained consciousness. To his horror, he found himself covered with banana leaves inside a basket. He could guess that his sisters had thought him dead and left him. He looked for them everywhere and kept on calling out to them.

'Soi'

'Soi soi la" he called out to his sisters.

'Soi, Soi'

'Soi, soi, la !!'

He called out hoping against hope Tayamma and Khiyamma would answer. Khopchilipa heard nothing. He got up, and walked into the jungle still vainly calling out to his sisters. Khopchilipa would go on to have his own adventures. He grew up to turn into a handsome young man, and married a powerful headman's daughter. At his wedding, he did manage to see his sisters one more

time but that's another story. The rains did come, and years later slowly there

people, headed back to the same old village as did Khopchilipa. Tayamma and

Khiyamma were never seen again and people felt sad that they did not get a

chance to learn the art of weaving from the two sisters. The spirits were kind to

the sons and daughters of man. Strangely it was discovered, whoever wanted to learn weaving only had to go to the hill top where the sisters had sat and woven their first blanket on the stone loom and pray with a humble heart to the spirits of the two sisters, and they would know what to do.

Many went up the hill top to learn the art of weaving. It was Khiyamma who

had woven the last blanket on the stone loom and it was also Khyamma who had woven the first bamboo casket for the dead before she had been transformed

into a wood pigeon called 'Haleso' in the local dialect. The villagers therefore,

named the hill top Halaeso Dara.

The rains did come and the harvest was good. During the harvest festival, the villagers gathered as usual for their biannual festival of Sakaela. They offered their harvest to the gods and celebrated the bountiful harvest with dancing and beating of drums and cymbals.

The villagers all returned but always hoped for the return of the two sisters

without whom the village was not complete. So, during the Sakela dance, the

dancers all keep calling to the sisters to tell them all is well with Khopchilipa their brother.

That the harvest was good and the villagers are well, and that people are warm in the cold nights thanks to them and that the dead also rest in green bamboo caskets all thanks to the two sisters.

The Sakaela is celebrated all over the hills twice a year. Midst the of clash of

cymbals and the booming of drums the loud cry of.

"Soi,Soi,"

"Soi, Soi la," still reverberates in the air as the descendants of Khochipilipa still seek to call out to Tayamma and Khiyamma, the first weavers of our tribe.

In their honour, the descendants of Khopchelipa the Khambus/Rais keep offerings of grain for Khyamma who turned into a wood pigeon and the pangra seed (Entada Rheedii) as an offering to Tayamma who turned into a Hornbill in their altars.

Strangely, the humble pangra or Entada Rheedi is also used by the indigenous tribes and their healers in Africa. The healers claim the plant helps them communicate with their ancestors effectively.

40. BHAILO AND DEWSUREY: THE STORY OF AN ANCIENT KIRATI FESTIVAL

Many years ago, there lived, along the foothills of the Great Himalayas a nomadic tribe called the Kirats. Many a historian and scholar have tried to trace their lineage to Tibet, China, Mongolia, and Burma..

There is mention of them in the great Hindu Epics, the Ramayana (where the vanaras are warned of traps set by the kirantis), the Mahabharata (where Arjuna uses his military might to rid Khandava Forest of the Nagas, the Kiratas and other forest tribes), the Vishnu Purana (that holds the story of the origin of the Burja Tribe) and the Markandey Purana (that explains why the Kiratas worship by night).

These nomadic wanderers, often referred to as "Barbarians" by various different historian and writers down the ages, have a marvelous history of how each clan came to be and shared similar language and customs. Their tales of the snowclad lands and mighty rivers and of tigers, pythons and yetis showed the extent of their travels.

In the beginning, armed with just bows and arrow and slings then later wielding the Khukuri, a blade that strangely resembles the Greek blade, the Kopis that meant 'to cut' in Greek 3500-2200 BC Copper Age. These barbaric nomads made war upon each other and won honour and respect as warriors and also had their fair share of bitter defeat and division of their lands and the dishonor of having to serve various masters in their own lands. Such times saw the birth of brilliant Haangs (king/Chieftain) like Baali Haang, Srijung Hang, Muda Haang, Yellambar Haang and others.

With the passage of time many stories were lost and many were retold so many time that bits of the story went missing or worse... 'borrowed' endings from the Panchatantra and the Hitopedesha (famous Ancient Indian Tales). More Tribes came into being, some tribes were lost, wars were waged, new kingdoms were carved and lost and won and lost again as time went by.

With the relentless march of time a lot of local knowledge, sacred practices and festivals disappeared. All we were left with were some cultural practices, rites and ritual that were difficult for many 21st century Kiratis to understand and accept. It did not help that there were truths and half-truths all around.

We were left wondering what our culture meant, and how we were to make sense of it all.

Among all this confusion about our heritage, religious and cultural practices, new ideas came to being. Ideas that were directly opposed to celebrating these ancient customs. These ideas were actively propagated and newspaper articles were published asking various Kirati Tribes not to take part in such festivities.

Maybe it was an effort to preserve the "purity of the Karati tribe" (By Voldemort's standards, I would definitely make it to the Top Ten in the Kirati Mudblood List) Maybe it wasn't.

Maybe it was a misguided and feeble attempt to create disunity among the various Kirati tribes by sending this unspoken message across that "we are more unique than you." This reminds me of my favorite line from Animal Farm : "All animals are equal, but some are more equal than others." Maybe it wasn't.

All I know is when my children ask me why we celebrate this festival or that, I must have an answer that makes them proud to be a Kirati and to see that the earth is a part of us and we are all a part of the earth. In fact, the whole world started off as Kirats... nomadic wanderers.

Marvelous fantastic wanderers who saw ancient forests and ancient skies, discovered, invented, destroyed, recreated, explored and made friends and allies.

Wanderers, 'barbarians', nomads who fought, bled and cried when they lost their dear ones, who thought up marvelous practices of inventing Spirit Brothers "Meeth" and thought of really very interesting ways keep the peace in a tribe, even when a man from the same tribe stole another man's wife (who was then honour-bound to avenge this insult). Wanderers who Lived, Loved, Lost and Laughed like the rest of the people of the world.

Wanderers who celebrated the days of plenty, prayed to the Spirits of the Trees and Rivers and Skies. Sometimes called heathens and pagans and Naturalists, Spiritualists at other times. Who somehow managed to come up with some really terrible ideas that were called "social evils" later on, faced unimaginable hardships, poverty, sickness and ignorance, yet managed and is still managing to keep growing amidst all odds the Human Spirit alone can prevail against. Yes, the Kirats are Unique.

Unique like the rest of Humanity.

This is a tale about one such cultural practice unique to us.

Let me begin this wonderful tale like I always do…

Long, long ago when the hills were no longer young, Man had learnt to live in villages and had managed to work together as a tribe. It was during this time there lived a pious man called Baali Hang. He was a noble soul and commanded great respect amongst the tribes for his military might as well as his pious god-fearing ways.

Baali Hang had grown up seeing how the tribes who spoke almost the same language and followed the same God fell upon each other and caused so much misery and pain. He had seen his elders fall in battles that could have been avoided and seen many cast out from their own various tribes for having something as simple as marry someone from the other tribe. It was no surprise then that Baali Haang with the blessings of all the good spirits and the power of Good managed to subdue his enemies and establish himself as Haang (King/ Chieftain).

He was a wise ruler and ruled his lands well. He unified the warring tribes and taught them to live in harmony and to be happy in each other's unique ways. His Chiefs and subjects respected him and were happy.

The Spirit of Good blessed him, and he was able to see clearly into the future and know when a man's time was done. Many came to ask him to tell them how much time they had to put their affairs in order and then move into the next world. This way, Baali Hang earned great respect for himself.

Many years passed this way and one day King Baali Hang saw that his time was near. He gathered his chiefs and held a meeting to decide how the land was to be governed and how things were to be managed after he had gone.

"The Spirits have blessed me with many things in this life. I have enjoyed victories and a long spell of peace. My ancestors have blessed me with great wealth of land, friends, people and fame. I have enjoyed my life here with your love and respect. The time has come for me to move on to the world of our ancestors,' he said. 'Now it is time for all those assembled here to put forward matters that need to be dealt with at once and also clear any doubts about matters regarding the welfare of your clans."

There was a loud clamour as many of the young chiefs jumped to their feet and shouted, they didn't believe this was true. They had grown up hearing their fathers tell them of the battles they had fought with the young Baali Hang and how they believed he was indestructible. They had heard stories of how their Haang had uprooted trees and lifted small hills to rain them down on his enemies when he had run out of arrows. The legends spoke of Baali Haang single-handedly fighting with a hundred men while archers had rained arrows on him, with all that he had survived to lead their fathers to victory after another. He had been their hero and their idol. They could not believe that the Spirit of Death would even dare take their beloved Haang away.

The older chiefs looked on in shock and disbelief as they tried to make sense of what Baali Haang had just said. They had seen battles with their Haang and had seen him fight for what he believed in. They respected his military prowess as well as his intelligence. They could not believe that they, who were now so old, were still alive while their Haang who was just in his fifties, was going to die. They had not known a single case where the Haang's prediction of death had not come true.

Baali Haang waited till the clamour had died down and spoke, "I know each and every man in this gathering, loves and respects me. Each of you has loved me like your own. Now it is time for me to leave, and for you to let me go with your prayers and blessings. Please do not grieve and weep for me. It is said that tears of loved ones block our path into the next world. Now let us concentrate on more pressing matters that need to be attended to."

Baali Haang continued, "let us start the discussion on matters that concern people's welfare. Our people hav lived in peace for a long time please remember they have to live here for a long time, before they move on to join their ancestors. We have to make sure there is lasting peace even if I am not here"

His words, for the first time, fell on deaf ears.

The oldest chief stood up and said, "Haang, I was as old as you are now when you conquered my lands. Even as a young man, you displayed such wisdom that unified us all. Without you, we will just fall out again and go back to our old ways. How can we think of matters at hand when nothing will ever be the same without you."

Another chief stood up and said, "You are a holy man, which is why the Spirit of Good walks here, without you our sins will surely bring destruction on us all. Without you we will never have the blessings of Kuwangti (the Spirit of Victory)."

A young chieftain spoke up, "We honour our ancestors, offer prayers, ask them for strength to do what is right, and ask for success in our ventures. We keep them in our Chula Dhunga (alter, which is actually a fireplace made of three stones). They can still guide us from the next world. When we die, our sons and their sons will do the same. You O Haang have no son because you refused the life of a householder for the Spirit of Purity and Good to live in your body. Where can we even turn to ask for your guidance? You cannot leave us."

One by one the chiefs stood up to point out why he could not leave. They just pointed out the various challenges they would be unable to meet without his guidance and presence. Some said they were willing to challenge Death itself. Some begged him to let them trade places. Some asked to accompany him as they thought it was their duty to accompany him. Many asked him to to use his powers and stop Death.

Baali Haang listened carefully to what each had to say. He understood that behind all their love and respect, lay the truth. The young Chieftains still needed time to grow and understand many things and the older Chiefs needed to be a little more time to learn to take independent decisions.

Finally, when the last chief had spoken, he addressed the gathering.

"What you have said is true, but it is not I who is leaving you. The Spirit of Death has decided that my time is up. Three days from now when there is no moon in the sky, and the world is in plunged in darkness he will come to take me. We can only pray to him to let me stay for some more time among you. Prepare to fast, pray and purify yourselves mind body, soul and pray to him for what you want."

The chiefs got their people together and asked them to bathe themselves and purify their homes fast. The first day they cleansed their homes and themselves, offered food, flowers and fruit to the crows who were considered the messengers of the Spirit of Death. The crows ate the offerings and flew away. The next day they cleansed their homes and themselves and offered their prayers, garlands and delicacies to the Dogs, who were also considered the close companions of the Spirit of death. The Dogs ate the food offered, and walked around proudly with their garlands around their necks and were pleased.

The third day, the people offered their prayers and offered cooked delicacies, flowers and fruits to the Bull. It was said that the spirit of Death used a black bull as his mount when he walked on earth, the people prayed to him not to help the Spirit of Death. The Bull enjoyed the attention, and ate all that was offered to him and was pleased.

On the fourth day, the people cleansed their homes, lit lamps and torches and lit up every corner and every dark spot in the villages. They did this so that they would be able to see the Shadow of the Spirit of Death as he came to take their beloved Haang away.

In a big hut, Baali Haang sat in prayers while his chiefs came fully armed with their men to stand guard. The Haang told them that arms were of no use in this case, and they ought to pray instead of trying to fight something that was not of this world. The chiefs then sat all around him in a circle, and started praying while the men stood all around the hut and prayed.

Night fell, the lamps were lit and the torches blazed lighting up every corner of the village. The young girls got together in a group and went from house-to-house singing songs to keep the women and children awake throughout the night. The menfolk being at the Haang's hut, the women were only too glad of the company and gave the girls gifts of grain and snacks. The girls went from house to house singing about how they should all help the Haang. (Let us help=Pha-l-lo which later became Bhailo) (REF: History of Kiratas by Shri Iman Sing Chemzong)

At around midnight just as the Haang had foretold the Spirit of Death was seen in the form of a dark shadow. Swiftly it flitted along the well-lit paths and made its way to where Bali Haang sat. The people set up a loud cry and like instructed, they started praying to the Spirit to let their Haang live.

The Spirit approached the hut and the men let him pass unchallenged like they were asked to. The spirit entered the hut where the Haang sat. The Chiefs in one voice started their prayers to the spirit and asked him to spare the life of their beloved Haang. They started their prayers as well, each man prayed to the Spirit and asked for Baali Haang's life. They told the spirit without the king they would all be lost, and everyone would start fighting among themselves. The land would be divided and chaos would reign. They wept and begged the Spirit to spare their leader.

Seeing so much devotion and love, the Spirit of Death was moved. In a loud voice he told the people that he would try and help them, but he had to do what he had to do. With that the spirit disappeared and Baali Hang's lifeless body fell gently to the ground. The people kept on praying steadfastly and repeated their prayers. The dark night waned, and dawn crept in and at the first cock crow, Baali Haang came back to life. Taking in a deep breath, he sat up slowly like one who has just woken up from a deep slumber. The people rejoiced, they had succeeded in saving their leader.

The next day, there was a big feast and after the feast, the men and boys divided themselves into groups and went far and wide, spreading the good news that all was well with their beloved Baali Haang. He had sent them to tell one and all, he had been saved by the devotion and faith of his people. The Priest King (Deusurey) sent his thanks and blessings to all his subjects.

Baali Haang lived to a ripe old age and promised the people he would live in the Chula Dhunga of all the people, give them guidance and help whenever they needed it. Some Kiratis call him Buda Haang (old king). His lands came to be known as the Baali Haang land.

The well loved leader lived to see his Chiefs and their clans grow from strength to strength. When his time finally came, he promised the clans that he would live in the Chula Dhunga of all the people and give them guidance and help whenever they needed it. Some Kiratis call him Buda Haang (old king). In many households of people hailing from the ancient kingdom of Limbuwan, they still pray to him. My mother's family still start their prayers with reciting the three names Buda Haang. Baali Haang, Kula Haang and Soona puri (the male and female diety of the house).His lands came to be known as the Baali Haang land.

About a hundred years, these lands were conquered and divided into three different kingdoms. Later in history, two very powerful Magar Kings are known to have ruled over these lands that were still populated by various Kirati tribes and sometimes King Baali Haang is referred to as a Magar King. There is also mention of one chieftain called Lochan, who led one of the Kirati Groups from Siman Garh, had a priest named Baali, and how the children of the priest Baali settled in a place called Lamichhan and came to be known as Lamchhaney. Lochan himself, had three sons Ghaley, Ghonde and Lama.

This is not true as Bali Haang's lineage was never discovered and no one really knows exactly to which Kirati clan Baali Haang actually belonged.

Old kingdoms fell and new borders were drawn and redrawn but the Kiratis never forgot their priest king. Every year, they celebrate Tihwar (Diwali in India) by cleansing their homes and lighting oil lamps all around their homes. In the month of Mungshir even today, the darkness of Aushi (no moon night) is dispelled by the lighting of thousands of oil lamps and Kirats in the ancient lands of Baali Haang keep their nightlong vigil while the sounds of Bhailo and Deusurey echo loud and clear like in the days of the priest king.

This is why, every year during Tihwar after Bhailo and Deusey have taken place. The Kiratis observe the ceremony of Bhai Tika (Brothers Day). Sister's fast and pray for their brother's long lives.

The ceremony may differ in small ways with each clan of the Kirats but there is one common practice where a walnut is placed in the brother's hand, while his sisters put the five auspicious colours (taken from Hinduism later on) on his forehead, and draw a ring around him with oil, and tell the Spirit of Death that he is not to come anywhere near her brother till the oil has evaporated and gift him a garland of Makhamali flowers because the Makhmali flower doesn't wither so soon and tell the spirit he can come only when the flowers have withered and died. This never happens because, the dried flowers are the seeds of the next generation.

Some clans do not believe in gifting garlands to their brothers as a garland of flowers is a symbol of marriage for them. After the ceremony is complete, she takes the walnut from him and places the walnut on a broom so it doesn't slip. She smashes it with a stone and throws the broken bits on to the roof. The walnut is a symbol of the Spirit of Death's head and it is considered very inauspicious if the symbolic head is not smashed in one blow.

Once this ceremony is over, the brothers give their sisters gifts of money or clothes, and the sisters break their fast and spend the day with their brothers. Married sisters wait for their brothers to come to their homes. Some send an invitation to their brothers with water and flowers. Some do not as it is understood that it is the brother's duty to go to wherever his sisters are.

Bhai Tika, a day when siblings put aside their differences and just be happy and grateful that they have each other in their lives.

It is a day of celebration, in honour of an ancient Kirati Warrior Priest Bali Haang.

41. RIKKUPPA AND THE GREEDY CRAB.

According to the Mundhum (song of creation) of some of the Kirat Rai/ Khamboos it is said, in the beginning there was only sky. The Sky was destroyed and the Earth was created. Then, the Earth was full of water. Many shamans do not agree with this, and say there was only water and nothing else. So here I am starting this tale with one version of the shaman.

In the beginning, there was only water everywhere and all that existed was a huge ocean. In the huge ocean lived a huge serpent and its mate. They frolicked in the water, and salty foam flew here and there. The foam collected in a place and froze and that is how the first rock was created. The foam kept freezing and the rock kept growing larger till it cracked a little. Tiny ferns (wasepi) slowly sprouted from the crack and thrived. The rotten leaves of the fern fell and termites appeared to eat them. The termite started to dig up and started piling up the Earth from the seabed of the Baikuwa sea.

The first plant mentioned in the Mundhum is wasepi (the fern). Then, grass started to grow and mushroom (deule) started to grow on the mud piled high. The Earth soon had earthworms and beetle larva (khumle kira).

Hadbade grass, dubo grass and chindo (bottle gourd) started growing. This plant bears gourd shaped like a bottle. Once the gourd is dried and cleaned, it is used as a container to hold water or alcohol during rituals.

Now I'm not sure about either the earthworm or the beetle larva. The shamans are not unanimous about this bit but, either the earthworm or the beetle larva gave birth to a female human child Ribhumma, and then male human child Rikkupa /Rikpa (pronunciation of the names differs from region to region).

The children grew up quickly, and when they turned two, Rikkupa turned his face towards the mountains and headed into the hills.

Ribhumma turned her face towards the plains, and made her way down towards the hot plains.

The years passed, and Ribhhuma grew into a fine maiden.

One day the thought struck her, everyone I see has a mate, how come I don't have one, where shall I look for one? She thought about this for a while.

One day as she was thinking about this again, she looked around and saw a pair of lapwings merrily playing. She called them to her and asked the lapwings. "Everyone I see around me, has a mate. Do you know of any mate suitable for me?"

The male lapwing replied, "I'm not sure but I have heard the river murmur tales of a human male Rikkupa somewhere high up in the mountains."

Ribhumma quickly got out some gold dust and smeared the lapwing's wattles with it and said, "Now that I have anointed you with gold, please be my representative and find Rikkupa and bring him here." The lapwing was happy to see its wattle glow bright yellow and flew as swiftly as he could towards the mountains. When he grew tired, he stopped by the river, and hopped on the stones and after recovering his breath, he spread his wings and flew again. He flew and flew higher and higher and higher, the air grew thin and it was cold, very cold.

The lapwing finally arrived at a very steep waterfall. He was already exhausted and weak. He couldn't make it over the waterfall. Sadly, he turned and went home.

Ribhumma was sorry to see the bad state the lapwing was in, so she told him to go home and rest.

She looked around again, and there she saw a river crab scuttling merrily across the sand, mumbling to itself. Ribhumma caught the crab and told him about her plight. She asked the crab to get

Rikkupa down to the plains. She put many gold rings on both its claws and promised it a copper cauldron, if he came back with Rikkupa. The crab mumbled something Ribhumma didn't understand and happily went up the river the lapwing insisted on accompanying him.

He travelled for many days and came to the waterfall, the lapwing hesitated but the crab didn't mind the cold, he stoutly moved ahead and dragged the lapwing along with his claws. Thus the two companions made their way to the mountains

After a while they found Rikkupa dozing by the mountain stream with his back against a rock.

The crab woke the man up and told him that Ribhumma had sent for him. Rikkupa did not believe there was another human somewhere in the plains. He asked the crab.

"Are you sure it is a human female that sent for me?" He asked.

The lapwing and the crab both managed to convince Rikkupa about Ribhumma and he agreed to go with them.

Well, the two humans met and liked each other and after many days of deliberation, they decided to wed.

Ribhumma, true to her words, gifted the crab a shiny new copper cauldron as a token of her thanks. The crab walked away still mumbling something she couldn't understand.

Rikuppa on the other hand, could hear the slightest whisper and he could understand what the crab was saying.

"A few golden rings and a stupid copper cauldron are all I get for my troubles."

"The lady is very stingy. I hope she has a bad marriage. I hope her husband loses interest in her and leaves her."

Rikkupa got very angry when he heard the crab grumble thus, he lifted his leg and stomped down on the crab who was carrying the cauldron on his back. The cauldron got flattened and the crab's body got trapped inside the metal. This is why we find crabs with flat bodies and a hard shell on them. This how the greedy crab was punished.

Another version of the tale narrates that it was Ribhumma who hit the crab on its back with a firebrand and the cauldron stuck on its back. This is why crabs have a flat, hard shell around their bodies, and we can see the gold rings on their claws while they go about mumbling under his breath near streams, and rivers in the hills.

Rikkupa and Ribhumma lived happily for some time, and soon became parents to a healthy beautiful girl. They named her Naimma. One day, Ribhumma came back with her usual pitcher of water from the spring. She heard Rikuppa rocking the baby to sleep and repeating the lines, "In a way I am related to you as your father, but in another life you will be someone else." Ribhumma walked in and asked him what he meant by those words.

Rikuppa only said "what words?" and went on rocking the baby to sleep. Later that night Rikuppa felt a strange uneasiness and couldn't sleep. He suddenly got up in the middle of the night, slipped away into the jungle and kept walking around aimlessly.

The ways of the jungle are mysterious and Rikkupa suddenly started crawling on his hands and knees, and slowly he was transformed into a boar (perhaps it had something to do with the crab's curse or maybe something to do with fate). After his transformation, he completely forgot he used to be a human and went about life as a boar.

One day he came upon the field of yams that Ribhumma had planted a few months ago. Greedily he dug up an entire bed of yams and ate to his heart content. Then, he rolled in soft mud and made a mess and trotted off in the dawn.

When Ribhumma discovered Rikuppa missing, she looked for him high and low. She became convinced that he had abandoned them and left for the mountains. She decided to stay in the same place and wait for his return. A few weeks later, she went to dig up a yam for Naimma, and was shocked to see the damage there.

Her sharp eyes made out the hooves print and she knew it was a boar that had destroyed her yams, without much thought she cut down a supple bamboo and fashioned many sharp stakes out of it. She dragged a heavy log, and placed the sharp short stakes in a row along the length of the log. Taking a strong vine, she secured the stakes and hoisted the log on to the branch of a tree and set a trigger trap for the boar. After covering the trigger with leaves and setting everything in place, she returned home with whatever yams she was able to find.

The next morning, she went to have a look at the yam field and found her trap had sprung, and a huge boar lay mangled and impaled in the sharp bamboo stakes beneath the heavy log that had come crashing down on its back once the trap was sprung.

She removed the boars carcass from the trap and dragged the beast by its tail to a clearing. She burnt off the hair and disemboweled the animal. She removed the heart, a bit of liver and cut off a whole ear and a bit of the nose and placed a few hairs of the boar on a leaf and walked the edge of the jungle with her offering.

If the forest gods decided to look for the boar, he would know she had taken the boar.

Ribhumma sprinkled a tiny bit of rock salt and smoked the meat. She took some fat and fried some bits of meat and fed Naimma and ate some herself. She took the bits, she did not use and threw them away and cleaned out the small intestines. She took a little bit of limestone powder from a nearby rock, mixed with water in a container, turned the intestine inside and out and soaked them in the lime water for a while. Then she threw the water away and washed them and hung them out to dry above her fireplace. Tired after so much work, she fed her child and went to sleep after her own meal.

The next morning, when she went to her fire place to start a fire, she saw a young male human squatting by the fireside.

He looked very much like Rikuppa but he also looked a lot younger.

She addressed him as Rikuppa as asked him where he had been.

She told him how a boar had destroyed their yams and how she trapped the boar and prepared its meat.

"I have smoked the meat dear husband, so it will keep for a while," she concluded.

The young human (the second human male on earth) Parhuha angrily replied "You evil woman, you cut me up, and ate me. I am not your husband Rikkupa. I am Parhuha, my friends also call me Salpa ."

He stamped his foot in anger and turned his face to the mountains and walked away.

Ribhumma realized sadly that Rikuppa was well and truly gone and this was a reincarnation of Rikuppa, but now he was no longer the same person.

She hastily gathered the intestines and threw them away and made a decree that none of hers or Naimma's descendants would ever eat the intestines of a boar /pig because a clansman had been born from the intestine. This practice is still prevalent even today among certain clans of the Kirati Rai/Khamboo Community.

It is interesting to note that many Kirati Rai/Khamboos keep a boar tusk in their altar as a mark of respect and reminder of their ancestor Rikkuppa, the first Man who walked the earth.

Ribhumma lived for many more years and saw her child Naimma grow into a beautiful, sure footed, strong, fearless huntress. Each time her bowstring twanged her feathered barbs hit its mark. Ribhumma knew her daughter would thrive and be safe even after she was no more.

One evening, Ribhumma slept a little earlier than usual and never woke up from her sleep. Naimma put her mother's body in a cave and conducted her last rites. She then heaped stones and boulders at the mouth of the cave, offered her prayers and moved away to another part of the jungle.

One day the thought struck her, everyone had a suitable mate except her. Where would she find one?

She looked around for someone to help her and saw the wind merrily playing among the trees. She called out to the wind. "O wind tell me, everyone here has a suitable mate but I have no one, can you help me find someone I can wed?"

The wind rustled and puffed and replied, "Dear lady, I am not too sure but the rains have murmured something about a human male Parhuha or Salpa who lives high up in the mountains near a turquoise lake."

"Can you go and tell him about me? Can you go and make him leave everything and come to me?" asked Naimma.

"I am sure I could," replied the wind and it proudly flapped its giant wings and flew towards the mountains. It flew here and there and after a few days it espied the turquoise lake nestled among the snowy peaks.

He flew straight down and across the lake to see Parhuha dozing by the lake with his back against a rock. "What brings you here?" roared Parhuha.

"My lord Salpa (Parhuha's other name). I have been sent by lady Naimma to lead you to her. She has been looking for a suitable mate but there is no one for her in the plains.

"Hmmm" said Salpa, "if she has sent for me then I must go."

He walked to the edge of the lake and looked at his reflection and stepped back hastily.

"I don't think I will go with you, I have changed my mind," he said suddenly.

"Can't you see how rough and unkempt I look. I do not think she will like me because I wear skins and I look so dirty. She will probably laugh and make fun of me."

"No, I am sure she won't," replied the wind.

"What if she does?"

"I would feel ashamed," I have lived freely and with pride here at my lake, what if she treats me poorly looking at my matted hair?"

The wind was so sure of Naimma, he told Parhuha. "My dear lord Salpa, if she ever treats you poorly, you may cut off one of my wings. I can guarantee she will treat you with respect."

With that assurance Parhuha took one last look at his beloved lake and mountains and set off into the plains.

Parhuha's lake is still there in a place called Dobhane village in Bhojpur district in Nepal. Many Hindu,Buddhist and Kirat pilgrims visit it every year.

It is called Salpa Pokhari (salpa's lake) and four festivals are held each year, on full moon days. The Baisakh purnima, Rishi Purnima, Kartik Purnima and Mangsir Purnima.

Parhuha left the snow clad hills with the wind, his dirty matted hair made him all hot and sweaty as he headed into the warm plains. His animal skin coat made him smell very bad and break out into a bad rash. He scratched furiously making it worse. The sweat and grime on his face left his face streaked with dirt and he looked terrible. He smelt terrible and he felt terrible. He was nervous and anxious, and the heat of the plains that did not help his temper either.

When Naimma first saw Parhuha, she made a face and involuntarily snorted at Parhuha being so grimy and laughed at him. Parhuha was furious.

In a fit of rage, he turned to the wind in anger and lopped off one of its wings. Ashamed and angry, he went on to dry up all the sources of water in the vicinity.

He went deep into the woods and found a large leaf where he left about two cups of water mixed with his semen and left for the mountains in a terrible rage.

Everything was dry and barren now. There was no water. Naimma felt very thirsty. She called the birds and asked them to help her find some water.

The birds flew in different directions but no one found a drop of water. The woodpecker was lucky enough to find some water dripping from some ferns on to a rock. He called the other birds who couldn't hear him at first, finally when they hear the woodpecker call and arrived at the stone, the woodpecker had already drunk most of the water. The birds all got angry but a few managed to slake their thirst with the little drips that were left.

Thus, refreshed a bit the birds flew far and wide once more until one of them found the leaf with water on it. They did not know that Parhuha had mixed his semen in it.

Carefully, they poured out the water into a clay cup and gave it to Niamma. She drank the water gratefully. After she drank the water it started to rain.

The rivers, the ponds and lakes all filled up once more and the plains became lush and green again.

Nine months later, Naimma gave birth to a baby girl. She realized she had made a mistake in judging Parhuha on his appearance, and asked the birds and animals to find Parhuha and bring him to back to her. She did not want her daughter to grow up without a father.

The birds and animals went to out far and wide to look for Salpa. They found him a changed man. After his rage had subsided, he had felt terribly ashamed of his behaviour. He knew it was all his fault. In his hurry to see Naimma, he hadn't bothered to stop at a stream and wash up. Not only that, he had taken too much pride in his powers, and felt like he did not have to make any effort to win Naimmas heart. He had decided to change.

He no longer had matted hair, he had learnt to make bamboo combs and now his raven black hair was neatly combed. He had learnt to use herbs and the river water to get rid of his rashes and kept himself clean washing his body with sweet flag.

He looked handsome and healthy when he came to Naimma, who promptly fell in love with him. The two decided to wed and had three more children.

They called their first born daughter Wailungma, the second born was a male tiger (Chaapchha Saya), the third son a bear (Barpa Saya) and the youngest was a human boy(Hoccha).They lived in peace and harmony for a long time while, Naimma created food grains and drinks for humans.

Wailungma and Hoccha learnt to make weapons and to track and hunt and weave baskets and build huts and grow grain.

As for the tiger brother and the bear brother, they were lazy and learnt nothing. What happened to the brothers after their parents had passed? We will leave it for another tale. We take our leave of Salpa and his family.

The reader must be wondering what happened to the poor wind.

The wind was not forgotten, Salpa went looking for the wind and found him hiding in a cave. He gently nursed the poor wind back to health and though he was not able to give back the wind his other wing, he blessed it and the wind was still able to fly around among the trees. This was a good thing because the wind lost, the strength to destroy everything with two flaps of its wings. It had not been not very kind to many forest creatures in the beginning. Now that it had lost its full strength and it grew kind and considerate.

He still loves playing among the trees, and whenever any descendant of Parhuha feels hot on a sunny day, it is said they only have to whistle in a certain way for the wind to come and gently fan them. The Nepalis /Gorkhali people still believe in this and many whistle for the wind while on walks and treks in the hills and mountains.

In Nepali culture, it is forbidden to whistle a tune inside a house (day or night) and whistling after dark is an absolute no no, as our ancestors believed, even the wind deserves some rest. So, it not to be called or disturbed at nights.

42. THE CLEVER MAN WHO WAS NOT SO CLEVER AFTER ALL

Many folk tales were told to children to teach them basic courtesy and manners, but within these tales there also lay the simple truths of life in general. The following is one such story that was often repeated by my grandmother to my sister, and me every summer.

Long ago in the hills, there lived a clever man. He lived on top of one of the three hills that looked into the wide valley below. He had built a big cottage on the small hill, as his yaks and cows would have the green grass of the hilltops all to themselves. The village sprawled out along the valley, and he found the village rather too crowded.

The village folk did come quite often to the hilltops sometimes looking for firewood, medicinal herbs, or mushrooms and they would stop at the Clever Man's house and share all the latest news and gossip, so the Clever Man always knew what was going on in the village even though he did not live there.

His wife and two sons helped him out and life was good, and they were all happy.

He had many cows and yaks and sold a lot of milk, butter and curd and made enough to live in peace. Had the Clever man been a little nicer, he would have thanked the Creator for his happy life and lived happily till the end of his days, but this was not to be.

As his cows calved and his yaks grew in number, Greed awoke in his heart. According to another tale, Greed, anger, hate and jealousy lives in the hearts of all the sons and daughters of Man, but sleep most of the time thanks to a little bird (see story of the robin).

The Clever Man wanted more money. So, he went far, far away for some time leaving his eldest son in charge of the home and came back a few months later. He had met some traders who had told him all about selling yak wool, cow hides and meat and skin and horns and tail.

After he reached home, he told his sons that they would no longer bury their dead cattle. All dead animals were skinned to be and their horns and tails were harvested. Their flesh was to be cut into strips and dried in the sun. All this would be kept in the Kholma (woodshed) and when the traders came, they would get a good price for the skins, wool, horns and yak tails. The Elder son was horror struck. He refused to help his father with the task. The younger son was his father's pet and though his mind told him otherwise, he helped his father with the grisly task.

The Clever man made more money but Greed who was now wide awake in his heart wanted more and more, he just couldn't stop. His Eldest son moved away as he grew a little older and went away to a very far off land. There he put together some cattle and sold milk, butter and curd.

He left because the sight of the dead cows and yaks being skinned sickened him, and he could not understand why the animal that had given the family so much were not given a decent burial. It was what everyone did.

Old cows, sows, old nanny goats were buried with some rice, flowers, coins and incense.

Why in some places even mother hens were generally left in peace and buried when they died? This is what people did everywhere and here was his father taking more from them even after they were dead. He could not stay with his father anymore.

The Clever Man did not care. He was just interested in making more money. His cattle grew in numbers and the work load increased. The absence of the elder son meant more work but he was happy.

One day, the Clever Man saw his wife give a glass of buttermilk to a thirsty passerby and that gave him another clever idea. In the evening when they sat down for supper, he told his wife she was to charge a coin for every glass of buttermilk that she gave away.

The wife was horrified at this suggestion. In the hills it was common courtesy to give buttermilk to people who stopped by and asked for water. She said she was not going to do it. Their house was up in the hill top and many passersby had to stop there and ask for water. The Clever man got angry and said he was ordering her to do so. She flatly refused. The Clever Man got angrier and angrier and finally in a fit of rage, he hit her.

The next morning, she was gone. She bravely set her face in the direction her First born had and left. She had had enough and was determined never to come back ever again. After travelling for many months, she found her son and lived with him in peace.

The Clever Man didn't care. Greed was his God now and he just didn't think about anything else. He started charging coins for buttermilk from the thirsty passersby. His younger son still stayed on, but found it more and more difficult to obey his father.

One day, the Clever Man asked his son about the number of hides and horns as the traders were due to arrive in a week or two. The son replied they didn't have any for the traders as the gods had been kind and none of the cattle had died.

Early next morning, the son was woken up by his father and told to hurry up with the morning chores. The Clever Man then asked his son to lead the old cow out, and together the father, and son slowly walked to the small meadow on top of the hill. The son left the old cow to graze wondering why they had come there.

The Clever man said the grass was greener near the edge and slowly led the cow towards it. The Son warned him to be careful as the cow could fall off the side, and go tumbling down the hill. To his horror, his father calmly led the unsuspecting cow to the grass near the edge, and with a mighty push, he sent the poor animal hurtling down the hill.

As the dumbstruck son stood with his mouth hanging open in shock and horror, the Clever Man told him this was what he was to do to all the old bulls and cows and yaks when the animals were of no use to them. The father and son walked down in silence and without any more talk the Clever Man set about skinning the dead animal.

Late at night the Son got up collected his weapon and knives and with his small bundle of belongings, he stepped out of his house and walked away into the darkness. He could no longer stay, and be a part of something so dreadful. It had taken him a lot of effort to skin and gut the dead animals but he had told himself they had died in peace, and had been able to follow his father's wishes. He knew he could not bring himself to do what his father asked.

We do not know how the Clever Man felt when he discovered his son gone, but we do know he never went looking for him. Years passed and the Clever Man grew older and richer. He still charged coins for buttermilk from the thirsty people but he found less, and less people passing by.

One day a whole ten days passed without any one passing by. He decided to find out. He walked for a while to a point in the hill where he could see the entire fields and villages below. He could see one or two people climbing up the hill, but instead of taking the usual route that led towards his house, they turned a bit to the right and then walked up. Determined to find out he walked down to the new detour.

A tiny trickle of water had been found among the ferny black rock just above the new path. The grass had all been cleared away. Water seeped and dribbled down the sheer black rock to form a tiny little pool at the foot of the rock. A two-inch wide channel had been scratched at the side of the tiny pool which led the clear water to two and a half feet piece of bamboo that had been split, and fashioned as a pipe to carry the trickle of water to the passerby on the path. It wasn't much but to someone who has been walking uphill in the sun, it was a god send.

The Clever Man got angry and understood why people did not walk up to his house for buttermilk any more. He made up his mind to do something about this.

As dawn was breaking the next day, he made his way through the brambles to the top of the black rock, and swiftly cut away all the grass, ferns and greenery. He did this every dawn before any one was up and slowly in a few weeks he cleared away all the greenery and destroyed the source of the water seep.

The tiny trickle dried out and people had to take the old route once more. The Clever Man was happy again.

It was said that when a person is born, the creator keeps two empty pots in his name. Into one goes all the good deeds and into the other goes the bad and after a man dies, he is judged for his deeds both good and bad. It is also said that sometimes when a person is too evil, the pot is unable to hold much more and it breaks while the person is still alive and that is the time the Creator steps in.

This act of deliberately destroying a water source made the Clever Man's Pot of Bad deeds full to the brim. The pot would not be able to hold another drop more. The Creator saw the man had a long life yet and decided to step in.

Disguised as a poor old woman, dressed in rags, the Creator made his way up the hill, to the Clever Man's house.

It was beautiful morning and the green hills smiled at the cloudless sky. The Clever Man watched the old crone slowly make her way to his house where another thirsty passerby already sat drinking buttermilk. The Clever Man eagerly sat the old woman down, and told her the price of buttermilk. The toothless old crone laughed and laughed and asked him who had ever heard of anyone buying buttermilk. After all, it was just water that was added to the cream and curd when butter was being churned, so it was just water.

The other man drinking his glass of butter milk laughed and the Clever Man got very angry. He said it was his buttermilk, and he would do what he liked with it. He would not give it for free. The old woman laughed some more and said she did not want buttermilk she just wanted some water. The Clever Man said he didn't have any. The old woman asked him to not get angry, and that she just wanted a little water and she would be on her way.

The Clever man still refused to give her water, and said he didn't have any water anywhere. The other passerby reminded him that water was not to be denied even to an enemy and asked him not to get angry. The Clever Man still refused to give any water. Finally, the Passer by decided to go inside the Clever Man's house, pour out the water himself and give it to the old lady.

He poured the water out and just as he was giving it to the old crone, the Clever man who had worked himself into a tearing rage, came up and struck away the water pot from the old woman's hand as she lifted the water pot to drink. The force of the blow, and the weight of the bronze water pot caused the old woman a bad nose bleed.

The kind-hearted passerby ran to get Titae paati (Indian Worm wood) to stop the bleeding. This final act of cruelty caused the Clever Man's pot of evil deeds to shatter and the furious Creator threw off his disguise.

He cursed the Clever Man and disappeared.

When the kind passerby came back with the herb, he found no one there. No one ever saw the old woman or the Clever Man.

It is said the Creator turned the Clever Man into a bird and cursed it with an unquenchable thirst. As the bird flies desperately in search of water, all the springs, ponds and streams look like pools and streams of blood to the bird. All day it screams in desperation and thirst and the terrible thirst plagues it through the night.

It is only the very early mornings it is able to drink a few drops of dew from the grass before the sun comes up.

The people of the hills call this bird **Kaa- Kaa-li- Koo- Kooli** chara (meaning bird).

The ancient people of the hills believed one of the greatest sins one can commit is denying water (even to an enemy) or destroying and desecrating water bodies.

My sister and I we never saw this bird, but after we were told this tale let me tell you, we were both very hospitable and made sure we offered water to anyone who landed up at our house.

Of course, there were days that we felt a little lazy when someone wanted a glass of water, we would not feel so enthusiastic about closing our favorite comic book. During those times if someone just casually mentioned name of the bird, it was enough to make us hurriedly close the book and make our way into the kitchen. I guess this story did ha have its use with many parents in the hills till the days before video games and mobile phones.

As for slaughtering of female animals, it was the practice of all tribes not to slaughter females. Even today in many villages in the hills, dead cows (not bulls) are given a proper burial with prayers, rice and flowers and incense.

I don't know how it is now but when Nepal was under the rule of the late king His Royal Highness Birendra Bir Bikram Saha Dev, I did witness a police raid on a local meat shop in Battisputali Kathmandu. The local mutton shop owner had apparently slaughtered a she goat, and the police came and picked him up while all the meat was taken down and buried in a deep pit the policemen had dug. The man was let off with a fine and a warning. The locals were forbidden to dig the meat out and feed it to the dogs. The Law forbade the slaughter of female animals.

Among the various hill tribes, many eat beef but only males are slaughtered. All male animal, whether pigs or goats or bulls, that are set aside for slaughter are neutered. People used to believe that once an animal has created life it could not be slaughtered.

This practice is now steadily dying in the hills. Slaughter of female animals started about ten or twelve years ago. However, in most villages even today, people still do not slaughter any animal once it has given birth.

In some rural homes (very few of them left now) the ducks and hens that have hatched chicks are also left in peace.

People used to believe that slaughter of animals, although a necessity for their survival, had to be done with care and prayers and indiscriminate slaughter of animals was never the norm.

www.ingramcontent.com/pod-product-compliance
Lightning Source LLC
LaVergne TN
LVHW061608070526
838199LV00078B/7212